If It Wasn't For That Dog!

By Michael Forester

Published in 2008 by YouWriteOn.com

Copyright © Text Michael Forester

Published by YouWriteOn.com

Hearing Dogs for Deaf People is a registered charity which selects and trains dogs to respond to specific sounds which hearing people often take for granted, such as the alarm clock, doorbell, baby cry, telephone and smoke alarm.

Instead of barking, the dogs alert the deaf person by touch, using a paw to gain attention and then lead them back to the sound source. For sounds such as the smoke alarm and fire alarm, the dogs will lie down to indicate danger.

Whenever possible, the dogs are selected from rescue centres, but they are also donated by breeders and members of the public, with the remainder coming from the Charity's own breeding scheme. Size and breed of dog is usually unimportant, but every dog selected must be between seven weeks and three years old with an excellent temperament and a willingness to please.

The practical value is obvious, but the therapeutic value should not be underestimated. Among reported benefits, many recipients find their increased confidence and independence encourages them to go out and participate in activities which they previously avoided.

The charity has placed nearly 1500 hearing dogs since its inception in 1982 and has two training centres in the UK. Each dog is supported by a group, company or individual, happy to raise the £5,000 needed for its training – which can be broken into two parts of £2,500. Hearing dogs are free to deaf applicants. For further information on supporting the Charity, applying for a hearing dog or supporting your local branch please telephone 01844 348100, email info@hearingdogs.org.uk or visit www.hearingdogs.org.uk.

Preface

I was woken at six this morning; not by the alarm clock – I never hear that. Instead, at the sound of the alarm a small, furry, black and white form leapt onto the bed and walked all over me until he got a reaction. Then, as soon as he knew I was awake, he came up and started licking my face. He knows that always gets me giggling. The only way to get him to stop is to give him the biscuit he is entitled to for waking me up. Mind you, I have to be careful. The AD's an artful little creature, and he does love to get the day started. Sometimes he tries it on, and wakes me before the alarm goes off. In the early summer sunlight, it's occasionally been as early as 4.30am! As a consequence, I have learned to keep two clocks on the bedside table. One sounds the alarm that he responds to but that I can't hear. The other displays the time in large, illuminated red letters so that I can check he isn't cheating.

When I'd made the early morning cuppa we went down to the little bothy in the garden which is now my study and I went on line to get my overnight e-mails. The AD curls up at my feet patiently while I do this, but somehow he always seems to know when I'm ready to head back to the house. That uncanny sixth sense tells him I'm done before I make any kind of conscious move, and he'll always get up from under the desk and look at me expectantly as if to say "Get a move on- it's time for my walk!"

Last evening the doorbell rang. I didn't hear that either, of course, but he did. He's supposed to alert me with a formal prearranged signal of putting his paws round my knee, but usually he's so preoccupied with the unmitigated excitement of someone being at the door that it's all I can do to get him to jump at me at all to tell me what's going on. It's much the same with the phone, but I think the excitement there comes from knowing he's going to get a treat for telling me it's ringing.

Now, all this auditory work is pretty remarkable. But you know, the most amazing changes that he's brought into my life have nothing to do with the sounds he hears and tells me about. You see, when you begin to lose your hearing you tend to lose your confidence along with it. You're afraid that you'll make an inappropriate response to other people, because you've not heard what they've said. And gradually you begin to withdraw. You become reclusive. Eventually you simply stop communicating.

A little later today when we drive into Fordingbridge, the most important gifts he gives me will become evident. I'll put Matt into his distinctive maroon jacket and halte collar, and he'll go through an instant personality change. Gone will be the excitable, ebullient dog with his overwhelming curiosity and love of life. In his place will be a poised, alert professional who will walk smartly by my side ready to tell me if a sound occurs that I need to know about such as a fire alarm going off. And simply by being there in full dress uniform he will announce my invisible disability to the world. In doing so he'll draw me into any number of different conversations with the strangers who want to stop us and talk to him or ask me about his work. And that's why in the first year that Matt was with me I had more impromptu conversations with other people that I had in the whole of the ten years preceding his arrival. So yes, whilst the sound work is important, much more important to me is the incredible impact this little creature has had on my ability to and, indeed, my wish to communicate. He has quite literally drawn me back from isolation into a world that I now find wants to go out of its way to talk to me. A few years ago, neither I nor the people around me would ever have believed that this was possible – and if it wasn't for the dog it would not have been. That's really why I'd like to tell you how it all happened – how Matt came into my life and what happened as a result of his doing so.

But in order to do that we have to go back to 2002 - because it all started with Sage.

Michael Forester
The New Forest
October 2008

Sage and Time

Actually, to be specific, it all started with Methuselah, a horseshoe, and Sage.

It was September 2002, and I was sitting in a classroom, waiting to meet the fourth consecutive person in twelve months who was charged with responsibility for teaching me how to read lips. We were a group of perhaps fifteen people, arranged in a horseshoe of chairs around the edge of an uninspiring room in the Lymington Community Centre. Truth to tell, I didn't really want to be there at all, and I was feeling impatient. The average age of the group seemed to me to approximate to Methuselah's (well, he was young once, you know) and, being in my mid 40s, the amount I had in common with the rest of my fellow lip readers could be written on the edge of a mal-nourished paper clip. Not, of course, that I have anything against those older than me. No doubt, even in my mid 40s, I would have been regarded by many as antediluvian myself. I fidgeted in my chair, waiting for the show to get underway, already looking at my watch, wondering how I'd cope with the two hours of anticipated boredom until it was over. I began to concoct excuses for leaving early – business meetings… auntie Hilda's birthday (she died fourteen years ago)… a prior with the grim reaper… grandmother's third funeral (so you've never heard of exhumation?) – anything would do really. Attending at all had been a seriously bad idea – maybe I'd just cut and run and not bother with this lip reading lark any more at all. For most of us this was our first morning together and the silence of unfamiliarity and embarrassment hung heavily over the horseshoe.

Just before 10.00am there was a scuffling sound just outside the room (yes, I've still got enough hearing to pick that up). I watched the door handle turn. As the door inched open, through the gap there squeezed a large golden Labrador, carrying his lead in his mouth. A woman followed shortly behind the dog, her face obscured by the tall pile of boxes and papers she was carrying in her arms in front of her. She tottered into the room and dumped the boxes down on the teacher's table with a sigh of relief. Beaming a very genuine smile, she looked around the assembled multitude to discover who she would be teaching this academic year.

The Labrador, by contrast, had his own routine. Sporting a maroon jacket on which were printed the words "Hearing Dogs for Deaf People," he had made his way into the room in a laid back, "I'm-pretty-cool" kind of fashion and paused in front of the class member nearest the door. She smiled, nodded slightly, petted him and offered a few admiring words. Then quite slowly and deliberately, he made his way on to the next person who did the same. The Lab proceeded systematically around the room, stopping at each class member in the horseshoe of chairs. In front of each he paused and presented his lead, which also carried a label that bore the same words – "Hearing Dogs for Deaf People." Solemnly, and quite deliberately, he presented the lead to each member of the class in turn and awaited an appropriate acknowledgement. The meaning was clear. He intended for each of us to understand and acknowledge that he was a consequential dog, a dog of no little importance. Finally he reached the end of the horseshoe where I was sitting. He paused one final time, and with some amusement I introduced myself, confirmed that he was indeed a remarkable dog. Satisfied that all the assembled multitude were aware of his formidable status, the Lab (whom I was later to be informed was called Sage) strolled nonchalantly up to the teacher's desk where his owner was watching with a eye-rolling, "seen-it-all-before" kind of smile on her face. Sage looked up at her intelligently, head slightly to one side. When he had established to his own satisfaction that she had no further instructions for him, he settled himself down on a blanket under the desk, put his nose on the floor and went to sleep. From this position of tense, poised alertness, he did not re-emerge until coffee break, when it became obvious that he considered himself off duty. For from that moment until the end of break, Sage roamed the chatting congregation, trying to cadge biscuits. This was one unusual and seriously funky dog – and what's more, he knew it.

Boredom now well forgotten, I concentrated on getting to know the teacher, Sam, and the class members a little better. I also managed to make some progress with my lip reading. But the star turn of the day that left the really clear, lingering memory was Sage. Later I was able to talk to Sam, our conversation focussing on Sage, with the result that I began to receive my first exposure to what the concept of Hearing Dogs was all about. Of course, this was September 2002, and at that time I had no way of knowing that about 18 months later I would come face to face with my own hearing dog, who would change my life immeasurably and for ever.

Going Deaf? Wot, me?

I've heard it said that deafness is in some respects the most difficult disability to cope with insofar as it differs from other disabilities in one key respect. If you're walking down the High Street and you see a person coming towards you in a wheel chair, you get a very clear signal that this individual has a disability of some sort. How you react depends on a large number of factors, which can range from embarrassment that makes you look away, to excessive friendliness in an attempt to compensate, to acting perfectly normally (hopefully in the majority of cases), as you would with anybody else.

What makes hearing loss or deafness different is that you can't see it. Because, generally, there is nothing about the appearance of a deaf person that visually suggests a disability, you tend to assume they are the same as you, and you therefore expect the same responses from them that you would give yourself. The problem arises when you don't get them. For when someone responds to us in an unexpected manner, we ourselves tend to react strangely, defensively.

I first became aware that I was losing my hearing in 1989 when I was working as a management consultant. I remember the first day I noticed something different. I was running a training programme for about a dozen people (also arranged in a horseshoe shape!), when I suddenly realised that I couldn't tell from where in the room individual voices were coming. By the time I'd located a particular person speaking, they'd often finished what they were saying and I therefore had to ask them to repeat themselves. By the end of the day that was getting pretty frustrating for all of us. A conversation with my (then) wife about it that evening resulted in a decision to visit the doctor. This led in turn to a series of consultations with an ear, nose and throat specialist in Harley Street, who confirmed that I did indeed have a hearing loss. In fact, so marked was that loss, that he felt the need to test his audiology machine just to make sure it wasn't at fault! So there and then, in the summer of 1989 I was packed off to a hearing aid company to have a private hearing aid fitted. No counselling; no support; no explanation of how I might feel, no discussion of where this all might lead. In

13

fact, a huge emphasis on the technical aspects of hearing loss and the technology that might compensate, but not the slightest cursory glance at how it might feel to be facing a life-changing loss of one of the five senses.

From my unprepared state, my reaction to impending deafness, as I learned much later, was much the same as most people's. At first I wanted to pretend it wasn't happening – particularly the possibility that it might be progressive and that some day I might end up profoundly deaf. So I had the very smallest hearing aid fitted that I could possibly obtain, and went about my business, pretending, as far as possible, that nothing had happened.

But you can't cheat nature. She just goes on in her own sweet way, regardless of what you'd like her to do. As the early 90s slipped away so did my hearing, leaving me emotionally in denial about the consequences. By 1996 I'd been forced, painfully, to begin to face reality and had changed my occupation. It's not too easy to look impressive enough to win consultancy contracts if you can't hear the chief executive of a company when he's muttering into his coffee cup. So we'd taken the decision to buy a residential home for the elderly, partly on the basis that as I lost my hearing it would be easier to sell rooms than it was to sell consultancy.

The changes in my work circumstances were challenging enough. But the really difficult changes were taking place in my home and social circumstances. Perhaps it was of minor consequence that the TV was set each night at a volume that drove every other member of the family from the room. Perhaps it didn't matter that I had to ask friends and family to repeat themselves ad infinitum. Perhaps it didn't matter that I sat quietly at the kitchen table, missing the banter and the punch lines of normal, happy family conversation. But more significantly I'd all but withdrawn from social interaction. Why? Because when you can't be sure that you've correctly heard what's been said to you, you're never certain if you're giving the right response. And most people going through this process find it too embarrassing to keep asking for a speaker whom they don't know well to repeat themselves, perhaps several times, until they get the message. This will be particularly so against the hubbub of cocktail parties, or the pub, or noisy groups in whatever social situation you find yourself. On a number of occasions I'd not heard what was said under such conditions, smiled sweetly and given a completely inappropriate response, sometimes with disastrously embarrassing consequences. The result was that I, like most other people going through this process, withdrew from all unnecessary social contact. Much to the frustration of my rather extrovert wife, I would refuse invitations to dinner parties, moan at the prospect of attending family gathering and sometimes simply disappear when we were due to go out. The effects of hearing loss don't stop with the person losing their hearing. Everyone else around them feels the pain of the change as well.

By the end of the 90s I was still working, though now in the very different field of managing care homes for the elderly. As the Millennium turned, I was coping reasonably well with voices at work, because on the whole people speak in a much more measured and controlled fashion in a work context than they do socially – particularly when speaking to the boss! However, my social life was effectively over as a result of my self-imposed exile. Added to that, I was having growing difficulty hearing daily sounds – the telephone, the TV and so on. It's remarkable how much we rely on sound to tell us what's going on around us – try putting ear muffs on for a day and you'll see what I mean.

In 2001, I found my marriage over, and I guess I'll never really know the extent to which the frustrations imposed by hearing loss contributed to that sad event. But whatever the reason, I was facing the prospect of living alone and it was clear that life was going to change significantly at many levels. However, I was clear about one of the changes I would have to make: I was resolved to manage my deafness proactively and much more effectively than I had done so previously.

Back to School

As a result, September 2001 saw me start lip reading classes. The term "lip reading" in this context is something of a misnomer, because these groups teach a great deal more than just the skill of lip reading. In essence they train you in coping with hearing loss, and give you a whole host of strategies that you can employ to make life work better for yourself. So in those first few months, I learned everything from how to select a restaurant table intelligently (if I sit with the light behind me it falls on your face, making it easier for me to see and to lip read what you're saying), to the technological devices available to boost what hearing I had (the TV's volume control was saved from an untimely demise by the addition of an induction loop to my sitting room), to assertiveness in deafness (asking for the music to be turned down in a public place really is an option and often everyone else in the room appreciates the fact that I've asked!). But perhaps most important of all, that class at the beginning of September 2002 introduced me to the concept of a hearing dog.

Why on earth would I need a hearing dog?

I watched Sage for the first couple of weeks of that new class. Each Tuesday morning he would follow the same pattern, seeking acknowledgement around the horseshoe before positioning himself under the teacher's table until the biscuit tin appeared at coffee time. At that point he would revert, as if by magic, to the 'I'm-just-a-sad-ol-Lab-an'-if-you-love-me-you'll-give-me-a-biscuit' routine. Not too many weeks into the programme I approached Sam, to find out a bit more about what Sage did for her. He was trained, she told me, to hear the sounds that were significant in her life – her telephone bell, her doorbell, her alarm clock, her smoke alarm and so on. When any of these sounds occurred, Sage had a special signal to give Sam – he'd sit by her and put one paw on her leg. She'd then ask him the question "What is it?" opening her hands in a gesture of enquiry, and he'd lead her to the source of the sound. In the case of a danger sound like the smoke alarm, instead of taking her to the source of the sound, he would instead drop to the floor to indicate danger.

But quite apart to his sound related work, Sam enthused about the effect that Sage had had on her socially. She had experienced the same reclusiveness and reticence to talk to others that I was familiar with, but Sage had changed all that for her. His prominent coat attracted attention when they were out and about, and given that she could take him places others dogs are not permitted (supermarkets, restaurants etc.), he had become a focal point for conversations for her in such situations. So much was this so, that sometimes when in a hurry, Sam actually needed to leave Sage at home, because she knew that wherever she went he would become the celebrated focus of attention!

I went home to ponder all this, and the implications it might have for me. I'd not owned a dog since I was seventeen years old. How would I adjust to one now? The sound work Sage did was interesting, but quite honestly, technology was doing ok in keeping up with the deterioration of my hearing. In the little flat I'd moved to after my separation I had had a doorbell installed that made the lights flash. I also had an amplified telephone bell, amplified phones on which to talk to people and an induction loop to make the TV talk straight into my hearing aids. But the issue I just couldn't get off my mind was how good it would be to start having normal conversations with people again. A dog like Sage would act as a catalyst to bring me back into the social loop, as it were. One to one conversations were still fine if taken reasonably slowly, and if held with people who knew me and understood the circumstances. What was missing was the opportunity for those momentary unplanned interactions most people have with others during the course of the average day, which are so much a part of most people's lives they never even notice them. A hearing dog would clearly offer me a compensating advantage in a hearing world in which I was suffering so many disadvantages. There was definitely something in all this I needed to explore further.

Thus intrigued with the possibilities, in late September 2002 I wrote off to the charity Hearing Dogs for Deaf People ("Hearing Dogs") for their brochure and information pack. From that point forward, the well-oiled machinery at Hearing Dogs ensured matters proceeded at a clearly defined pace.

A week or so after I wrote, the brochure pack arrived. This gave me much the same information as I'd already gleaned from Sam and Sage. It was full of explanations of how hearing dogs were trained, how they can help people with hearing loss, and so on. But in particular, it contained numerous case studies of how "recipients" (as Hearing Dogs term the people who actually use their dogs) found their dogs helpful to them. People emphasised various aspects of sound work, explaining how they used the dogs for every purpose from hearing the doorbell to telling them when pans were boiling over on the stove. But the theme that was common to every recipient was the social impact of having the dog. Yes, the sound work was important, yes, they became loved and trusted friends, but most of all, the dogs enabled their recipients to connect with a world of social interaction, acting as a clear indicator of deafness, and becoming a much admired focal point for conversations with friends and strangers alike.

Encouraged, I decided to make my application. As with virtually everything else in life, there was a form to fill in! Apart from the usual bits of personal information like name, age, address and so on, it asked me to define my degree of hearing loss as mild, moderate, severe or profound. Not really knowing the technicalities, I ticked on the line between moderate and severe, and sent off the form. A week or so later, back came a letter saying a report was needed from my audiologist, since hearing dogs are only allocated to people with severe or profound hearing loss!

Over the coming weeks I awaited further news until finally towards the end of the year I heard from Hearing Dogs once again. My audiologist had confirmed my hearing loss as severe and I did indeed qualify for a dog. I would hear from Hearing Dogs again in due course, I was told, with a date for an interview.

The Interview

Over new year 2001/2, I packed myself off to California for a holiday (I'm something of a globe trotter, and the significance of this for having a dog had not escaped me). In my incarnation as a writer, John Steinbeck is something of a guru to me, and I wanted to see America's National Steinbeck Museum in Salinas, and some of the places he wrote about in Monterey and the adjacent parts of California.

By May I'd had news from Hearing Dogs and it felt as though life was picking up its heels a bit. An interview had been arranged for me. I would be visited at home for an assessment as to my suitability for a hearing dog. 23rd May 2003 saw the interviewer arrive at my flat. What, I wondered would she be looking for? I was keen to make this happen now, and wanted to put my best foot forward, as it were. I need not have worried. Kate was a charming individual, and well versed in conducting such interviews. She wanted to satisfy herself on the suitability of my hearing loss for a dog (of course) and that I fully understood what I was letting myself in for. Then there was the question of what sort of dog would best suit my life style. Some fare better in urban contexts, others in rural. Some are more exuberant and love exposure to as many people as possible, others are quieter personalities and prefer the company of fewer people. Crucially relevant is the question of whether there are any other pets in the household. Kate also wanted to discuss what sound work I would want to use the dog for and to tape the relevant sounds such as my doorbell and my telephone, so that when the time came Hearing Dogs could train the dog to those specific sounds. We settled on doorbell, telephone, smoke alarm, fire alarm at work, and cooker timer. Being a naturally early riser, I reckoned I didn't need the dog to wake me in the mornings (Intriguingly, when I started writing this passage at 7.00am this morning, Matt, was still snoozing away upstairs on his warm and comfy sheepskin! Sometimes you have to wonder who's here for whose benefit! When Kate was done, I asked if she thought I'd be accepted. She wasn't permitted to tell me on the spot, but the little wry smile she let slip gave me hope that the response might indeed be positive).

Getting Back to Work

With the first hurdle on the road to a hearing dog now cleared, my focus of attention switched during the coming weeks, as we neared the date for my formal acquisition of my ex-wife's shares in our jointly owned Nursing Home, Hurst Manor. The subject of Hearing Dogs receded to the back of my mind, as I began to get to grips with a more clearly defined personal and work-related future.

I should explain that we'd owned Hurst Manor since 1999. For a while it had been one of two care homes we'd run, but the other had been sold back in 2002, essentially because neither of us could afford to buy the other out. Regrettably, and to our joint shame, our preoccupation with the divorce had meant we'd not paid the remaining home nearly enough attention. Over the years it had grown somewhat shabby and in need of attention. The date for formal handover was set for 30th June and my honest admission is that I had butterflies over the commitment I'd made. But there again, I always do.

I consulted with my good friend, Caroline (a petite, pretty and spiritually aware lady, of an age I'm not allowed to disclose), who offered to come down to Somerset with me for a day and tell me what she thought of the place, purely as a lay person. So one day in early July we jumped into my BMW convertible, dropped the roof to take advantage of the sunshine, and headed off towards Somerset. On arrival, I parked and showed Caroline up the path to the front door of our listed Georgian manor house, rang the doorbell and swallowed hard – what would she think of what lay inside?

The door was answered by Mandy, one of our longest standing care assistants. Mandy had worked at Hurst Manor for seventeen years and was a pillar of strength to management, staff, and residents alike. Opening the door wide and standing aside, she beamed a smile at us and invited us in. "Good start," I thought, beginning to let hope of approval build. We stepped into the hallway and Caroline looked about her, gazing up at the high ceiling, the enormous doors and the wide corridor. She nodded, and looked at me enquiringly.

Out & About

We spent the next hour exploring the home. Each time we passed someone in a corridor, Caroline stopped and talked enthusiastically, endearing herself to each in turn. When we came across Matron Sue, it might as well have been love at first sight! There was an immediate rapport between them, and it was obvious the two would become firm friends. Caroline peered around every open door without imposing on the resident in the room. Upstairs, downstairs in and in several ladies chambers, she cast an enquiring eye, but all the while betrayed nothing of what she was thinking.

After a full and detailed internal inspection we headed out into the garden, for a look at our outside facilities. Then we finished up in my office, which in those days was housed in a wooden chalet in the garden. Needless to say, the chalet, like the rest of the home, had seen better days. In fact, having had a roof leak the previous year and having remained undecorated for quite a few years before that, it was in a bit of a state, to say the least. We seated ourselves down with a cup of tea and I awaited Caroline's feedback.

"Well," she started, speaking thoughtfully and choosing her words carefully, "I'll tell you what I think. When we arrived at the front door, I was struck with two things. First, the décor in the hall's a bit dowdy, but much more importantly, we were welcomed with real warmth. If I were looking for somewhere for my mum to live in her declining years, I'd be much more concerned with the quality of care she's receive than with the decorations, so I'd be paying most attention to how people behaved towards me, and the staff here are wonderful. Then we walked around the home and I began to realise that the whole place is a bit lacking and needs sprucing up. But if I were looking on behalf of mum, I'd think to myself, 'Not to worry, the people here are lovely and mum will be well looked after.' " At this point, Caroline stopped and looked me straight in the eye with a rather grave expression. "Then," she said, "I'd come over to your office to meet you, the owner. And I'd look around in here, with the ceiling stained brown with the water damage, the furniture worn out, and the whole room looking like it hadn't seen a paint brush since Florence Nightingale last visited. Then I'd think 'There's no way I can trust my mum to someone who's prepared to work in these conditions, and worse still, prepared to make his staff work in them'. So I'd thank you for your time and disappear. Then I'd go and find somewhere that I really believed would look after mum well."

Caroline sat back, smiled at me sweetly and waited for a response.

Re-birth at Hurst Manor

Oh brother! I'd asked for feedback and wow, had I got it! I turned red with embarrassment and flustered through a few words – I don't even remember now what I said to her. But I had to admit she was right and we needed to make changes. The home was not well occupied at the time and there wasn't much spare money to play with, but nevertheless, something had to be done. So the next day I went to B&Q, armed myself with paintbrushes, paint, rollers, and all manner of other decorating hardware. Then, the following weekend I arrived at the home unannounced, literally rolled up my sleeves and proceeded with the decoration of the chalet. Given that my usual work had to go on as well, it took three weeks to complete the job. And then the pristine decorations showed up the shabby carpet and furniture. So from somewhere we found the money and re-carpeted and re-furnished as well. And it was this single project that set the standard and tone for the next two years. For it's a well known fact that if you re-decorate one room in your house it shows up all the rooms that you've not done. And whilst the staff had been hugely impressed that I was prepared to roll up my sleeves and work personally on the chalet, they were keenly aware of the need for changes in the home itself.

So there and then I asked Caroline to stay and work with us in capacity of interior design consultant, and we commenced a refurbishment and development programme that started in June 2003 and continued until 2007. Month by month we worked our way steadily through the place – repainting, re-carpeting, re-furnishing and re-equipping as we went, all under the guiding hand of Caroline's colour and spatial awareness.

Living, as I do, in the New Forest, and with Hurst Manor being in Somerset, generally I needed to stay over during my visits, which in those days normally lasted for three days each week. So, for the first ten months of the refurbishment programme, until we had funds to renovate an old flat at the top of the house, I found myself sleeping on an old fold down chair on the floor of my office. The whole programme served to remind me that I had to work for a living, and I had to pull the business round if I wanted to make a living from it. But little by little, as the work proceeded and the appearance of the home began to change, we found spirits lifting amongst staff and residents alike, and the atmosphere became more and more positive. In the village people began to talk about the changes that were taking place at Hurst Manor. "Has the home changed hands?" asked the woman that ran the mobile library service when she visited. "Everyone's saying how different it is."

"No," answered Matron Sue, "But the hands that own have been doing some long overdue work!"

Dogs and Shopping

As the weeks proceeded, I gradually came to feel that I was once again on top of the business. Gradually, I began to find space in my thinking for matters unrelated to work. And a lot of the time my focus would drift to the subject of hearing dogs – would I ever hear from Hearing Dogs? How would I use a dog? Could I sensibly have a dog come to live with me in my little third floor flat?

One of the conclusions I had more or less come to already was that I could see no benefit in taking a hearing dog – should I ever finally acquire one – shopping with me. After all, what could a dog do, other than slow me down? That was until one evening when I went shopping for tiles in B&Q. It was gone 6.00pm when I arrived, and the place was virtually empty. I was browsing around the shelves, sorting out various bits and pieces I needed to buy for the refurbishment of a bathroom, when quite without warning – or so it seemed to me - I was suddenly grabbed by the arm and bundled unceremoniously out of a side door. No, I wasn't being mugged. My "assailant" was a shop assistant. Evidently, the fire alarm had gone off, and, despite the fact that I was wearing my hearing aids, I hadn't heard it. I stood around outside the store for a while as the fire drill proceeded, watching with some amusement as various members of staff in sight restrictors or wheelchairs wandered about representing disable people in need of assistance from the shop staff. I found myself wondering how they would have represented deafness if I'd not been in the store. Ironically, when I tried to tell the manager that I couldn't hear the auditory alarm, and perhaps some visual alarm system was needed, he wasn't terribly interested. After all, he had his fire drill to attend to! But nevertheless, the whole event was a salutary reminder of how little hearing I had left at certain frequencies, and how much I really would need that dog with me when he finally arrived. I drove home thoughtfully, now fully convinced that I had done the right thing in applying for a hearing dog.

Flats and Dogs and Houses and Visions

Perhaps it was that experience, or maybe it was just the passage of time, but over that summer I began thinking more about the impending arrival of my dog, and the suitability of my living arrangements. During most of my adult life I have, from time to time, been prone to dreaming significant dreams or occasionally seeing visions. For much of that time I have also practiced meditation, which I originally learned at the suggestion of my doctor, who said it would help reduce my blood pressure. Whether it ever did

I'm not sure, but I do find it has a calming and centring effect on me, sharpening my perception of what is going on around me.

One Thursday morning I was at home in the flat, meditating. Without warning a vision appeared, and a most unusual one at that. Believe this or not as you choose, but an apparition of a dog came to visit – a Springer Spaniel. Now, for those that do not experience such things I know how strange this will sound, but I can only report reality as I experience it, and on this occasion I was being visited – or so it appeared – by the spirit of a dog, whilst I was in trance. This rather large, diaphanous creature appeared on the other side of the room, sniffed the air, then walked over to me wagging its tail. Then it jumped up, placing its paws in between my legs on the sofa on which I was sitting (remember this for later). It sniffed around me just as dogs are prone to do, and I responded by talking to it and reaching out my hand to it. Then I told it to go and have a look around the flat. It bounded off inquisitively and for a few moments I waited, amused, for its return. Seeing it nose its way around, it was evident to me that a dog this size in a little flat like mine would be a problem. Assuming it to be the spirit of the dog I would be getting, I said to it "I don't think I can have you here – you're too big!" If this indeed was to be my dog I was thinking I would delay accepting it until I moved. It then sniffed me again and promptly disappeared!

Strange stuff, you may think, and you may well be right. But it did get me to thinking how far from ideal my flat was for a dog. The only real solution would be to move home. In reality I didn't regard this as too onerous a task, since when I'd moved into the flat in April 2002, some 16 months previously, I had intended to live there for only a year while I sorted out my life and direction following my divorce. The fact that I was still there in Summer 2003 was largely due to my preoccupation with the refurbishment and rejuvenation of Hurst Manor. Moving home was therefore actually quite an attractive proposition.

It was only a month or so later that I had my second vision of the year, once again while meditating. This time I saw a house, an L-shaped thatched cottage, looking down over fields, and I knew in my mind it was associated with a place called Godshill. Now, I did know a Godshill – it's at the northern end of the New Forest, close to the little country town of Fordingbridge, on the River Avon. But I had no connections with the place, and I knew of no locations in the Forest where you would have a view down a hill over open fields. The New Forest is all trees and heather land. In the seven years I'd lived in the area I had never seen a view remotely like the one in my vision. So I noted what I'd seen and carried on with the rest of my life – including some house hunting. In reality though, I wasn't very focussed on it, still being preoccupied with what was happening at work.

Got to have that dog

I was innocently pottering round the flat one morning attending to this or that largely insignificant task, when the post dropped through the letterbox. Being the nosey type, I always open the post as soon as it arrives if I possibly can, just in case I've won the lottery (which I don't do) or the premium bonds (which I don't own) or a rich uncle (which I don't have) has left me a fortune. Well, we can all dream, can't we? So there I was, working my way through the brown ones (definitely bills – put aside to open with a double strength coffee later) and the little white ones (mostly mail shots, not worth opening, but let's see just in case) to the big white ones (definitely junk mail selling gas fired artichokes or guaranteed return investment bonds in the Strangeways stock market). Eventually I reached the bottom of the pile of big white ones and tore open the last envelope. I extracted a pile of papers including a covering letter which was upside down. As I turned it round to read it, out of the pack dropped a photograph which froze me to the spot. It was a picture of a dog. My next thought was:

Got to have that dog.

Black and white and seated obligingly for the photographer he gave exactly the impression you'd get of small boy having his first school photo taken, tie badly knotted, collar open and cap on lopsided. The appeal was overwhelming.

GOT TO HAVE THAT DOG.

His head was slightly to one side and his lip seemed to curl up in a wise-guy kind of smile that said "I'm on best behaviour – please adopt me.

GOT TO HAVE THAT DOG!!!!!

I was riveted to the floor. I stood there motionless for a few minutes just staring at the photograph. At this stage I couldn't think straight enough to read the letter. But I presumed that I was being offered a chance for this endearing scruffy urchin of delight to become my hearing dog. And from that point forward it was exactly like falling in love. Nothing whatsoever else mattered. I had

GOT TO HAVE THAT DOG!!!!!!!!!!!!

Finally I managed to get myself back into a normal state of self-management and I read the letter. It started:

"We are pleased to enclose a photo of Matt, an eleven month old Spaniel Type Mongrel We would like you to come here to The Grange Training Centre, to meet him at 11.00am on Monday 8th March 2004. The rest was routine administrative stuff about how matters would move forward after we met, assuming we both liked each other. It felt like a dating agency had just arranged for me to meet a woman whose picture had left me completely bowled over! I re-read the letter several times, tying to get my head around the practicalities. They were wholly beyond me at that moment. All I knew was the effect that the picture of this little creature was having on me. And if his personality turned out to be anywhere near similar to that implied in the picture, I'd be prepared to do whatever it took – and I do mean WHATEVER – to ensure he came home to live with me. So yeah, you could say I was just a tad smitten.

Later that day – in fact quite a bit later when I'd calmed down – I thought again of my vision. Matt wasn't actually a Spaniel, but he was referred to in the letter as "Spaniel-type." So what was the connection, and what was the vision all about anyway? I filed the question away in pending until I'd actually met the dog.

The letter had arrived on a Friday towards the end of February. At least I had the weekend to get back into a normal frame of mind before going to work on the Monday. But when Monday came I (of course) took the photo to work with me. To each of my closer colleagues I told the same story. I'd fallen in love over the weekend. We'd not met – I'd only seen a picture, but it was love at first sight and I was sure this was THE ONE. When I showed the picture to Brenda, our Training Manager, she was as smitten as I was. She grabbed it out of my hands and put it straight into the photocopier. The resultant copy was immediately mounted on the wall in front of her desk where it resides to this day. I tried the same ploy on Caroline. Before I finished she squealed "It's a dog!" jumped at me and threw her arms around me. From everyone's behaviour you'd honestly have thought that I'd truly just got engaged, such was the power of the image of Matt. I made absolutely no provision at all for the possibility that he might not be at all like his picture or that – horror of horrors – he might not like me! But nevertheless, this was how it was – I was now living in anticipation of meeting Matt. And in my time habitual worrisome fashion, I began to think of all the things that might go wrong. Hearing Dogs might give him to someone else after all; they might say I couldn't have him in the flat and re-allocate him by the time I'd moved (I resolved to phone the solicitor and make matters happen faster); I might not cope with the training. The list of worries built steadily until everyone around me was close to screaming point with me. "Will you please shut up about that dog. It's gonna be fine!" was the pretty constant theme of the next two weeks.

Matching Matt

Slowly and painfully, creaking and groaning, the time inched forward to the day when Matt and I were to meet. Having read the information pack through several times, I was now aware that this was a serious and crucial step in the process of my receiving a hearing dog.

Hearing Dogs go to enormous lengths to match the right dog to the right recipient. During the year while I had been waiting as patiently as I could while my name had gradually been making its way up the waiting, list a great deal had been going on. Naturally, a whole lot of other people were way ahead of me on the list. Each in their turn, they were all having their circumstances considered and having suitable dogs located and allocated. In fact, I'm told that quite a few people at Hearing Dogs have a hand in the allocation process. Essentially, they're looking for a lifestyle and personality fit. And now it became clear as to why all those questions were asked at my first interview about what I do with my time, how and where I work, what my left inside leg measurement is (not really, just kidding). For obvious reasons, not all dogs are suited to all environments. Your naturally quiet and retiring dog isn't going to take too well to a recipient whose life is lived actively around town, on and off trains, on and off buses, in and out of offices or shops. Of course, having monitored the dogs closely from the point at which they are accepted for training, the selectors know them well. But they know us, the recipients, less well and must glean the information they need about us from that first interview and the questions they asked, to which the answers were so meticulously recorded.

So how, you might wonder, do dogs get accepted for training as hearing Dogs in the first place? Many come from rescue centres and are selected for their level intelligence and suitability of temperament – as well, of course, as their hearing! Others are donated by, for example, breeders, and come under the care of Hearing Dogs from a very early age. A few, as turned out to be the case with Matt, are bred specifically for the characteristics of particular combination of breeds. I was later to find out that Matt was a cross between a Cocker Spaniel (chosen for intelligence and capacity to be trained) and a Havaneese (chosen for the non-moulting coat and also intelligence). Spaniels are well known as a breed, of course, but Havaneese less so in this country. The breed is regarded as South American, developed from dogs taken to Havana by Dutch traders and merchants. Relatively unusual in the UK, they are a similar size to small terriers and have characteristically flat faces. Once I'd made the connection, one of the features of the combination that came to intrigue me was that crossing a Spaniel with a terrier sized breed gets you a dog that's considerably smaller than a

Spaniel. And of course, there was that little matter of my strange experience in the flat when I'd told the doggy apparition who visited that he was too big for me to have in the flat…. I'll leave you to make of that whatever you will.

A Havaneese bitch had been donated to Hearing Dogs and they had decided to breed from her some time back. In fact, Matt was from the third litter of Havaneese cross that they'd bred, having found the two previous litters extremely successful. So it was that at seven weeks of age, and completely unbeknown to me, Matt was allocated to his socialisers, Brian and Wendy. He was to spend the next six months with them.

Puppy Days

Brian, Wendy and their teenage daughter Lynn live in Luton. They had become socialisers for Hearing Dogs after seeing a demonstration of the work of a Hearing Dog at a local dog show several years earlier. In fact by the time Matt came to them, they'd been acting as socialisers for over three years. Indeed, by the time I finally got to meet them and thank them, they had been doing the job for over five years. Matt was the tenth dog they'd worked with, but only the second that Hearing Dogs had actually taken on for further training following socialisation – a clear indication of the very high standards that Hearing Dogs have to achieve at every stage in the process of their training. Indeed, because the standards are so high, there's always a long waiting list of people wanting to take these "Fallen Angels" that, for one reason or another, are not suitable for onward training.

The puppy socialisation process is considerably more than simply baby-sitting a young dog until it reaches an appropriate age to be trained. Socialisers have to follow a closely specified programme of activity over a fourteen week period to ensure that the growing puppy is exposed to a wide range of circumstances, varying from visits to the home by adults and children, through walking along a street without becoming frightened by the traffic, to remaining calm in crowds. In addition they attend puppy classes at The Grange, where the basic training disciplines (sit, walk, stand, stay, come, etc.) are instilled into the dog. The ultimate objective is to ensure as far as possible that the puppy grows up to be a confident dog and therefore able to be placed in a variety of different circumstances. All this, of course, is in addition to the basic requirements of acting as host family and enjoying and loving him (considerable fun) and teaching house training (not nearly so much fun).

Brain, Wendy and Lynn had worked diligently through the programme with Matt for fourteen weeks, finally handing him back a little sadly for his sound work training which was to last a further sixteen weeks at The Grange. Thus, by the time Matt reached 37 weeks of age, he had been in training for the whole of his life bar the first seven weeks! I was to meet him when he reached eleven months of age.

Meeting Matt

Between the arrival of the letter on 27th February inviting me to The Grange and 8th March when I was due there, I was like a kid waiting for Christmas – only there was no advent calendar to open each day. So instead I plagued friends and colleagues with "Only five days to go... only three days to go," until everyone around me was bored silly. But when the choruses of "Shut up, Michael" flew my way, all I had to do was smile sweetly and flash *that picture* at the assembled multitude and all concerned would swoon in besotted happiness, controlled by the strange spell cast by this remarkable creature's photograph.

Eventually, 8th March arrived and I set off bright and early from the Forest for The Grange at Princes Risborough. As I drew nearer and nearer, my nervousness increased. Would they decide he wasn't suitable for me for some reason I couldn't be aware of?

got to have that dog

Would they decide not to allocate me a dog until I was settled in a new home?

got to have that dog

Would they decide he hadn't reacted positively enough to me quickly enough?

GOT TO HAVE THAT DOG!!!!!!!!!

And so the list of implausible reasons why I might not be allocated my already beloved Matt lengthened, until I finally pulled up in the drive and switched off the engine.

Looking around me, I took in the sights of what The Grange is all about. Originally a farm of 27 acres, it had been the subject of much development over the years. To the original 16th century farmhouse had been added numerous other blocks to accommodate the rapidly growing organisation. As I was later to be told, the site contained several staff houses, a restaurant block, four training houses, a kennel block, a reception and administration building and a training block. Indeed while I was there, the construction of yet another new building was underway that was to house recipients who were at the Grange for training as – unbeknown to me at this time – I would shortly be.

As I made my way from the car park to reception, the busyness of the place made itself felt. From one side came someone with a dog on a lead, smiling a "Good morning" at me. In the corner of the car park the tail gate of an estate car was open revealing several dogs in the back. From out of the restaurant emerged two young women in sweatshirts sporting the Hearing Dogs logo – trainers returning from coffee break no doubt. If I'd not known before, by the time I left the car park it would have been impossible to miss the fact that this was a seriously doggie-orientated organisation.

Reception was housed in a sympathetically designed barn-type building clad in black wood. Evidently Hearing Dogs had gone to considerable trouble to retain the character of the site they were expanding – that or the Planning Department were as tough on them as they are on the rest of us! I opened the plate glass door, and slipped round it, feeling strangely out of place and full of anticipation. From behind a high reception desk a lady receptionist looked up and smiled. "Can I help you?" came the traditional greeting.

"Hi there, I said," trying to make myself feel more confident. "I'm Michael, here for a first Meeting with Matt."

The woman looked down at her pad for a moment. Oh yes, she said, you're meeting Fiona. I'll call over for her now. Please take a seat." She motioned to several comfortable looking armchairs behind me. As I awaited the arrival of Fiona, my eye was caught by a video running in the corner of various aspects of the work of Hearing Dogs. A selector was being interviewed on the tape, discussing how he went about choosing appropriate dogs from the rescue centre. He was playing with a little terrier cross as he explained how he looked for potential candidates with intelligent, enquiring minds and good hearing. As he talked to the camera he pressed a little squeaker of the type you'd find in a child's soft toy. It was hidden in his hand and the dog was going near crazy with inquisitiveness, trying to work out what was making the noise. The selector concluded to the camera that yes, he would probably accept this charming little fellow for training. But even then nothing was guaranteed, for Hearing Dogs eventually reject and re-house about 50% of the dogs they initially accept for training. I was also later to learn that the innocent looking little squeaker that was engendering so much interest from the dog would be crucial to its later training.

My preoccupation with the video was broken by a touch on the shoulder and a "Good morning, Michael." I looked up a little surprised, having become completely absorbed in what I was watching. Standing before me was a slightly built young woman in her early twenties. "I'm Fiona," she continued, "and I'm going to introduce you to Matt. If you're ready, would you like to come with me to the restaurant for a cup of coffee?"

'My kinda way to start an interview,' I thought as we made our way over to the restaurant block. When we were settled down inside the bright and airy refectory, Fiona proceeded to tell me how we would be spending the morning. The first priority, she explained, would be for me to meet Matt and spend some time alone with him. Assuming that went well enough, I would then get to take him for a walk in the grounds and fields of the farm, all owned by Hearing Dogs and used extensively for walking and training the dogs. Then I'd have a chance to see a demonstration of training in order to give me an idea of how my own training with Matt would be conduced. At the end of all that, we'd then have a final discussion about how the day had gone and a decision would be taken as to whether Matt would be the dog for me. I tried not to show my tension, but the last time I'd felt like this was when I was seventeen and being interviewed for a place at Oxford University. I truly could remember nothing in my life before that I had wanted as much as I wanted a positive decision that would lead to that little dog coming to live with me... and I'd still not even met him yet!

"Well, if you're ready..." came Fiona's voice, breaking my distant train of thought and bringing me abruptly back into the room. It truly was now or never. On the edge of an experience that would change my life for ever, I was just as tense with the anticipation of what it would mean as I was with the possibility of it not proceeding at all for some unfathomable reason. As we left the restaurant and made our way over to the training houses I could feel my heart rate rising.

Fiona opened the front door of one of the houses and showed me into a lightly furnished lounge. When we were seated she continued. "Ok, I'm about to go and get Matt. You may find when he arrives that he's not terribly interest in you at first. Dogs bond with their trainers, and he's likely to show a preference for me. But don't worry about that. If this all goes ahead as we're all hoping, within a week or so of you starting training with him he'll have fully bonded with you. Really, there's nothing to worry about."

'Uh huh,' I thought. I wish I had a fiver for every time I'd heard that phrase before.

"Now," Fiona continued, you just hold onto these." She passed me a handful of small pieces of what looked to me like dried dog food.

"What is it?" I asked, somewhat distastefully. I wasn't used to handling doggie stuff. Clearly there were adjustments to be made!

"Special treats," she answered. "Matt loves his food." How right she later turned out to be. "When he comes in you can attract his attention with the treats." It sounded like a sensible enough strategy. So off Fiona went to retrieve Matt, while I sat by the fire, feeling like a prospective bridegroom awaiting a first meeting that was expected to lead to an arranged marriage.

A few minutes later she returned. The door opened and round it came a small black and white dog, about eighteen inches at the shoulder, with long floppy ears like a Spaniel's but a squarer, flatter face, more like a terrier. His tail was held high in alertness and he was straining at the leash to find out what might be new and interesting inside the house. He caught sight of me and tugged 'til Fiona was inside the door. She shut it carefully to bar his exit should he be minded to make a bid for freedom. Then looking at me to make sure I was ready, she released him from the leash. He made an immediate dive across the room for me, jumped up putting his front paws on my knees (remember that vision?) and sniffed all over me. I giggled. "Hello Matt." I said. He lifted his face towards mine. A long tongue flopped out of his mouth and he gave a pretty good imitation of a grin back at me. I stroked him and fondled his head and ears. Satisfied I had nothing else of interest to offer, he then made a bee-line back to Fiona.

"OK," she said, "call him back, then tell him to sit while raising your hand like this." She held her hand out, palm upwards, and lifted it about six inches in a clear unequivocal motion. "When you've got him sitting, offer him a treat."

That sounded straightforward enough for even me to manage. "Come here Matt," I said, holding out my hand in the prescribed manner. To my amazement he did exactly as asked. I offered him one of the bits of food. Now, that clearly made all the difference to the level of interest I offered as defined by Matt! He nuzzled my hand and I opened my palm. The treat was quickly gone. He looked around for another, so I gave him a second. Then, satisfied there was no more food to be had, my rating on his interest-ometer fell back to zero. He rushed immediately back to Fiona again, where she stood watching with interest and amusement on the other side of the room. With her encouragement I called him back again, going through the same sitting procedure. He returned again for another treat. And so we continued with this game over the next few minutes, his natural bond with his trainer giving way to the bribe of food, only to become his dominant driver as soon as the food was gone..

Fiona was satisfied that things were going well enough to move to the next stage. "Right," she said. "I'm going to leave you alone with him for about half an hour to see how you get on. Don't be surprised if he cries for me when I'm gone. That's quite normal. He'll bond with you soon enough. I promise." She offered me another handful of treats which I could use to keep Matt amused, and then slipped out of the door when he wasn't looking. But as soon as she closed it behind her, he rushed to it and jumped up at it, immediately distressed, whining and crying for her.

"Look Matt!" I said, trying to sound enthusiastic. I held out another treat and he dutifully came trotting back. We went through the 'sit' routine again and he looked up expectantly for his treat. As soon as it was gone he made another rush for the door, pining for Fiona. I wasn't much encouraged, despite Fiona's confidence that this would change as soon as he got to know me. And so the next ten minutes continued in precisely in this vein. He'd run for the door and cry. I'd encourage him back with a 'sweetie.' As soon as said sweetie was consumed he'd revert to pining mode and sit forlornly at the door waiting for Fiona to return. Writing this now in full knowledge that he tends to do exactly the same when I'm away from him, it seems not in the least strange that he should have exhibited such behaviour. But at that time I was as new as it was possible to be around dogs, and virginally inexperienced. My concern that he didn't like me and possibly never would, was crushing. After ten minutes all the sweeties were gone and he showed absolutely no interest in me whatsoever. His only wish was for the return of his beloved trainer. When she finally did come back

and walked through the door I must have looked crestfallen.
She didn't even stop to ask how we'd got on. "Oh dear, she
said," seeing the look on my face. "Well, I did tell you this
might happen. But don't worry it will soon pass. In fact, next
week I'm moving up to Hearing Dogs' training centre in
Yorkshire, so a colleague of mine, Hannah, will take over his
training here. By the time you next meet Matt he will be as
bonded with Hannah as he is now with me."

'Fine,' I thought. 'Just so long as you don't mark us
down for this.' I was still determined to make this
relationship work.

GOT TO HAVE THAT DOG!!!!!!!!!

The rest of the day passed in similar fashion. I had an
opportunity to walk Matt around the fields and to spend a
little more time with him on my own. Then all too soon our
allocated time together was over, and he was returned to
kennels while I went to see a demonstration of how trained
Hearing Dogs undertook their sound work. Finally, with the
afternoon drawing to a close, Fiona and I returned to the
training house where I'd first met Matt. I was surprisingly
tired from the newness of it all – a foretaste of what was to
come.

It was crunch time. Fiona by now would have made
up her mind as to whether Hearing Dogs was willing to move
forward with my training and Matt's placement with me. I
needed to know the verdict. We sat down and I looked
enquiringly at her. "Well?" I asked. "Do you think we're
going to be OK together?" I awaited her response with bated
breath.

"Oh yes, she said casually, I'm sure it will be fine.
Assuming you're happy to proceed, I'm content that your
relationship with Matt will work out fine, and we'd like you
to come here for training with him."

I held on tight inside, afraid to show too much of a reaction. "Wonderful." I said, finally. "When do we start?"

"We'd like you to come here for a week's training on 19th April," she answered. "Then you'll get to take him home for a weekend, and a Placement Officer will come to work with you at your home the following week. We just need you to sign some papers to confirm you can afford to insure him and that you understand that you'll never actually own Matt." I'd known all along that Hearing Dogs always retains legal ownership of its dogs in case of the extremely unlikely eventuality that one of them is mistreated and has to be withdrawn. It was one factor that made me a little uneasy about getting close to and emotionally involved with a particular dog, but I did understand the thinking and accepted that it was reasonable. Besides, by that stage, frankly, I'd have been prepared to sign anything short of a confession of matricide to ensure Matt came to live with me. His magic spell over me had not weakened despite his lack of interest in me. I trusted that in time I'd be able to win his affection…

GOT TO HAVE THAT DOG!!!!!!!!!!!

The Oaks

With all now proceeding well with regard Matt, it was back to the drawing board in terms of finding somewhere for us to live. And now that I actually had a date for bringing Matt home, what would be the effect of a delay? I'd skirted round the issue when I'd visited Hearing Dogs for that first meeting, in fear that my 'almost-no-fixed-abode' status would bring the matter to an abrupt close. When I finally came clean on the subject would they tell me I couldn't have him unless I had somewhere suitable to live? Would they want to postpone letting me have a dog until I was settled in a new house, in which case would I be allocated some other dog? My heart was lurching at the prospect of losing him – pretty strange behaviour considering we had only just met and that I had little idea of what life with him would be like. Of course, the best solution to all of this would be to have found a house by the time I next visited The Grange for my week's training with Matt and to have a firm moving date. That would minimise the chance of this becoming a terminal issue.

That Friday, somewhat in trepidation, I bought the newspaper which carried house sale ads for the northern part of the New Forest – now my preferred location. I flicked past dozens of ads for houses old and new, large and small, nothing particularly grabbing my attention. Then - and you know how this goes if you've ever bought a house – I turned the page and froze (yup, freezing was getting to be a pretty regular experience for me). Sitting unassumingly on the page and looking out innocently at me was an L-shaped thatched house. My eye dropped to the wording of the ad. Could it…? Might it be possible….? Was it at all feasible that it was in Godshill? I read the text over slowly. "New Forest, Godshill" The house in the ad cocked its head to one side, raised its eyebrows and smiled enquiringly at me.

"Now lets not get tooooo excited here." I thought. You're a house and you happen to be L-shaped. And err… by the way… you're twice the price I can afford."

The house looked disappointed, but didn't say anything. It just kept looking at me in a sulky kind of a way. I looked back, desperate to allow myself to believe that this could be happening. I looked at the top of the page where the agent's details were listed. Seeing a web site reference I rushed into my study and typed in the "www…." Sure enough the agent's site came up. I typed in the house details. Up came the full particulars… starting with a picture taken from a location some distance back from the house and clearly up a hill… and the hill continued down past the house… to open fields in which horses were grazing. The house cocked its head to one side once more, smiled at me again and said "Vision?" in an enquiring tone. For the second time I was smitten. Now, lest you get the wrong impression, I'm not really the kind of guy who gets smitten terribly often. I prefer to think of myself as poised and controlled, the very epitome of the cool, clear thinking businessman, a powerful force to be reckoned with, lest anyone should think to under-estimate me. Ok, so maybe I need to do some self-re-evaluation when it comes to dogs… and houses… and maybe some other stuff as well. All right you've got me. I admit it. I'm a fully paid up card carrying member of the Softies Club. And long may it last.

I took the elevator down to cloud eight and read through the agent's particulars of the house. 'It is difficult to know how to describe The Oaks," began the blurb. "Delightful; unusual; wonderful; it certainly is all of these, but also so very much more.' I nodded, and stuffed my lolling tongue back into my mouth. A thorough reading of the details wafted me gently down to about cloud four and half where precipitations of reality commenced, making me realise that The Oaks was *far* too big for me. Then I went into free fall, hitting ground level in the middle of an emotional hailstorm when I looked at the price again.

"Buy me," smiled the house when I'd picked myself up, rubbing my elbows.

"Can't," I answered, "Aint got the dosh."

"**Buy me**," the house repeated insistently.

"Ok, here's what I'm prepared to do," I replied, going into my 'I'm-a-cold-hearted-businessman-in-negotiations' mode. "I'll come pay you a visit, and when we're both agreed that you're totally unsuitable for a single man…

"A single man *and* a dog," interrupted the house.

"..and when we're both agreed that you're totally unsuitable for a single man *and a dog*," I continued, "We'll shake hands and agree to go our separate ways. OK"

"Deal," said the house, smiling knowingly, in that way women do when they've made you think you've got your own way but really you're doing exactly what they want you to.

I phoned the agent and arranged a viewing for 29th March 2004.

The date duly arrived, and I left home early for the agreed appointment, knowing that I might have some difficulty finding the house. Making my way across the open heather land, I took the road leading down under the A31 and watched the traffic whizzing over the top of me as I entered the northern section of the Forest. It wasn't exactly foreign territory to me, but the A31 is a very definite boundary running East to West across the Forest, and up until then my life had been lived very much to the south of that boundary. There was something refreshing and new about entering into this rather more secluded and less tourist-frequented area.

Finding the village of Godshill was a matter of following maps and road signs, but you have to make sure you don't blink or you'd miss it. Downtown Godshill consists of about three and three quarters houses plus the Sandy Balls holiday park (alias the Fleshpots of Godshill), which also boasts the one and only shop in the village. Finding the house was much harder. Eventually, having circled the area several times and still not managed to make sense of the agent's directions, I phoned and asked for the telephone number of the owners so as to get correct instructions 'from the horse's mouth,' so to speak. With some considerable reluctance (presumably lest we somehow do a deal without him and thus avoid his commission), the agent relinquished the phone number. I dialled, and a friendly voice answered the phone (if you're wondering how I cope with the phone given my deafness, the answer is that I have specially adapted telephones with modified amplifiers – doesn't do much for the privacy of phone calls to have your conversation blaring out at 30 decibels and audible to everyone within three hundred paces, but it achieves the objective of communication!). The friendly sounding voice provided the correct directions, with the result that I soon found myself driving up a narrow, bumpy forest track to a location I'd never have found on my own. The Oaks was certainly secluded – definitely a plus point in my estimation.

Parking on open Forest land behind the house, I got out of the car and made my way to the gate, where I stood staring down over the garden and the valley sloping away beyond it, similar to but not precisely the same as in my vision. I was confused – was this the image I'd seen the previous summer or not? At the gate, I was greeted by the owner, who introduced himself as Barry, together with two large golden retrievers. Clearly the house was suitable for dogs! Barry and I shook hands and I said, "Just one question before we get started. Why would anyone want to leave here?" The question was justified. This was the archetypal rural idyll – a beautiful, part thatched cob cottage with a range of outbuildings on a large site, lost deep in a part of the New Forest that attracted relatively few tourist visitors. Life really didn't get any better than this.

Barry's answer was straightforward. "We've been here twenty-two years now," he said in a considered tone. "We're older than we were, and its time we moved somewhere a little easier. Besides, our daughter wants us to move closer to Salisbury so we can be on hand for babysitting!" The answer was as justified as the question. No worries about potential hidden dangers raised their ugly heads.

Within ten minutes Barry and his wife Annette had invited me in and we were chatting animatedly about dogs and the Forest and deafness and reincarnation – as, of course, one does with prospective vendors. ☺

We ended the afternoon by taking a walk around the immediate Forest area that surrounded the house. We walked along the side of the valley, with the hills rolling upwards to one side and the grassland dropping away below us to a bridge crossing a little stream on the valley floor on the other. It was the perfect image of an ancient river valley and I could easily visualise the mighty waters crashing and rushing down to the sea, all those millions of years ago, across the very spot where The Oaks now lay. I mused upon the briefness of our time here. But for the time we were here, it was delightful, and I could see that both Barry and Annette would find it hard to leave this wonderful area. At the garden gate we shook on the principle of the deal, and I left.

Leaving Barry at the garden gate, I initially returned to the car. Then I thought better of it and climbed the hill behind the house. Even on that late March morning the ground was still mushy with the winter rains, but not sufficiently so to prevent me climbing up to the point where the estate agent had taken his photo for the particulars. I looked down for a long time – for a very long time – on precisely the view that I had seen in my vision the previous summer.

Waiting for training

From that point forward, life took on a kind of 'phoney war' status. I knew that I had to go on living in my little flat until the transaction on the Oaks was completed, including survey, searches and the various other legal and financial formalities were finished that always accompany buying a house. At work we were proceeding at the usual pace of two steps forward and one and three quarters back, towards completing the renovations and getting ready to start the new building work that would complete the rejuvenation project I had taken on. And in addition to all that, of course, there was the looming prospect of my visiting The Grange in the second half of April for my week's training with Matt. In truth, this was where my attention was really focussed when it wasn't fixed on some specific piece of work that needed doing in conjunction either with the business or the house transaction.

The days slipped slowly past, inching their way towards the 19th April when I would go to train with Matt in The Grange in Princes Risborough. I wasn't the only one who was excited. At work we had now succeeded in building a closely-knit management team all of whose members were as much friends as they were colleagues. Several of my friends there had taken photocopies of the photo of Matt that I'd brought to work with me, and those photocopies were now adorning various desks around the building. As I went about my daily activities I'd get regular comments like, "Not long to go now," or "Just another few days," and "Are you excited?" coming from every corner of the building. I was indeed excited, but I was getting to the point where I wished I could go and get on with the blessed training and get everyone to shut up about it!

By Monday of the Appointed week I'd taken a quiet weekend to prepare myself for my visit to The Grange, reading my joining instructions and buying every conceivable item I could think of that I might need whilst away. Then once again I stepped into the car and headed off, this time up the motorway to Princes Risborough.

As I passed the sign that announced that I'd arrived at The Grange, home of Hearing Dogs for Deaf People, I tried to put all other thoughts out of my mind. For the next few days I needed all my concentration for the learning I was about to try to absorb.

Training at The Grange

In truth, though I'd received joining instructions some weeks before, I had little idea of how my week at the Grange was going to be spent. In particular I had no concept of the incredibly steep learning curve that I was about to face and the number of times during the week I would feel like dropping out through frustration. As far as I was concerned, when I arrived at 11.00am on Monday morning I was going to spend a relatively relaxed, relatively quiet week with a few very earnest, doggy-type people getting to know a new doggie. It all seemed a bit over the top, truth to tell. 'Well,' I thought, 'they need to keep it all professional of course, but I really can't see what all the fuss is about.' Uh huhhh. It would take me significantly less than twenty-four hours to find out.

I went through the déjà-vu experience of parking the car, smiling 'hellos' to the various people passing busily about the site and announcing my arrival at reception. By this time Fiona, who had been Matt's trainer when I had come to visit the first time, had handed over to Hannah, whom I had met briefly on my previous visit. I waited in reception for her to come and collect me. I remembered Hannah as a slightly built young lady in her early 20s, with short dark hair and a serious, reserved disposition. I guessed that it would hardly be surprising if a significant proportion of people who worked for an organisation such as Hearing Dogs were drawn more to the company of animals than to that of people. Hannah soon appeared in reception and walked me over to the old farmhouse that I'd noticed on my previous visit. This was to be my home for the next five days. "I'll let you get settled in," she said, "then I'll come back at say, 12.00 and we can discuss what's going to happen."

'Fine,' I thought, 'we're clearly going to take this week at a pretty relaxed pace!' Off Hannah went, leaving me with Vici the housekeeper who showed me to a bedroom. The farmhouse was sixteenth century and really looked the part – low ceilings supported by gnarled oak beams, inglenook fireplaces with hundreds of years of soot at the back, little winding staircases behind secret panel doors – you'd pay a fortune to stay there as a holiday home – but there again, this was no holiday! There would be various comings and goings by others during the week, Vici explained to me, but I'd be the only person staying at the farmhouse for the whole time – except of course for Matt!

Hannah returned an hour later, weighed down with an odd assortment of items – a large bag of dog food, a weighing scale, a maroon dog coat with an odd looking dog lead attached to it and an extending lead – but no dog! We sat down in the enormous beamed lounge in front of the inglenook and shared a coffee, while she explained how we would spend the week. Shortly I would meet Matt again, then after lunch we would commence sound training. A little later in the day I'd then receive instructions in how to deal with Matt overnight. Tuesday would be devoted to further sound work and a visit into High Wycombe to begin to get me used to taking Matt around towns. Then on the Tuesday evening my elder daughter, Naomi, who suffered from dog phobia, was due to visit us for her first meeting with Matt. Wednesday would be devoted to more sound work (I was getting the idea that this sound work stuff was pretty high on the agenda), some instructions on grooming, and an appointment with the photographer. Unusually, on Thursday I'd need to change trainers, and a lady called Nikki would take over, because Hannah was shortly to leave the organisation. With Nikki, Matt and I would then take a train trip as well as doing more sound work. Finally, on Friday we'd finish up with (yup, you've guessed it) more sound work and lunch in a restaurant. After lunch, all being well, Matt and I would get to go home together.

Well, there was quite a bit to get through, but none of it sounded too complicated and I was assured that there would be many breaks in the programme and chances to absorb the learning. "So," said Hannah, "If you're ready, I'll go and get Matt." This was it. Training was about to start in earnest.

First Meeting at The Grange

Just a few moments later, around the edge of the door came the little black and white form with which I was already familiar, straining at the leash and panting with excitement to discover what new and exciting distractions might be inside the room. With Hannah in tow behind him, Matt made an immediate beeline for me and, just as he had done on my last visit, jumped up and gave me a comprehensive licking. "Hello Matt," I said. He showed no real signs of recognition though, and in a few moments I was discarded as being of far less interest than the various toys that he had already discovered lurking in the corner of the room.

While Matt busied himself with high priority matters, Hannah explained the various items she had brought for me.

The dog food was obvious, but the weighing scales less so. "You need to feed him twice a day," she said. "Make it as close to 8.00am and 6.00pm as you can, and give him 90 grams of the dried dog food. He shouldn't need anything else and if you over feed him you'll find his weight will go up." That was all pretty clear. Hannah then proceeded to show me how to put Matt into the maroon jacket. On the side it read "Hearing Dogs for Deaf People – in training. It reminded me of the L-plates on my first trip out as a learner driver back when I was seventeen! The lead, or halte collar as it is called, was more complex though. Hannah explained that it was a specially developed dog leash that went over the dog's face. Although it didn't hurt him, it afforded considerably more control in directing him than a simple lead attached to a neck collar would do. "You'll notice a change in his behaviour when we put this on him," said Hannah. She then proceeded to show me how to slip the halte collar over Matt's snout and attach it with the clasp at the back of his neck. Though it was clearly not his favourite piece of equipment, he showed little resistance. When that was on, we put the jacket on him while Matt waited patiently. Then it all came off again to give me an opportunity to try putting it on myself. The coat was no challenge, fastening with rip zips on his flank and under his chin. But the halte collar was more difficult than it looked. Though Matt stood patiently throughout the process that was very evidently familiar to him, I fumbled about, all fingers and thumbs, becoming more and more irritated at my own inability to execute a seemingly simple task. I looked helplessly at Hannah.

"Don't worry," she said. "You'll soon get the hang of it. Everything's new at the moment and you just need to give it a little time." Finally I succeeded in attaching the halte collar, somewhat chastened by my own clumsiness. It was to be a continuing problem for some weeks to come, with the result that I tended to avoid using it unless absolutely necessary.

Clearly all this was familiar territory to Matt, though. When I finally had him properly attired in full dress uniform he looked uncannily professional, standing poised and sober, waiting for instructions. All his normal exuberance had completely disappeared the moment he went into uniform. The training that he had received for all but the first six weeks of his now thirteen month life positively glowed through his alert, professional stance. For, though whilst under other circumstances he was a perfectly normal and highly ebullient puppy, when put into his formal uniform he suddenly became professional – mild mannered Matt Kent had changed into Superdog, so to speak!

"We'll walk him over to the training house in uniform to give you a chance to get used to controlling him," said Hannah. As we left the farmhouse for the few yards walk to the training house, I felt strange and conspicuous. Matt, of course, was perfectly behaved, and did not so much as stop to sniff the grass or pay attention to the various dogs and people we passed on our way. When we arrived I was shown into one of a series of timber fronted terraced houses built on the site for the purposes of training the dogs in different home environments. The one we were to use was sparsely furnished with odd sofa and chairs, a largely empty kitchen and a bed or two. It felt decidedly little eerie, being a house that was never intended to be anyone's home. There was no time to focus on how it felt though, as we were to get straight down to business.

When I'd first been interviewed by Hearing Dogs, the interviewer had taken recordings of various sounds around my flat, to ensure that the dog eventually allocated to me could be trained to my specific sound needs. When I'd visited The Grange for my first meeting with Matt we'd agreed on the sounds on which he would actually be trained. Hearing

Dogs will cope with up to eight different sounds if you need that many. With Fiona's help I'd settled on my home telephone, my door bell, a cooker timer, a standard smoke alarm and the fire alarm at work. In addition, we had agreed that Matt would be trained to respond to a call. Now it was time to begin to put his training on all those sounds to the test and – equally importantly, to teach me how to work with him in his recognition of those sounds.

Hannah first got me to remove Matt's uniform – no problems there – taking the halte collar off was much easier than putting it on! Then she asked me to sit in the lounge and handed me a little plastic squeaking device, like the ones used by the dog selector I had seen on the video in reception when I first visited The Grange. Hannah explained that this was the first sound that the dogs were trained on, and that they never forgot it. So, if I ever found Matt reluctant to respond to a sound, I was advised to use the squeaker to encourage him. "Take some pieces of food to use as a reward," she said, "and press the squeaker. He should alert you, by putting his bottom on the floor and both paws on your knee. He should stay there till you release him," she explained.

I did as I was told. Squeaking the squeaker got precisely the planned response – but for Hannah, not for me! Quite naturally, since Hannah had trained him all these weeks, Matt started out by wanting to alert her to the sound of the squeaker. She shook her head and motioned towards me. Matt soon got the idea. When I pressed the squeaker again, he immediately dropped back onto his hind legs next to me, then lowered his bottom to the floor, putting his front paws around my knee, looking straight up into my face for reward and instruction. I was elated and amazed at how it was possible to instil desired behaviour in a dog through training, I rewarded him with a piece of food. "Good boy," I said warmly, meaning it completely, for I was truly impressed with what he'd done. We tried this a couple more times until Hannah was satisfied that Matt and I were working properly together.

"OK," she said, "that seems fine. Now let's try him with the cooker timer." I'd already been told that I could use this little device to time just about anything – there was no reason it should be restricted to cooking. I'd even been told that one recipient set his cooker timer when his train left Waterloo at the end of the working day. He then went to sleep, so that his dog would wake him just before they pulled into his home station! I was not prone to sleeping on trains and had no applications for the device that I could immediately think of, but it nevertheless seemed a pretty useful implement to have around – maybe for, err… cooking?

We set the timer first for thirty seconds, showing both the device itself and a treat to Matt. Then we watched while the seconds ticked away. When the thirty seconds had elapsed, the device bleeped. Matt's response was instant. He immediately followed the established routine of dropping onto his back legs, bottom on the floor, with front paws around my knee. I rewarded him again with praise and an item of food, genuinely impressed with his capabilities once more. "What is it?" I asked him, opening my arms in an enquiring gesture on Hannah's instruction. Immediately he ran to the cooker timer making sure I was following. "Good boy!" I responded spontaneously again, as I rewarded him with another small food treat. Once more I marvelled at the skill that had gone into training and the enthusiasm of dogs for doing what was asked of them. And so the afternoon proceeded with various other elements of the sound work – doorbell, telephone, smoke alarm and fire alarm, both in the lounge and with me feigning sleep in the bed up on the first floor of the training house. Here Matt varied the routine for alerting me by jumping on the bed until I got up to ask him again "What is it?" Pretty simple work for me, you might think, and it was certainly undemanding physically. But amazingly, by the end of the afternoon I was exhausted, and couldn't understand why. Learning new patterns comes more slowly to us than we might think, particularly if they are in a previously unexperienced context.

At the end of the afternoon, Hannah asked me to practice putting Matt back into his halte collar and jacket. As she stood back and left me to it, I turned the collar this way and that, trying to remember which way was up and which down, which was front and which back. It took me several attempts to find the right combination of straps and clasps, with Matt standing patiently all the while for this rather inept human to complete what he had hitherto considered the simplest of tasks. I feel pretty foolish! Finally, I had the collar correctly fitted and slipped his jacket over his back. It was fairly obvious from the writing on the side of the jacket which way round this item went and it attached under his middle with Velcro strips. Even I could manage that one! But the halte collar was to remain an issue for me throughout the week and was to become a very major bone of contention when I was visited at home the following week by Matt's placement officer. Was it really as difficult as it seemed to me? Who knows, perhaps I'm just a slow learner. But the issue was later to be the cause of my coming within a hair's breadth of cancelling the whole training process and walking away, however highly I thought of Matt. How strange that so often our destinies and futures are held in the balance by the simplest and smallest of issues.

Matt and I said goodbye to Hannah and set off back to the farmhouse where I was under instructions to ensure I gave him several opportunities during the evening to get outside to do what doggies normally do outside! Other that that, my time was my own. Truth to tell, my head was reeling from the newness of it all. There was so much to remember, all of which apparently had to be done just so. I'd never have expected to find myself so tired from doing what superficially seemed to be so little, yet the precision of what was required was alien to me. Each step had to be learned and discharged perfectly. There seemed to be little if any room for variance from the approved path. Perhaps in truth my state of exhaustion was also partly attributable to the work related concerns that had been on my mind – who knows? But the net result was that I was more than glad the day was over and beginning to wonder if I was going to last the course. 'Only three and a half more days to go,' I found myself thinking. It wasn't that there had been any particular problems other than the awkwardness of the halte collar. Everyone I'd met had gone well out of their way to be pleasant and helpful. But I had totally underestimated the steepness of the learning curve and the effect that climbing it would have on me. Perhaps Hearing Dogs as an organisation had underestimated it too – but then they had a lot pf people before me to discover that from.

After Matt's dinner we went for a walk around the fields that belonged to The Grange. The light was falling and it was the time for the rabbits to come out to play. Matt enjoyed himself, pulling hard on the lead to get further, faster in the normal manner of young dogs. But by bedtime I'd still not managed to generate any apparent connection with him.

In consultation with Hannah, I had decided that Matt would sleep outside my bedroom on the landing whilst I stayed at The Grange, since that was my intended arrangement at home. Subject to the bedroom door being left open, Hannah was entirely agreeable that there was no real reason for him to sleep actually inside the room. I wasn't used to dogs at this time, and the idea of him sleeping in my bedroom didn't appeal to me. Matt himself was to change that arrangement soon after we arrived home. But for now, his sleeping place was outside the open door of my room, on a comfortable dog mattress on the landing. As I settled down for the night I felt perplexed and a little frustrated that I'd not managed to engender any interest from him, let alone achieved this 'bonding' thing that Hearing Dogs people talked about. 'Ah well, I thought as I drifted off to sleep, 'tomorrow's another day.' I could only have been asleep a matter of moments when a certain little four-legged creature came rushing into the room, put his front paws on the edge of the bed and started to lick my face. Matt had finally realised that I existed and was wondering if I'd like to play!

Frustrations and Progress

Tuesday, day two at The Grange started early – at about 6.00am in fact, with Matt once more deciding that since the light was up it must be time for both of us to be up. We were, after all, wasting perfectly good playing time! Actually, being an early riser anyway, I didn't much mind the fact that he scampered around the bedroom until I was awake. 'Right,' I thought. "First job: early morning pee.' – for the dog that is, not me! I threw some clothes on quickly and took him down to the back garden on his lead where he communed with nature in the anticipated manner. 'Fine for now, I thought, 'but what happens when we get home and we're on the top floor of a block of flats. Presumably I'm supposed to take you out to the nearest patch of green to achieve this objective, before I'm permitted so much as a cup of tea.'

He didn't actually answer, but if he had it might have been 'Yup, unless you'd prefer I undertook natural functions on the lounge carpet.' Wise guy!

With Matt's dues appropriately paid to nature, I entered into my own morning routines, finally finishing with Matt's 90 grams of breakfast at precisely 8.00am. 'I'm getting the hang of this doggy thing,' I thought to myself. Maybe day two would be less of a strain on me than day one.

At 9.00 it was time to get him into uniform and set off to the
restaurant for breakfast – my first visit there with Matt. Once
again I fumbled my way over the halte collar and jacket while
Matt stood, coping patiently with my inexperience. I found
myself wondering if all this was *really* necessary for a short
walk over to the restaurant. I knew the answer though.
Perhaps it wasn't strictly necessary in itself there and then.
But what was necessary was that I got the methodology of
getting him into and out of uniform right for the innumerable
occasions in the future when I would need to be able to do it.

Arriving at the restaurant, I placed my order at the
service bar, and went to find a table. "Sit," I said confidently
to Matt. He stood, looking at me blankly. "Sit," I repeated.
There was still no response. I looked around the room for
support. There was none to be had. I wondered what I was
doing wrong. When he failed to respond a third time, I gave
in from frustration and let him stand there while I sat at the
table with the newspaper, waiting for breakfast to arrive. As
one is suppose to, we were clearly establishing who was boss
in the relationship. Matt, of course was quite satisfied that the
boss role was rightfully his!

About 20 minutes later Hannah arrived. She greeted
me with a "Hello," then turned to Matt who was still standing
by the table. "Sit!" she said confidently. Matt immediately sat
down. Yup, we were now completely clear about who was
boss. I sat there a little confused, wondering when it would be
my turn to be boss! Breakfast over, Hannah explained that
we'd start the day's work with some more sound exercises in
the training house, then head out to High Wycombe to give
me some exposure to walking Matt around town. It all
sounded fine to me – but then as I was already demonstrating
admirably, what did I know?

The sound work passed off quite satisfactorily in
much the same vein as it had the previous day. Matt was
particularly enthusiastic in responding to the doorbell, out of

sheer delight at the prospect of seeing who was on the other side of the door. In this he has never changed. A ring at the door even now elevates him to a level of animation that nothing else can achieve. We are not a household that receives a large number of visitors, but boy, when we do, are they welcomed enthusiastically!

"Right," said Hannah at the end of the morning's work. "You go off and take Matt for a pee break, then have your lunch, and I'll meet you in the restaurant at 2.00pm to take you out to High Wycombe."

"No problem," I replied, and Matt and I went off to have a few minutes wander in the fields, suitably equipped with a supply of little plastic bags (use your imagination!). Mission accomplished, we returned to the restaurant where once again I placed a food order at the service counter and went to find an empty table to a chorus of "Hello Matt," from the assembled staff of Hearing Dogs. Clearly this was one well-known doggie! When we found a table, I hesitated, looking down at my new-found friend. Dare I try again? "Sit," I instructed, trying to sound just like Hannah. My gaze was met square on by those deep and mysterious eyes that seemed to hold the wisdom of the ages – and which also seemed to say 'get stuffed'! There was no response. "Sit!" I repeated, trying to sound extra-specially authoritative. There was still no response. I looked at the dog in considerable frustration. He looked back at me patiently with no malice or rebelliousness in his eyes, but still not sitting. "Look kid," I found myself saying, "If I can't get you to sit, right here in the hub of the Hearing Dogs empire, how do you think we're gonna cope with the more liberal environment when we get home?" He didn't answer. Once again I sat down to await the arrival of my meal. At some point when my attention was distracted Matt must have arrived at the conclusion that obedience was best for both of us, for when I next turned to him he was lying quietly under the table. As I gazed down at him trying to understand what passes through a dog's mind at such times, he gazed back up at me, trying equally hard to understand what passes through a human's mind at such times! We were getting to know each other, certainly, but it wasn't exactly a refined example of man and his faithful friend working together with breathtaking rapport! Hopefully an afternoon in High Wycombe would help us move forward a little towards the much craved for perfect harmony.

Lunchtime passed and Hannah duly reappeared for the trip into town accompanied by a (human!) colleague in training. The Grange is about fifteen minutes drive from High Wycombe, and I was about to get my first taste of the complexities of safely taking a dog anywhere in a car. I'd been provided with a car harness the previous day, but this was the first opportunity to use it. We walked Matt over to Hannah's car where she showed me how to place the car harness on him. Following my difficulties with the halte collar I was more than a little apprehensive. But the harness was marked so as to make it obvious as to which bit fitted where and it wasn't nearly the lofty challenge that the halte collar constituted. Next Hannah had Matt jump easily into the back seat and attached the harness to the safety belt. 'Nothing could be simpler,' I was tempted to think, 'except getting a dog to sit on command!' Still, if I was going to have trouble with this it wouldn't be while I had an expert with me, would it? Hannah drove us into High Wycombe with little communication passing between us. Though totally professional, she was clearly a quiet and retiring young woman who preferred to keep the social niceties to a minimum. I wasn't over bothered though, since I had more than enough to be thinking about. Climbing the hearing dog learning curve was, as far as I was concerned, only slightly less challenging than tackling the South face of Annapurna without ropes or rock boots.

Hannah pulled into the car park and switched off the engine. "You'll find people around here are used to Hearing Dogs," she said. "We bring them here for training all the time. So, if you're ready, get him into his halte collar and lead, then take him out of the car and put his coat on him." I assumed she meant the dog, not her colleague! In my inexperienced, fumbling all-thumbs manner, I eventually fulfilled the appointed task, thinking all the while of what patience Hearing Dogs trainers must have in order to work with novices like me. I'd be tempted to do everything for the trainee myself – but then I'm not a Hearing Dogs trainer. Eventually we were ready, and off we set to the shopping precinct. First stop was Boots where we walked slowly around the isles, ensuring that Matt walked professionally by my side. "Put him on a shorter leash," instructed Hannah. I looked back blankly. "Hold the lead a little lower down its length so as to shorten it," she explained, "so he has less lee way, in case he's tempted by the smells on the shelves." I complied, but there seemed to be no real need, for Matt was acting incredibly professionally and showing no signs of distraction by the gloriously smelly contents of the shelves.

Then it was out into the main street to ensure he would cope properly with both crowds and traffic. Everywhere we went we were greeted by benevolent smiles and requests to talk to Matt. I felt like I was walking around town with a celebrity! Later I was to learn that this was, to some extent, typical, for Hearing Dogs in their colourful coats attract attention, particularly when seen in places other dogs are not permitted. However, I was also later to learn that Matt attracted well more than his fair allocation of attention, even for a hearing dog. Certainly it's due to some extent to his appearance, for he has a cute face and is by appearance and temperament everyone's childhood dream of what having a doggie is all about. But it seems to me that there's something else going on with Matt that extends well beyond the physical as well… something about the strange spell that this particularly special animal seems able to cast on virtually anyone who comes within his orbit.

"OK," said Hannah evidently satisfied with his performance both in Boots and out and about generally, "that was really good. Now we'll try him in a supermarket. So it was off to Tesco's for a walk around the isles where Matt was no more tempted to sniff the shelves than he had been in Boots and where we faced no fewer benevolent smiles and received no less celebrity-level attention than had come our way elsewhere during the earlier part of the afternoon. But as we returned to The Grange in the car, I was drawn inwards yet again, aware of how strenuous I was finding the process of learning the management of a hearing dog, and frankly wondering if the results in the end could possibly be worth the work and the continuing inconvenience that having a disability dog would impose. It was a question that I would be facing for some time to come.

Bi' Do'

That evening, my elder daughter, Naomi, was due to visit The Grange in order to meet Matt. Though she no longer lived with me at that time, she was and still is a frequent visitor to my home. Her visit to The Grange was particularly significant, since she was dog-phobic and had previously been known to utter the words "If you ever get a dog I'll never visit you again!" The phobia was as curious as it was unfortunate, for ironically her first words at eleven months of age had been "Big Dog!" or as she expressed it at the time "Bi' Do.'" These she had spoken whilst out in her pushchair one day, in absolute delight at our passing what was, indeed, a rather large mongrel dog. But sadly we had needed to move house shortly after that, and when her school days arrived her route to school required that we pass a high fence, behind which was a rather yappy little dog. It was completely unpredictable as to whether it would be behind the fence or not on any given day, and hence the foreboding concerning the yapping was intensified by the uncertainty as to whether it would actually occur or not. Uncertainties and experiences loom large in the mind of a four year old, and unfortunately dogs were classified by Naomi thereafter as something to be frightened of, particularly if they were prone to barking. As we make our way through childhood we remember less and less of the reasons that lie behind such fears, but often we retain the fears themselves, regardless of how irrational we might consider them to be when we become adults. Accordingly, it had taken much thought on Naomi's part as to how she wanted to handle my acquisition of a hearing dog, albeit one that almost never uttered a bark. Before meeting Matt all dogs were classified in Naomi's mind in a universal set – and that set was something to be avoided if at all possible. Nevertheless, much thought and discussion had led her to the conclusion that the best way of her dealing with Matt would be to meet him at the earliest possible opportunity and under the most advantageous circumstances possible. That, of course, meant coming to The Grange to meet him. On this she had placed two stipulations – he was not to jump up at her (which accorded with Hearing Dogs preferred behaviour any way) and if he barked at her she would need to leave the room.

After our day in High Wycombe I was feeling pretty positive, for everything had gone well. The morning's sound work and the continuing sense of newness of all I was needing to learn was still leaving me feeling wiped out, despite the relatively small amount of time we'd spent on active training each day. But Naomi and her younger sister Vici hold a particularly high priority for me. It was important to me to ensure that both of them received a positive impression of Matt and that his presence in my life did not lead to any reductions in the frequency of their visits. When your children are small they want as much of your attention as you're willing to give them. But as any parent of adult children will tell you, when they're grown up, your biggest problem lies in persuading them to spend time with you as often as you would like! I didn't need anything in my life that would make either of them feel reluctant to come to visit me. So, with the day's active training behind us and with Matt walked, fed and toileted and held safely on site for me by Hannah, I drove off to High Wycombe station to collect Naomi. She arrived on time, and even before we spoke I could see that she was feeling doubtful about her decision to come. "You won't let him jump up at me, will you?" she asked, reiterating the rules of engagement we had previously agreed.

"No, of course not," I replied, as I went on to explain to her all the comings and goings of the week so far. Soon we were back at the old farmhouse and Naomi was comfortably settled in the lounge, admiring the large black beams and the sooty inglenook fireplaces. "Right, I said, "if you're ready, I'll go and ask Hannah to bring him in. She smiled me her unspoken and non committal reply. I went off to find Hannah. For the first time Matt greeted me as someone significant, if in a slightly more restrained manner than he would his trainer herself. I walked with them back to the farmhouse and took a deep breath before entering the room. The look on Naomi's face as we rounded the door said it all. This was a clear point of danger. She was, almost by definition, frightened of him. How would he deal with that? Hannah held him back on the extending lead, giving him enough of its length to get close to her and sniff her a little, but not enough to enable him to jump up. "Don't worry," I said, trying to sound not quite helpless, "give him a few moments to get used to you and he'll settle down." But already I could tell something rather strange was beginning to happen. Though Naomi was clearly wary of Matt and evidently would not tolerate him jumping at her, she was also evidently very drawn to him. Tentatively, she reached out her hand for him to sniff at, and showed obvious delight at the interest he in his turn was showing in her. It seemed to me that she was experiencing two different reactions to Matt at once. On the one hand she was feeling all the old dog phobia that had caused her to give dogs such a wide berth in the past. On the other, this little guy was so endearing, that he was clearly weaving his magic web about her in precisely the same manner as he was to do with just about everyone else I know. Naomi was succumbing to the relentless charms of Matt. Given the reactions to Matt's picture at work, she was already not the first of the people in my life to do so. Nor was she to be the last

As predicted, after a few minutes investigation, as far as Matt was concerned Naomi was no longer new and therefore not particularly of interest. Shortly, he settled down to chew on some favoured toy and paid us scant regard for the rest of her visit. Hannah withdrew to allow us all some time together. Periodically, Naomi would seek to catch Matt's attention and he would get up, tail wagging to greet her. But for the most part, if she left him alone he left her alone. After a dinner and a walk around the fields together, all too soon it was time to take Naomi back to the station. I deposited Matt back with Hannah and retraced the journey to High Wycombe station. By any standards it had been an inordinately tiring day. There had been successes too, though. Perhaps the light at the end of the tunnel really was daylight. But my nagging uncertainties concerning my ability to manage Mat and get the behaviour I needed from him left me wondering if, after all, that light was indeed the headlight of the approaching express train. As I turned into the drive at The Grange, the phone on the seat next to me vibrated, recording another message. I hardly needed to look to see that it was from Hurst Manor. Another resident had passed away that evening. We had now lost five in quick succession with all that implied, emotionally and financially. At the business level we were down to eighteen paying residents and my company was now loss making. There was no way of telling how much further the virus had to go, not how long it would take us to rebuild the energy levels and fee base at the home. It was anything but the perfect end to the perfect day.

The Light at The End of The Tunnel

Wednesday dawned to the same routine as had Tuesday. Matt and I were becoming more familiar with each other, but we were not yet, as the parlance has it, bonded. He regarded me as a semi-interesting new presence in his life, useful for treats and play, but quite honestly I don't think he'd have particularly noticed if I had returned home that day and never saw him again. As for me, although I found him endearing and I was beginning to get a feel for the social and communicative benefits his presence might bring to me, my awareness of the situation was overwhelmingly focussed on the amount of learning and behavioural change that was coming my way. I was becoming rapidly worn down emotionally and physically by the level of responsibility I was taking on and the need to comply with a very large numbers of pernickety procedures which in many cases I could see no obvious need for. In short, though the physical demands were minimal, I was rapidly becoming exhausted.

A walk in the fields and Matt's 8.00am breakfast led on to the first challenge of the day - getting him to sit or lie down in the restaurant. I'll not labour over the grim details since they were very little different from what had happened on Tuesday, and for that matter on Monday! Frustratingly, Hannah once more came to meet me at the appointed hour and found no trouble in getting Matt to sit down immediately upon her instruction. I was beginning to get the idea that this problem was all about me and not at all about the dog. But was I capable of changing in whatever way I needed to in order to achieve the desired response from him – and was I in fact willing to make whatever changes were needed? It was 9.00am on the morning of day three and I was close to being ready to throw in the towel. Yet something told me not to – that if I pressed on with this exhausting and frustrating process, benefit would come of it. And that same something also told me that if I did give up prematurely I'd regret doing so for the rest of my life.

Wednesday, Hannah informed me, would be devoted to a grooming talk, an off lead walk in the park and yet more sound work. It would also be the last day I would spend with her before Nikki took over the training programme. I was frankly not sad at the prospect of change. Although Hannah had been fine at the technical level of the training and perfectly polite, she seemed distant and I found her impossible to engage personally. Understandably, since she was leaving Hearing Dogs in a couple of days, her mind was on other matters. But from my point of view I needed not just technical support but also personal and emotional support. I remembered exactly the same pattern from 1989 when I'd first been diagnosed with hearing loss. The technical support machine had swung efficiently into action to get me fitted with a hearing aid, but no one had actually taken any time to explain to me what the frightening process losing my hearing would feel like, or to offer me support through that process. Now something analogous was happening. The organisation was super efficient at ensuring I was properly trained in the technicalities of managing a hearing dog, but no one seemed to be paying any attention to the emotional implications of what was, in all fairness, an enormous change in my life. I am told that since my experience Hearing Dogs has begun to devote considerably more time and attention to helping trainees with this adjustment process. But right at that moment I had a growing feeling that I was trying to undertake something that was beyond me, and which eventually would beat me. So as the events of Wednesday wore on, I was increasingly forming the representation that, come Thursday morning when Hannah left, I would leave too. It would be with an overwhelming sense of failure and dejectedness, against the advice of the inner voice that was urging me to stay, but nevertheless, I was all but resolved to leave. It was actually to be the experiences of Thursday and the intervention of Nikki which changed everything.

By Thursday morning the struggle at the breakfast table had reached its fourth repetition. Once again, I told Matt to sit. Once again he looked at me with a look of not so much defiance in his eyes, as an apparent complete lack of understanding. "Look Matt," I found myself saying to him, "If you can't do this one simple thing for me, how on earth are we going to work together as a team in the future? If you don't sit down for me now, we're all finished and done. I'm going to hand you back to Hannah or Nikki or whoever and pack my bags and leave." Not surprisingly, he stood looking uncomprehendingly at me. So that was it. The halte collar, the dog's unwillingness to respond to instructions, the seemingly pointless requirements to comply with the minute of approved methodology had all banded together to achieve something most unusual – my decision to give up. I'd have to go home and face relatives, friends and colleagues with the disappointment of their anticipation, but that was as it had to be.

"Good morning Michael." My despondent thought process was interrupted by a touch on the shoulder and a friendly confident voice. I turned around in my seat. Standing beside me and smiling down at me was Nikki. I looked up dejectedly.

"Hello Nikki. Sorry to tell you this, but I'm just about ready to give this up and head for home. I've failed. It's not Hearing Dogs' fault. For whatever reason, it's mine.

"Oh, don't say that," she replied, looking sympathetic. What's the problem? I'm sure we can get it sorted out."

"Well, for starters, "I said, I've sat here for the last four mornings and not once have I been able to get this blessed dog to sit or lie down on command."

"Oh, you don't want to get upset about that," she replied. "I'll show you how to do it. Just hold on." Nikki walked away from us for a moment in the direction of the restaurant door. She bent down over a small pile of blankets by the door that I'd not even noticed before, picked one up and brought it back to the table where she spread it out on the floor in front of Matt. "Try him again," she said cheerfully.

I looked up at her wistfully, feeling anything but confident. Turning to the dog, I issued the command "Sit," in as confident a manner as I could muster. For a moment there was no response. Then Matt looked at me briefly, stepped onto the blanket and sat down. Without further ado, he then proceeded to lie down and went straight off to sleep.

I looked up at Nikki, amazed. "How on earth did you do that?" I asked incredulously.

"I didn't do it," she said, "You did it." It's not so difficult when you know how. You just have to make sure that the dog is clear about what you want, and you have to give him time to respond to your instruction. You need to realise that he really does want to please you. You just need to give him enough information to be able to do so. I looked back at Nikki with continuing amazement and gratitude. The desire to give up and flee was still there, but it was beginning to recede.

Nikki sat down at the table. Soon we were chatting away like old friends. Without any criticism of Hannah being implied, the contrast was amazing. Here was someone to whom I could actually relate, and who was prepared to take the interaction beyond the immediate formalities of teacher and pupil in the way that was so very necessary for success. In short, here was someone who was prepared to engage at exactly the human level I needed in order to make the personal, non-technical changes that were required to enable my relationship with Matt to succeed. Later in the day I was to discover that before Nikki came to Hearing Dogs she had been the owner of a small business. Perhaps it was there that she had learned that when we are customers, or on the receiving end of an organisation's service, we treat the matter of *how* we are dealt with as being of equal importance to *what* we are receiving. Hearing Dogs was, to be sure, all about the supply of Hearing Dogs. But an empathetic, supportive style of interacting could make all the difference to the total experience a recipient had of the organisation. And in my case it made the difference between leaving The Grange alone and early, with my own metaphorical tail between my legs and leaving successfully with Matt at the end of the week. I had been wrong. The light at the end of the tunnel was neither daylight nor an oncoming train. It was the most professional and supportive of railway workers swinging a welcoming lantern to encourage me to press on towards the station.

Homeward Bound

The last two days of the training were as pleasant and positive as the first three had been difficult and demanding. The difference, of course, was very little to do with changes in Matt, and very greatly to do with changes in me. Given the encouragement and support I needed, given proper explanations of why things needed to be done in a particular way, the whole of the learning experience was positive, enjoyable and accessible. And as a result I was able to make the changes needed to enable me to achieve the growing rapport with Matt that made the partnership work. So much was this so, that even when things went wrong it was possible to share a giggle and to move on to getting it right. That day, for example, we were due to take Matt on the train. He'd been specifically exposed to train work as part of his preparation for coming to live with me, for I'd anticipated the occasional need to take him to London on the train when I visited Naomi at her home in Battersea. Nikki, Matt and I had got onto the train ok, but when the time came to get off, the carriage had been crowded and we'd not managed to make it to the doors before they were closed. Accordingly, with much shared mirth, we had had to proceed all the way to High Wycombe before the opportunity to turn around and come back presented itself. I was becoming a frequent visitor to High Wycombe station – perhaps Network south East would give me discount! Matt, for his part, took everything in his four-legged stride, in this case walking on and off the train as confidently as if he'd been passing through a static doorway. Nothing seemed to phase him.

Thursday merged painlessly into Friday, when the key event of the day was a restaurant visit. For this, Nikki chose the café at Sainsbury's in High Wycombe. It wasn't exactly haute cuisine, but it was definitely more than adequate for the purpose. Lunch passed uneventfully. There wasn't even an objection to Matt entering the restaurant and nothing to foretell for the battles that were later to come over the question of his entitlement to entry to food premises. For now that was a good thing. I had had two days of supportive, enjoyable training from someone who was prepared to step into the realities of the training process as I was experiencing them on the receiving end - and that had made all the difference. If it hadn't been for Nikki I am quite certain I wouldn't be in a position to tell this story. I hope that in due course she reads it and gets a great big kick out of it. Nikki, you dun good, kid!!

Well, Friday afternoon finally arrived. If there had been any discussions taking place about the development of the Matt and Michael partnership behind closed management doors at The Grange, I had not been party to them. I'm sure, though, I'd come across as a more than averagely difficult person to work with. Perhaps I'm a tad more emotional than Mister Average. Perhaps I just like things being properly explained. Perhaps I lack confidence. Perhaps I'm just an awkward bugger (yup, definitely that one). Perhaps all of the above are true. Nevertheless, we'd completed the next stage in the process and I was authorised to take Matt home for the weekend. We would have two days alone getting used to each other in my home before the placement officer, Abigail, visited us for further training on the Monday. At the end of the programme, I packed the car, and placed Matt in his harness in the back behind the passenger seat where he could see me and where I could turn briefly to him at appropriate moments such as when waiting at traffic lights. I was about to leave when a final thought occurred to me. "Could I," I asked Nikki, travel home with the roof of the car off?"

Nikki didn't know the answer, so she went off to find out. She returned a few minutes later. The decision was no, I could not, since even with his harness firmly attached to the safety belt, if he moved slowly enough Matt would still be able to get at least partially out of the car when it was moving. The roof of the BMW convertible stayed firmly in place all the way home. It didn't take much thinking during the journey to arrive at the conclusion that if I was keeping the dog then there wasn't much point in keeping the car. But then there was no contest really, was there? The car would be exchanged at the next possible opportunity.

The Five Fundamental Laws of Living With a Dog For The First Time

We got home to my little third floor flat about suppertime on the Friday after a two and a half hour drive. Matt's behaviour had been impeccable all the way – something that was to be repeated on virtually every car journey he has ever taken since. Some dogs just like the car, I guess, and he is one of them. When we get into it each day, he has no idea whether we're taking a ten-minute run up to the park for a walk or a six-hour drive to the Lake District. In fact, it really doesn't seem to matter to him. He always settles immediately and goes to sleep for the duration.

I parked the car and eased Matt carefully out of the back on his extending lead. Grabbing one or two items in my other hand I struggled to the entrance door of the block and fumbled my key into the lock. Matt, of course, was somewhere new and immediately wanted to find out what lay behind the door. He tugged me into the hallway where we summoned the lift. First challenge: I'd not been in a lift with him before – how would he respond to it? Whether he himself had been in one before or not, I had no idea. As soon as the door slid back he stepped across the threshold into what must have appeared to him as simply a tiny room. As the door slid shut in front of us and the lift began to move, I held my breath. If there was to be a reaction, now would be the time. But there was none. Again, he showed not the slightest sign of discomfort. At the top floor we were out and across the hallway to my front door with no hitches. Further fumbling with keys gained us entry, and Matt ran in ahead of me enthusiastically to explore a new environment. I shut the door behind us and slipped the lead from his collar, allowing him to run freely round the flat. It didn't take long, since the flat was tiny! He rushed round, nose to the floor, exploring each new sight and smell briefly before hurrying on to the next. I stood back in the hallway, amused at the child-like display of enthusiasm that was so similar to what I had observed in my vision of a doggy visitor to the flat all those months previous. It had not been him, for the visitor was somewhat larger, but the behavioural similarities were remarkable. Eventually he decided that there was nothing else to be investigated, and we moved into the kitchen to make a drink. I filled an aluminium feeding bowl with water and put it down on the floor in the hall while the kettle boiled. Matt lapped at it enthusiastically, sending water spraying all over the adjacent carpet and wall.

Back in the 1950s the science fiction writer Isaac Asimov specified three fundamental laws of robotics. In similar vein, and on the basis of my first year of living with Matt, I feel obligated to highlight here for the benefit of all mankind and dogkind, the five fundamental laws of living for the first time with a dog:

> **Law One of living for the first time with a dog: protect the décor and carpets– they will get ruined anyway, but you'll feel much worse about it if you've made no attempt to prevent it.**

I made a mental note to buy some plastic carpet guard material on my next trip out. Then I settled down on the sofa with a cup of tea and left Matt to wander round the flat at will. A few moments later my attention was caught by the fact that he was running round excitedly in the hall. Intrigued, I went to investigate what he'd discovered to animate him so. As soon as I got up he ran towards me, jumped at me and, believe it or not, smiled at me! Later I was to learn that "smiling" or bearing of teeth in a clenched jaw, is something common to Spaniels when disturbed. It took no time at all to discover the reason why. Right in the centre of the hall carpet Matt had made a large deposit – and I don't mean a financial one. The running round in circles was an indication that he knew that this was inappropriate behaviour and the smiling and jumping was an attempt to apologise. Fleetingly, the thought passed through my mind "'Now, I wonder who's supposed to clean this up?' Then the assembled multitude appointed me as a sub-committee of one to deal with the problem. Less than wholly enamoured with the start we were making to our new relationship in the home environment, I located the necessary materials and dealt with the offending item in the time-honoured manner. This brings us to the **Second Law** of living for a first time with a dog:

Law two of living for the first time with a dog: The dog's toileting needs take absolute priority over your need for a cup of tea, whatever time of the day or night it is.

With wistful thoughts of stable doors and bolting horses, I put his extending lead back on him and we made our way back down in the lift. The next question to answer was, of course, 'Where do I toilet him?' Armed with a supply of little plastic bags (now probably superfluous, of course) we crossed the road and walked the fifty yards or so to the nearest patch of grass which just happened to be by the station car park. Matt was delighted to be outside again and thoroughly appreciated my generous gesture of finding him some grass to sniff around. He had, however, absolutely no requirement for said grass from the bladderal or rectal perspective. Somewhat bemused, I led him back to the block.

The evening's efforts were far from over though. 'Now,' I thought, 'how do I get all our stuff up from the car to the flat? Or more specifically, what do I do with you while I'm bringing it up?' I grabbed another couple of items out of the car in my right hand while holding the lead in my left (I'm left handed, by the way), and we made our way back up to the flat. By the time we arrived I realised that there was no practical solution to unloading the car other than to leave Matt shut up in the flat while I did so. And of course, I had no idea as to how he would react to being enclosed for an indeterminate period in an unfamiliar environment. As far as I knew, if I left him alone, he could run amok from sheer terror, tear the place to shreds and do himself considerable

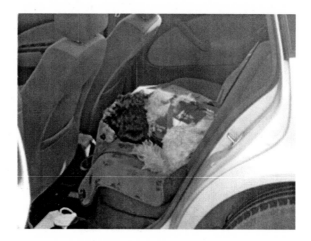

Travelling by car has never been a problem

harm in the process. Nevertheless, the only options were either to leave him in the flat or put him back in the car. I opted for the former. In order to minimise the time I was leaving him on his own, I worked out a system of ferrying everything from the car to the lift door, then making a single trip up in the lift before emptying all our possessions out on the landing floor outside the lift. From here I moved it all to the door before opening it and finally dumping everything unceremoniously inside.

Mission impossible was accomplished satisfactorily, and Matt had harmed neither the flat nor himself while I was gone. At the earliest opportunity I collapsed on the sofa with my now cold cup of tea, feeling thoroughly bemused. Was it really going to be as difficult as this to live with a dog? I should have taken better account of **Law Three**:

Law three of living for the first time with a dog: all the dog's needs come before yours…always!

So, with the cold tea remaining unconsumed, I unpacked all Matt's possessions and tried to arrange them in the hall in such a fashion as to make him feel at home as quickly as possible. His bed went down just outside my bedroom door, his toys were laid out on top of it and his feeding bowls were within a few feet by the front door. I then weighed out 90 grams from a large bag of dog food that Hearing Dogs had supplied me with to tide me over until I had a chance to place an order myself with the suppliers. Matt tucked into his dinner greedily. Maybe two hours after I arrived home I finally got around to looking in the freezer for something for my own dinner. As I sat down for the evening I felt like one of those cartoon characters who gets batted about the head and sees little flies buzzing around them in dazed confusion. It had taken precisely no time at all to demonstrate to me that my personal routines had to be subordinated to Matt's, that my home had been liberated to the purposes of doggie preferences and that my life was very definitely never going to be the same again!

After dinner I put the TV on for a while. In front of it was an old sheepskin rug that had been lying there forever. Matt promptly laid claim to it. I'd not invited him to establish territorial rights over the sheepskin, but then again, I hadn't taken account of **Law Four**:

**Law four of living for the first time with a dog:
unless you specifically instruct otherwise,
in the dog's opinion, whatever is on the floor
belongs uncontrovertibly to the dog.**

Now residing at the foot of my bed, the sheepskin has remained Matt's personal possession until this day!

Later in the evening, I went into the second bedroom of the flat, which I'd turned into a small study, in order to log onto the Internet and check my e-mail. In the study, I had an large, reproduction mahogany pedestal desk, which has been my constant companion since my parents gave it to me as a twenty-first birthday present rather a long time ago. I settled down at the desk and turned the computer on. As I concentrated on the screen, I felt a little furry form brush past my legs. Matt, who had been sitting on his bed out in the hall had decided to take up residence between the two pedestals of the desk right at my feet. I presume that there was something about the enclosed, cave-like space that resonated back to the wolf pack and gave him a feeling of security. It also had the added advantage from his point of view that it brought him close to me. The environment we were in, though home to me, was new to him and hence did not offer the sense of security he was used to at The Grange. Although I would not have expressed it this way at the time, the move into my territory was accelerating the bonding that was taking place between Matt and me. Anyway, I didn't see any reason to move him, and I later went on to place there the bedding I had originally intended for him to use to sleep on at nights. He has taken up residency under the desk when I am working ever since. In fact, the greater part of this book has been written with Matt snoozing securely at my feet in his cave!

Eventually bedtime approached. I was sufficiently into the routine from my time at The Grange to remember that I needed to give him a last pee-break before heading off to bed. If I'd been tempted to have forgotten or skipped it, **Law Two** and the afternoon's confrontation with the results of failing to take account of it would have kept my mind firmly focussed on the benefits of regular toileting! The difference between home and The Grange, though, was that we were now three stories up in a block of flats and the nearest green space was fifty yards away. I knew that, all being well, within a relatively short time Matt and I would be moving to The Oaks with its large garden and its gate opening directly onto the forest. But for the next eight weeks or so we would have to cope with making the trip to the green patch several times a day as well as undertaking longer walks at least once a day. Thus, the last job of the evening was to take him down in the lift and out across the road to permit him to discharge the necessary obligations of the physical frame before I could truly say that my day's labours were over.

The task having been duly accomplished, we returned to the flat, where I made ready for bed. Then, leaving the bathroom light on in order to illuminate any nocturnal wanderings I might need to make, I came back out into the hall way and told Matt to go to bed. He understood immediately, did a doggie three-point turn on his bed and apparently settled down for the night. Leaving the bedroom door ajar, I settled down in bed myself, turned out the light and made as if to go to sleep. A moment later I was disturbed by an increase in the light level in the bedroom. Matt had pushed the door open a little further and was standing by the bed wagging his tail. "Come on Matt," I said just a tad irritably. "It's bed time, not play time." I roused myself out of bed and led him back into the hall where he repeated his three-point turn and once more seemingly settled down for the night. I returned to bed with the door ajar as previously. This time I waited, not even attempting to go to sleep. A few moments later my anticipation was rewarded with the door once again being pushed wider to permit the entry of a small furry frame into the bedroom. Once more he stood wagging his tail by the side of the bed looking most pleased with himself.

I was getting less amused by this ritual by the minute. However, I knew full well that to shut him out of the bedroom in the hall would be breaking the rules and would ultimately work to my disadvantage. When I'm in bed with no hearing aids in, I am all but profoundly deaf. In particular, I can't hear smoke alarms and I can't hear fire alarms. Permitting Matt access to me at all times is fundamental to the work he's with me to do, and preventing him from doing so could one day cost me my life. With no Nikki on hand to turn to for advice, I decided to give ground gracefully. I put the light back on, went into the lounge and picked up the sheepskin that he'd taken a fancy to earlier in the evening. Then, returning it to the bedroom I put it down on the floor at the side of the bed. Matt gazed up at me with soft eyes. "Ok," I said, you can sleep there if you want to." He needed no further invitation. He made a final three-point turn over the sheepskin and settled down for the night. I turned off the light and we both went to sleep, now fully cognisant of **Law Five**:

Law five of living with a dog for the first time: you get more sleep if you give in gracefully!

Michael Forester

Auntie Penny

I remember clearly at what time the sun rose the next morning – it was 5.40am. The reason I remember is that Matt had decided that it was important for both of us to witness this historic event in person. Accordingly, he began scampering round the bedroom at about 5.30am. I wasn't over concerned, since I'm an early riser anyway, and I thought we might as well get the first pee-break (his of course, not mine!) of the day in early. After all, I had no notion as to his bladder capacity or the related length of time it was possible for him to go without an opportunity to empty it. I threw on some clothes and, noting that in acknowledgement of **Law Two** I'd not even taken the time to address that most basic of human requirements, the early morning cup of tea, led Matt out of the flat on his extension lead. At the bottom of the stairs we exited through the front door to find the street cleaner, Davy, standing under the canopy of the block, eating his breakfast break. As I said good morning to him I realised that at least I wasn't the first person out of bed in New Milton that morning. This made me feel a little better about the unfairness of being dragged downstairs and outside without the fortification of even so much as my early morning cuppa! There are few requirements more fundamentally important to the efficient functioning of the middle aged, adult male human than an early morning cup of tea. However, it is equally clear that this requirement is subordinate in the efficient running of God's universe to the **Second Law** of living for the first time with a dog, as stated above. Accordingly, Matt attended to his requirements and we returned to the flat. Everything seemed to be going fine so far.

I sat on the bed and wondered what to do with the day. Unusually for me, and due to overwhelming preoccupations with the practicalities of getting through the week at The Grange, I had planned almost no activity for the weekend. After all, it was supposed to be a quiet time for Matt and I to get to know each other. The one exception to this was that we were due to visit my good friend Penny that evening. But for now I had most of the day to kill. Having been asked to undertake no professional or sound work with Matt that weekend, I was limited as to where I could go. Any shopping would need to be undertaken without him, and I was reluctant to leave him on his own. So having consumed that much desired cuppa and readied myself for the day, the next appropriate event seemed to be a walk. Living where I did, I was spoiled for choice as to dog walking locations, since within a five minute drive I could be either in the New Forest or on the sea front. On our first morning I opted for the latter. So, with the rest of the world just beginning to rub the sleep blearily from its eyes, Matt and I took the lift down to the ground floor once more and made for the car. I was well familiar with his car harness by now, and only the halte collar and lead were still giving me trouble. But since we were not going anywhere we'd need it over the weekend I didn't trouble to take it. A five minute drive in the car took us to the cliff tops at Barton on Sea, where a very excited Matt fell over himself to get out of the car at the earliest opportunity and dragged me full pelt down the path to the sea and the sea birds, the latter being an instinctive matter of interest.

Our walk successfully completed, we returned home and I pottered about the flat for the day, interspersing the pottering with frequent doggie pee-breaks none of which, it seemed to me, required the use of the halte-collar that was causing me so much difficulty. The day passed pleasantly and five o'clock finally arrived. It was time to go to visit Penny.

Penny and I had met on the Greek island of Skyros some eighteen months previously. Along with most of the people on that holiday, we had both been at turning points in our lives and decided to take a holistic holiday that was

83

structured to give opportunity for inner reflection as well as tanning on the beach. I had noticed Penny within twenty-four hours of arrival as someone to whom others were instinctively drawn. It appeared to me that it was because she seemed to value everyone who came within her orbit. I watched in considerable fascination as person after person became easily engaged in relaxed conversation with her – conversations that for each one seemed to be satisfying and fulfilling. Not surprisingly, I had decided to make the attempt get to know her myself. Now, bear in mind that in 2002 I was still suffering from deafness-induced social withdrawal. Going on a group holiday and getting to know people were not within my normal repertoire of behaviours. But, attracted to the sense of acceptance Penny seemed to project to everyone around her, I took the risk. As a result we found ourselves spending a considerable amount of time together and forged a friendship that survived the ending of the holiday.

Penny worked as a senior local government officer for the London Borough of Richmond. However, she had reached that stage in her career where she was wondering if all the stress and the rush and the pressure were truly worthwhile. She had come to the conclusion on Skyros that they were not, and that her wish was to downsize and move away from London to somewhere she could have another dog. In fact, quite independently of me, she had come to the conclusion that what she actually wanted to do was to move to the New Forest. I say 'have another dog,' for it was only three months earlier in June 2002 that she had lost her beloved Meg, a black Labrador who had been her companion for thirteen years. Penny was looking forward to the time when she would once again want to have a dog in her life, but without the constraints imposed by living in London and working at a high octane public service occupation. Accordingly, in Summer 2003 she had taken a less demanding job in Bournemouth and moved to Ringwood, some thirty minutes drive from where I was living. Our friendship seemed destined to continue, and to include a particular focus on the matter of dogs. I had helped Penny decorate her bungalow that Summer and Autumn. She in her turn had taken a great deal of interest in my deliberations concerning the possibility of applying for a hearing dog, and had been able to advise me comprehensively on the practicalities of living with a dog, in whatever context. Penny, by any standards, was an expert on dogs. She had paced me through the uncertainties and elations of the application process with Hearing Dogs, had become besotted with Matt's picture in much the same way as everyone else had (though, it has to be said, had done so whilst maintaining a certain objective realism about the practicalities I would face which others had largely ignored). She was now waiting to meet the Star himself in person. She had also, it ought to be said, had a new carpet laid throughout her bungalow the week before. Amazingly, Penny seemed not to be aware of **Law 1**.

Matt and I drove to Ringwood, parked the car outside Penny's bungalow and walked up to the door. Ever inquisitive, Matt was pulling on the leash to discover what new and exciting distractions awaited him inside. Penny opened the door to us and with the minimal of 'hellos' to me, dropped immediately to Matt's level and let him clamber all over her! When he was satisfied that there was nothing else new to be investigated about this unfamiliar person, Matt's attention turned to the house that lay behind the entrance porch. "Well aren't you going to let him off the lead?" Penny asked me.

"What about your new carpet?" I asked uncertainly.

"Oh, you don't want to worry about that," she responded immediately. "You can't be house proud if you're going to be aunty to a dog!"

I suppressed the urge to question this apparent bout of temporary insanity. I let Matt off the lead and awaited commencement of World War III. Our four-legged hero dashed past us into the house with Penny in hot pursuit, also on all fours! Now, you have to realise here that we are talking about someone who, in a work context, can stop the charge of a fully grown adult male local government officer with a single withering look from thirty paces. I could only conclude that the all fours thing was a new and avant-garde technique for bonding with a dog of which the experts at The Grange were still unaware. I followed at a somewhat more leisurely pace (still vertical, still on two legs) until I found the two of them in the kitchen pulling a large collection of doggie toys out of the toy box. Penny was giggling helplessly and Matt was snuffling her and jumping all over her in excited confusion. Penny had clearly decided that she was going to be Matt's number one auntie. There was nothing I could have done to prevent it, even if I had wanted to.

As the evening proceed and the atmosphere calmed, Penny sealed her relationship with Matt with a particular treat that had the most remarkable effect on him: dried liver. I don't know whether he'd ever tasted it before, but as soon as Penny offered him the first small treat he was totally smitten. I think he'd have done just about anything for her that day, so long as she kept up the regular fixes of dried liver. Whatever else was achieved that evening, Penny had imprinted herself sufficiently on Matt's mind to ensure that on every subsequent visit he would go bonkers with excitement as soon as we get out of the car in her drive way.

Eventually, of course, he calmed down for the evening, and contented himself with dozing at his beloved Penny's feet as we chatted. I debriefed Penny on the elations and depressions of my week at The Grange, my anticipation of continuing difficulties in achieving the best results with Matt and my hopes for the assistance I was to receive for the next three days from the Placement Officer who would be visiting me to work further with us on the training. "Don't worry," I remember Penny saying, "Everything will work out fine. You'll be able to work through all your difficulties with the Placement Officer and I'm sure she'll put your mind at rest."

How wrong she was to be.

The Alpha Male

Saturday had now been successfully negotiated as our first full day together at home, and we set off back to the flat, where we spent an uneventful night. The next morning, Matt, the sun and I all rose at approximately the same time, and once more I deliberated on where to take him (Matt, that is, not the sun) for his morning walk. This time we headed into the forest, where I was careful to keep him on his lead as he explored the new sounds and sensations, and took particular interest in the ponies.

If you don't know the New Forest, I need to tell you that its beauty and energy is almost indescribable. Like many people, having come to live here in the 1990s, I have found it all but impossible to leave, such is the sense of peace and tranquillity that the place impresses upon you. The land here has remained almost unchanged for a thousand years, since William the Conqueror designated the area his 'New Forest' and forbad all hunting other than his own. Over the centuries it has evolved a truly unique method of governing itself, ascribing forest rights to the many homes that lie within its boundaries. Amongst these rights is the entitlement to graze animals freely over the land. Hence, though all the cattle and ponies here are actually owned by one of the many New Forest Commoners, they roam freely as if wild. Matt, of course, had no interest whatsoever in the legalities of the

Forest – but he did have a considerable interest in its four legged inhabitants! As we walked through the trees and the open land he strained at the leash to get as close as he possibly could to investigate.

So well did our walk go that morning, that I decided to return later in the day and, within the safety of a forest enclosure, let him off his lead for the first time. He scampered away happily to investigate just about everything, when round the corner in the opposite direction came a woman with a Labrador. I held my breath. This would be Matt's first encounter with another dog off leash. How would he react? How would the other dog respond? I need not have worried. On seeing the Lab he immediately slowed his frenetic pace, dropped his shoulders and advanced slowly. So did the Lab. Clearly, there was some kind of sizing up process going on. Each dog advanced a few paces towards the other, then dropped to the ground in what I was later informed was a gesture of non-threatening behaviour. When they were just a few yards apart they rushed towards each other like long parted lovers. Then it was all scampering and sniffing and wagging of tails.

The Lab's owner and I watched our dogs with contented amusement. Not surprisingly perhaps, we fell into conversation – about dogs, naturally! I explained to Marjorie, as she introduced herself, that this was all new to me and this was the first time I had let Matt off his lead.

"Oh," she responded, "you don't want to worry. You're his pack leader. He'll come to you and do what you want him to so long as he regards you as leader of the pack." Not being the aggressive, forward type, I was faintly amused to find myself cast in the role of Alpha male. Later I was to read Jan Fennell's book, 'The Dog Listener.' In it she describes how dog behaviour essentially resonates back to the wolf pack, where the survival of the whole pack depends on the selection of the strongest dogs as Alpha male and female.

Every other dog then discovers and maintains its place in the order of priority. It is even the case that the Alpha dog will assert its authority over other pack members by arching its head over the vulnerable head and shoulders of the other dogs. The lower status dog will permit this behaviour in an act of submission to the Alpha.

With me suitably educated, we ended our conversation and set off in opposite directions. As I walked, watching Matt carefully for signs of running off or other concerning behaviour, I marvelled at what had just happened. Though this encounter would have been nothing special to most other people, I had just undertaken virtually the first informal conversation I had had with a stranger in perhaps ten years. So significant does the reclusiveness become when you loose your hearing, that there is enormous reluctance to enter into any kind of exchange with a stranger, lest you mishear and therefore respond inappropriately. Without realising it, Matt had just begun to reverse ten years of self-limiting behaviour and belief. If I gained nothing else at all from the relationship we were now forming, this alone would be more than enough to justify his presence in my life. Thank you, Matt, I owe you an enormous amount. In fact, if it wasn't for the dog, where in earth would I be now?

Abigail

I was by now suffering the strains and stresses that the learning curve of canine management was imposing on me. A week of intensive training at The Grange had been followed by a weekend of flying solo with Matt at home. I had been tempted to give up on numerous occasions on the grounds that the whole process was simply too demanding and I was just not up to it. But with enormous support from the team at

The Grange, I had emerged from what I was assuming to be the most demanding period of the training process. It had not been easy, but nevertheless I was still there – and more importantly, Matt was still with me. By the Monday morning I was beginning to feel that this whole thing could actually work and that, despite the challenges and inconveniences of having a dog in my tiny flat for a short period, it was all going to be worthwhile in the end. And besides, I now had a further three days help and support coming from the placement officer, Abigail (which for reasons shortly to be come clear, is *not* her real name!).

One of the features of the week I'd just spent at The Grange was the frequent gaps that were slotted into the days when nothing was happening. I had come to presume that these were there by design, for the periods of sound work, outdoor work, town work and so on, were as demanding as they were new. But those gaps also gave me considerable opportunity to think about the process I was undergoing. Having been trained and practiced as a management consultant for many years before my hearing had declined, it was hardly surprising that I came to Hearing Dogs with a management consultant's eye. My observation in doing so, was that Hearing Dogs had a culture, similar to that of many of the organisations I'd worked with over the years, that was 'product focussed,' rather than 'customer focussed.' By this I mean that I found the organisation to operate superbly in anything to do with the dogs themselves – their welfare, their training, their management. But if there was a weakness it was in its awareness of its customers, or its ability and inclination to think through the experience it was creating for those on the receiving end of the organisation's processes. In other organisations such people are called customers. In Hearing Dogs they are called 'recipients' and they are people such as me.

Hence (and I've since discussed this at length with Hearing Dogs' management, so I'm not telling tales out of school) whilst I was at The Grange a great deal of time was spent on teaching me the rudiments of dog management – the obedience work, the grooming, the health management, the sound work etc., but not so much thought seemed to have been given to how I was coping with the whole experience of being pulled (in my case, kicking and screaming) up the learning curve of dog awareness and management. And if an organisation's culture is product focussed, it stands to reason that its employees will exhibit the same patterns if they are to identify with the culture of the organisation. Looking back, I can see now that my experience of training at The Grange had changed fundamentally and become dramatically more positive when Nikki had stepped in as my trainer on the Thursday. Nikki was not just a very experienced and competent trainer, she also had an instinctive people focus that somehow gave her an extra degree of awareness of how I as recipient was experiencing the training. She was able first to empathise with the frustrations I was experiencing and then, having gained my confidence, to help me through those areas that were causing difficulty. With the trainers I'd worked with previously at The Grange, I had done so out of necessity, for I recognised my need for a hearing dog. With Nikki, the learning process had become a pleasure. How intriguing that these are the very considerations that need to be borne in mind when training the dogs themselves!

So there I was that Monday morning, sitting in my little flat with Matt, anticipating the arrival of Abigail in the innocent hope that working with her would be just like my last couple of days working with Nikki at The Grange. Sadly, it was not to be. Now, I've thought long and hard about what I'm about to tell you about my experiences with Abigail, because the last thing I want to do is give you a negative impression of Hearing Dogs, or, if you're a potential recipient, to put you off applying for a Hearing Dog yourself. Remember, I'm now out of the other side of this process and I'm still saying that living and working with Matt is one of the most rewarding experiences I've ever been privileged to undertake in my entire life. But to give the impression that getting here was all plain sailing would also be to misrepresent reality. Of course, it also has to be said that I may not be the easiest of people to work with when I'm in the passenger seat. I guess I've been occupying the driving seat of my own life for long enough now that being told what to do doesn't come too easily at times, particularly when the telling is, shall we say, less than wholly tactful.

Well, 11.00am on Monday morning duly, arrived and as anticipated the doorbell rang. My lights no longer flashed, as I'd now turned off the device that warned me visually that there was someone at the door. But Matt was on good form and immediately came to alert me in the approved manner - bottom to the floor and paws on my knee. There at the door was Abigail, a diminutive young woman of perhaps 22 or so. We'd been introduced briefly at The Grange the previous week but had had no real opportunity to talk before.

"Hello Mike," she said as she stepped across the threshold.

Lesson one in dealing with a recipient: I don't like being addressed by my first name, particularly in its diminutive form, unless I have invited the other party to do so. Am I alone in this? I, at the age of 48, would normally expect to be addressed as Mr. Lawson by a person in their early 20s until such time as I invited the use of my first name.

Nevertheless, I swallowed my irritation and stood aside for Abigail to enter. She breezed passed me into the lounge where I invited her to sit and went through the normal pleasantries of offering coffee and so on. The necessary preliminaries completed, she slipped noticeably into professional mode and began to outline the proceedings of the next few days. Each day would entail some further sound work, but would also include a component of some other nature. During the first morning we would do some shopping. On the Tuesday we would visit the vet's and on the Wednesday Abigail wanted to inspect my place of work.

"Right," she said, becoming bolder by the minute. The first thing we need to do is phone the vet to arrange an appointment. Would you like to do it yourself or would you prefer me to do so for you?"

I thought for a moment. "Well," I responded, "Since most vets' receptionists are female, and since I have particular difficulty with female voices over the phone, and since you're offering, I'd be grateful if you'd make the call."

Watching her face at that moment was like seeing storm clouds gather over an otherwise clear blue sky. Evidently, I had said the wrong thing.

"Oh Mike," she said with considerable irritation, "How sexist!"

I stiffened, and all the sense of easy relaxation that I had assumed was appropriate disappeared in a moment. "That was not the intention of my comment," I replied rather formally. You offered me a choice and I simply accepted your offer for what I regard as a very good reason." I felt cornered and defensive. An exchange that had been supposed to be about further progress in climbing the learning curve had suddenly turned into something quite different. I felt no sense of wrongdoing, but it was quite evident that the battle lines were now drawn. What should have been a positive, if perhaps challenging three days now threatened to be, to say the least, exceedingly frustrating.

And it was all down hill from there.

I tried to put the exchange behind me, but was now feeling I needed to watch every response, every remark I made, every question I asked, to ensure its political correctness. The form and presentation of our verbal exchanges rapidly took precedence over the substance and value of the training. We moved smartly onto sound work in which Matt performed impeccably and then it was out to the shops to see how he behaved in public. Unsurprisingly, he was faultless here as well. Considering my question carefully lest it cause further offence, I had asked Abigail if she would help me choose some suitable toys for Matt. I had one or two that I brought with me from The Grange, but he so clearly loved what he had that I wanted him to have some more. "Nothing with a squeaker," was her immediate, negative reply. I sighed inwardly at the continuing emphasis on what was not permissible, what was not acceptable over what was good and what was possible. I understood the need to avoid toys with squeakers of course, since Hearing Dogs are trained on these little devices and its essential to avoid confusing them. But it just seemed a shame to me that we had to come at all parts of life from the perspective of the impossible and the unacceptable rather than what was achievable and what opportunities were open.

At lunchtime Abigail disappeared for a break, which was a relief for both of us, indicating that she would be back within half an hour. After an hour of absence I became a little concerned. And after an hour and a half I began to think she must have got lost. Eventually the doorbell rang and Matt went through his normal routine. "Hello Abigail," I said as I opened the door, did you get lost?

"No," she said. She looked and sounded defensive. Evidently the day was proving to be as challenging for her as it was for me. "I've been on the phone to The Grange." No further information was offered or requested. I drew the conclusion that in some way it was me who was deemed to be at fault and that I had been reported for it at length. Still, we would see how the afternoon went.

In fact, matters proceeded rather well until late in the afternoon when Abigail asked about Matt's toileting arrangements. "Oh," I said, at the moment I just take him over the road to the patch of grass by the station. I hope that's ok?"

She nodded her assent. "I'd like to see you go through that routine with him please."

Fair enough," I said, slipping his extending lead onto him in my continuing attempt to avoid my difficulty with the halte lead when I could.

"Where's the halte lead?" asked Abigail.

"We're only going just over the road," I said. "I have trouble with the halte and we've no need to go anywhere we need it, so I just use the extending lead."

Abigail seemed to grow visibly before my eyes as she drew herself up to her full height. "As I'm sure you know, Mike," she said patronisingly, "if you take Matt out in public you *must* use the halte collar and his jacket."

I looked at her, simply taking in the information for a moment. "But that means struggling with the halte and jacket here, struggling to get it off again at the station, letting him do what he needs on the extending lead for maybe thirty seconds, then putting him back into the halte and jacket for a twenty yard walk home – and then take it off again."

"Yes," she said. "The extending lead might break and he might run into the road."

Was it really an expression of satisfaction that I saw steal across her face? Did she really feel that putting me under ever increasing amounts of pressure gave her the upper hand? Who can say? I suppressed my frustration as I sat down and struggled with the halte collar that I was still finding fiendishly difficult. No assistance was offered, no suggestion as to how to make it any easier. I completed the task and we left the flat in silence. I still remember the irritation I felt at this wholly unnecessary (as I saw it) imposition of difficulty as we headed down in the lift for the walk to the station car park where I went through the routine in reverse. A further thirty seconds later Matt had completed the necessaries and I found myself struggling in the street once more to re-attach the challenging halte collar for the short walk back to the flat. By the time we returned, the pent up frustration of the day combined with this final confrontation had now led to my being more than a little irritated.

"Right," I said as we came back into the lounge, "are we done for the day?"

"We are," came the formal reply.

"Well, you need to understand," I continued, "that there is no way I am going through that ridiculous process at 5.00am tomorrow morning when there is no traffic about and not a soul on the streets." I looked directly at Abigail and awaited a response.

"Sit down, Mike," she instructed.

"Abigail," I retorted, please remember that you are in my home at my invitation. If I wish to stand I will do so." She looked at me, uncertain of how to proceed. "If you are insistent on my following this needless and difficult procedure," I continued, then you'd better take the dog back now. It's simply more than I can face doing."

"We'll talk about it tomorrow," was her response and she left without further comment.

Looking back on what I've written, I'm far from proud of my part in that exchange, and its clear I should not have let my irritation get out of hand in the way it did. All I can say is that it was the result of the accumulation of considerable frustration at having been patronised all day long by someone less than half my age, and having to think about everything I said before letting the words out of my mouth, lest they be deemed politically incorrect. However you look at it, Abigail and I were at opposite ends of the spectrum with completely different life experiences and expectations of the process we were undergoing.

I also need to acknowledge clearly at this point that I was receiving an enormous amount of help completely free of any obligation to pay, from a charity whose vision is to assist people like me, and that certainly means a degree of tolerance is necessarily to be granted to even their most inexperienced staff. But however you express it, the second day of the training was going to be challenging.

A new perspective

I was a dog-inexperienced individual at the end of a confrontational day with an animal expert with very little life experience. Abigail had a degree in animal psychology, but it evidently had given her precious little understanding of human motivation. After her departure I telephone my own expert – Penny – and asked if I could visit that evening to discuss the position with her. Her answer was that indeed I could and, with Matt on the back seat in his harness I drove the thirty minutes to her house. Matt's reaction on arrival was one of unbridled excitement. Penny had clearly impressed herself upon his doggy mind more than adequately! As she opened the door he tore past her into the house, running round in excited circles looking for the toy box and treat bag. We could only giggle and look on, enjoying his unadulterated enthusiasm for life itself.

As Matt gradually settled down, we gravitated to the lounge where I poured out my tale of frustration and woe over a cup of coffee. Did Penny agree with the stance Abigail was taking? Had she ever known an extending lead to break? What did she think of the requirement to go through this nonsensical routine at 5.00 in the morning when there were neither people nor traffic on the streets? Should I maintain my resistance?

Penny sat and listened for a long time saying nothing. As my frustration gradually became a spent force and I ran out of things to say she finally had space to speak. Her answer came in the form of a question. "How long is it until you move to The Oaks?"

I thought for a moment. "Seven weeks give or take," I answered.

"Look," she said, "It really doesn't matter what I think, does it? The reality of the situation is that you've obviously got off to a very bad start with someone who calls the shots and could quite possibly be responsibly for taking Matt away from you if you don't toe the line. So whether she's been insensitive or whether you're unused to taking instruction and react badly to them really doesn't matter, does it? You're so close to getting through this process. There's only two days to go and after that you can ask for another placement officer if you really feel the need to. Then it's just seven weeks till you live in a place where Matt can run out of the front gate and straight into the forest without any kind of a lead on him at all. I suggest you just put up with it for a little longer. Go eat some humble pie, grit your teeth and get through this. It'll be worth it in the end."

I sat silently for a while, absorbing but not much liking this very sensible advice. Then I smiled, thanked Penny and went home with the intention of doing exactly what she had suggested. It really was the only sensible course of action. However frustrating I would find Abigail the next day, I would put up with it for the sake of the long-term benefit. And believe me, it was going to be frustrating.

Abigail – Day two

Abigail arrived about half an hour late the next morning. I could only surmise it was because yet further phone calls were being made about the situation. As I showed her into the lounge, I took a deep breath and without enthusiasm said, "Abigail, I want to apologise for my behaviour yesterday. Please put it down to tiredness. I will accept what you say and comply with your instruction."

She looked thrown. Clearly, some speech had been prepared that was now unnecessary. I could hope that we could put yesterday behind us and work together professionally for the next two days. Regrettably though, it wasn't to be as easy as that.

To start, we undertook some further sound work that this time apparently required me to stand fully clothed in the shower while Abigail observed Matt's responses to the door bell. I felt faintly ridiculous, but said nothing. Then it was time for me to show Abigail where I walked Matt. "I have a choice of two small parks," I told her, "one in the centre of town and one a little further out. Then of course, there's the forest where we go for longer walks.

We made our way to the first park, which was still suffering the after effects of misuse over the weekend. I have to admit it really did look pretty rough, with bottles and food packaging strewn haphazardly around. It came as no surprise when Abigail deemed it unsuitable for Matt. What did come as a surprise was what followed. "Mike," she said, "I don't think that you're treating the things I say with enough respect."

I looked at her surprised for a moment. "Really, Abigail?" I responded in genuine surprise. "I've told you I'm prepared to comply with all your instructions, haven't I?

"Yes," she said, "But I still don't think you're treating what I say with enough respect."

I could feel my shackles rising again, and took a moment to ensure that today I did not over-react. "Abigail," I responded, "it is my belief that each of us are due basic courtesy, and I hope you will agree that I have unfailingly been courteous with you during your visit. But respect? In my book that is something that we have to earn." I left the matter there. As instructed, I struggled to re-attach the halte collar for the short walk to the second park and we headed off to see if Abigail thought it more suitable.

This park contained a duck pond and, of course, Matt showed inordinate interest in the ducks. I look back now, having gained complete facility with both the halte lead and the extending lead and wonder why on earth I had so much trouble in those early days. But as I've said before, the learning curve was steep. I sat down on a bench a little way from the road and attached the extending lead before removing the halte collar. Abigail waited silently while I did so. Then we were off round the pond, with me trying to hold Matt back from his very evident interest in pursuing the ducks, which were giving him an appropriately wide berth. We were coming back full circle towards the point of departure when she stopped me. "Right," she said. "Put the halte collar back on him now please."

I looked at her in surprise. Then I looked back behind us some twenty yards to where there was a bench on which I could sit to do the job. "Not back there?" I asked enquiringly?

"No, here," came the retort.

Then I looked forward about thirty yards to the place where I'd sat to put on the extending lead and take of the halte. "Not there?" I asked.

"No, here," she repeated, without further explanation.

I shrugged and dropped to the wet ground earth on both knees. As I struggled on the ground with the halte one more time I could all but feel the Abigail's Alpha head and shoulders press down in a gesture of control over my own shoulders. Pack supremacy had been more than amply demonstrated.

That night I could not sleep. I felt I had been taken full advantage of, if not actually abused. I rose at three in the morning and wrote a long letter of complaint to Hearing Dogs about the way I had been treated. Then finally at about four, I slipped back into bed having discharged my frustration into the letter and fell asleep for a couple of hours.

My interactions with Abigail were better the next day. Whether it was due to her having adequately established the pack order in her own mind the day before, or whether it was due to the fact that we were at Hurst Manor, my place of work, I can't really say. But when Abigail left at the end of the day, I made two decisions. The first was that I would not post the letter. However frustrated I was I had to acknowledge I had contributed to the situation and I had no wish to damage this very young woman's career prospects in the way that would inevitably have followed. Secondly, I decided that when the dust had settled on her visit I would ask for an alternative placement officer. It was evident that management at The Grange were aware of the difficulty, albeit that they had heard only Abigail's version of the story. I anticipated that there would be no real resistance to my request. In fact, two days later I received a letter confirming my appointment some three weeks hence for a two-day visit by a placement officer. Her name was Sarah. Hearing Dogs had done the only sensible thing they could do in these circumstances – they had replaced Abigail as my placement officer. And Sarah was to prove to be a very, very different person.

Matt at Work

With Abigail's departure I was now flying solo with Matt and gradually absorbing all that living with a hearing dog requires and offers. But initially at least, every item of the training had to be remembered consciously, every routine undertaken slowly and carefully. There were times that I found myself tired, confused and frustrated. When I mentioned to Caroline about how difficult I was finding it all, her response was surprisingly unsympathetic. "Oh Michael," she said abruptly. "You're like a new mother with her first baby!" And here was someone talking who had, in her time, brought up three babies. She had little sympathy for a mere male who wasn't coping too well with a new dog. But when I stopped to think about it, actually, she was right. I was going through similar procedures and routines in looking after someone other than myself for the first time in many years. And seeing it in a comparable context to motherhood somehow made a difference. I redoubled my efforts and resolved to do whatever I needed to make the relationship work. It wasn't going to be effort free, but it was going to be overwhelmingly worthwhile.

Of course, a hearing dog at work was a new experience not only for Matt and me, but also for the colleagues with whom I work and for the residents of the nursing home. I began to make it a practice to take Matt into the lounge on each visit I paid to Hurst Manor, to give opportunity for the residents to see him and talk to him. It's remarkable how much difference a small matter like reaching out a hand to stroke a furry animal can make to the daily experience of an elderly person.

Good morning Auntie Brenda!

As far as the staff were concerned, Matt was universally adored from day one. As we walked round the corridors and rooms of the home in pursuit of a normal day's activities, the smiles of benevolence and questions as to his welfare and history were endless. Matt took all of this in his stride when in uniform, always looking poised and professional, every inch the working dog, alert to the needs of the person he was there to help. By contrast, once out of uniform he would revert to a very normal one year old, just-out-of-puppy-stage dog, with huge enthusiasm for life and all it offered. Friendly to everyone without exception, Matt did have, however, his favourites. In just the same way as he had attached himself to "Auntie Penny" at home, he was to form a lasting bond with "Auntie Brenda" at work.

Brenda is a much-valued colleague who works with me on the administrative side of the business. At the time Matt arrived at Hurst Manor, she and I shared an office in a wooden chalet in the grounds of the nursing home. Perhaps because of Brenda's proximity to Matt during the working day and the fact that he saw more of her than other staff members at Hurst Manor, he grew to become very attached to

103

Brenda. So much was this so, that as soon as we arrived at work on a Monday morning, he would strain at the leash to get to the office. If Brenda was already at her desk, he would rush across the floor at whatever speed the lead would permit and throw himself in excitement at her. Then it would be all licks and wags and cuddles for several minutes before he finally settled to a hard day's snoozing under my desk. The chalet has long since gone now, one of many changes resulting from the refurbishment and extension of the business. But Matt's connection to Brenda persists. And each Monday morning when we arrive at work he tugs me up the stairs to our new office where his first task of the week is to reacquaint himself with his dear friend with a level of enthusiasm that might suggest four months' absence rather than the usual four days!

Watch the Birdie

I've mentioned earlier that from virtually the first day I met him, Matt displayed considerable inclination to chase anything that moved. Though I'd been advised not to let him off the lead when I first took him home, it was evident from the first moments of walking on the beach that he had an instinctive interest in birds, and he did everything he could to get closer to them. Evidently you can take the dog out of the bird-retrieving environment, but you can't take the bird-retrieving instinct out of the dog. Walks along the beach in the early morning would often be punctuated by a sighting of a sea gull or raven. Matt would then display an unerring propensity to chase off towards it, until he came a little too close for the feathered creature's comfort. Typically it would simply stretch its wings unhurriedly, in full knowledge of the advantage conferred by its three dimensional movement capabilities as compared to Matt's mere two. Then it would soar into the air and out towards the sea, settling on the pinnacle of some inaccessible rock a hundred yards or so away, leaving Matt looking bemused.

The instinct ran a little deeper than simply chasing birds, though. From the time he came to live with me onwards, I noticed on many occasions that Matt had a deep instinct to carry something in his mouth, particularly when excited, and particularly when someone he knew well came to the front door. His habitual behaviour is to present a newly arrived guest with an offering of some sort. Items deemed appropriate for the purpose can be any one of his own toys, an old bone, a carelessly discarded slipper of mine or even, if nothing else is available that fits the purpose, a leaf. As for the deeply buried bird-carrying instinct that gives rise to this behaviour, we were later to have considerable trouble with Matt's propensity to chase at first birds and then just about anything else that moved. However, several months later, on the one occasion when I actually saw him corner a bird – when it became trapped in the greenhouse - he simply stood in front of it wagging his tail. I am quite certain that my little furry side kick represents absolutely no danger whatsoever to any form of animate entity on the planet – he simply takes the view that the purpose of his being alive is primarily to play, and that the rest of us have been put on the earth to assist him in this vocation. However, not long after Matt's arrival in my home the bird chasing thing was to get him into his first spot of trouble.

The previous summer Penny and I had begun taking Sunday walks exploring the Jurassic Coast – that stretch of coastline that runs from just west of Poole all the way down to Exeter. Designated as a world heritage site, it offers many fine walks for both enthusiastic fossil collectors and casual ramblers like ourselves. Living where I do, I'm spoiled for choice when it comes to walking. Accordingly, there had been very little incentive over the preceding few years to go

very far a field in pursuit of new walking territory. I
sometimes think you could live in the New Forest for a
lifetime and still walk somewhere different every day.
Nevertheless, we were now venturing down to the coast, and
Matt's arrival was a perfect excuse to step up the level of
activity in this department. One sunny Sunday afternoon we
ventured out for a walk in Studland, an area that lies between
Poole and Swanage. A pleasant walk along the coastal path
for an hour or so left us ready for the traditional late
afternoon cuppa, following which we were just about ready
to return home. It was then that Penny noticed Studland
Heath National Nature Reserve on the map. Since we were
close by and neither of had visited it before, we thought we'd
give it a quick look before turning for home and supper. As
we locked the car and made our way into the reserve, I could
see no signs that indicated dogs should be on leads, so,
naturally, I let Matt off his for another run. His youth and
puppy-like nature ensured at this time that he would throw all
available energy into the matter at hand and charge about like
a mad thing, later flopping asleep in complete exhaustion.
Well, that was the game plan anyway.

We followed the path downhill to a little pebble
beach. It was then Matt saw the birds… and saw them before
I had a chance to get him back on his lead... and saw them
before I noticed the sign that said "please keep dogs on leads"
A whole flock of sea birds were minding their own business,
roosting quietly on the edge of the water, perhaps a hundred
yards from where we had emerged onto the sand. Matt, of
course, did what the genes of generations dictated he must do
and made a bee-line for the birds, straight across yards of
intervening mud flats that lay between us and the roosting
flock. His initial confident, springy gallop took him down the
pebble beach, and then straight into twelve inches of thick,
black mud. Perhaps that wouldn't be too much of a problem
for larger breeds with longer legs. But when you stand about

two feet high at the shoulders, one foot of molasses-consistency mud is something of a challenge. Initially he tried to continuing pursuing his quarry. But instead of bounding forward as if he had springs on his feet like he normally does, each jump took him chest deep into the mud. The flock looked on in a superior, seen-it-all-before kind of way. Not one wing was flapped. Finally Matt got the message and stopped. Then he look round at us, decided that an honourable retreat was in order and made to return. Lollup. Lolloup. Lollup. Each bound took him chest deep into the black mud. Then finally he was out and dashing back across the pebbles to his master who, he presumed, would be so delighted to see him on his return and would like nothing better than for his faithful dog to show his affection and commitment by jumping up at him as high as he could possibly manage. There was nowhere for me to run. I gave in gracefully, accepting that every item of clothing on me would be consigned to the washing machine as soon as I arrived home. In fact, come to think of it, the washing machine has been working rather harder since Matt's arrival in my life than it ever needed to before. Can't think why.

However, a more immediate challenge was to get Matt home without transmogrifying the inside of the car into an uncannily accurate mock -up of a therapeutic mud spar. Mercifully, I had previously bought a large plastic sheet that sits on the back seat underneath Matt's blanket. Ginger carefully, I attached Matt to his harness, resolving to carry towels in the car at all times in future, and drove back to Penny's house. On the way back we discussed tactics. Penny was of the firm conviction that Matt should be given an immediate bath. I concurred, being in no position to argue. So I carried him into the house and held him while the ever patient and long suffering Penny ran a bath into which we gently placed one unbelievably muddy dog. Whether it was his first bath, naturally, I can't say. What I can tell you, though, is that he suffered it in evident miserable silence, making no attempt to get out until we released him. However, the moment he was free he leapt from the bath and rushed, dripping through the bathroom door, shrieking and squealing in animated excitement, and distributing copious quantities of muddy bath water round the bungalow as he went. I reckoned that if anything would sever my friendship with Penny this was it. But no, dogs can evidently do no wrong in Auntie Penny's book. Well, at least Matt can do no wrong anyway. Finally we cornered him and towelled him dry, making a clear mental note that Matt displayed no element of the traditional Spaniel water-baby nature whatsoever. An aversion to water and propensity to chase moving wildlife were to feature significantly on his agenda in the months to come.

Am-eazing Dog

The weeks were now rolling by towards the anticipated move to The Oaks in the summer that would finally rid me of the frustrations of managing Matt in the tiny flat. We were practicing sound work daily, taking trips out in full dress uniform (him, not me that is – I rarely vary from my own uniform of jeans and tee shirt). I reported Matt's progress to Hearing Dogs weekly (well, as often as I remembered to anyway), commenting on his progress in sound work, health and general behaviour. Matt's new placement Officer, Sarah, had been to visit in May and we had established a good quality rapport and working relationship. Sarah was a lady somewhat closer in age to my own than Abigail had been. She had, not surprisingly, considerably more experience of life in general and considerably more tact in particular. Matt and I were making good progress in working together as a team and Sarah had been pleased and perhaps a little surprised at how fast our competences were progressing. I had even developed a greater facility with the halte lead to the point where attaching and detaching it no longer represented an unpleasant experience. In fact, had we not needed to move home, I rather think we might have been given a final assessment and signed off as qualified by Hearing Dogs relatively quickly. My 'new mother' status was rapidly diminishing and Matt and I were becoming an effective working team, not to mention the best of friends.

My younger daughter, Vici, had visited and become totally smitten with Matt in much the same way as everyone else was. Her elder sister Naomi, having met Matt at The Grange during that first week's training, was now coming to spend her first weekend with me following Matt's arrival in my life. It was during this visit that Naomi first noticed that I would frequently refer to Matt as being amazing. Indeed, so noticeable to her was this, that it became quite a catch phrase for us that weekend. Whenever he did anything he'd been trained for, such as alert me to the fact that the phone was ringing, one of us would remark to the other, "Well, he is an amazing dog." And so, the title 'Amazing Dog' was born and became applied progressively more and more to everything he does. Now, I'm told that most dog owners will readily identify with the practice of speaking nonsense to their dogs, and over a period of time Matt's nick name became 'The Am-eazing Dog' – or 'The AD' for short. Just as heather progressively grows to cover the New Forest hill sides in the autumn, the term 'Am-eazing Dog' crept further and further into our daily vocabulary. So when he wakes me early, it is, of course, an am-eazingly early hour at which to be woken. My greeting to him in the morning after I've been licked into a state of wakefulness is "Good morning Am-eazing dog. Are you being am-eazing today?" Regarding the answer as self evident, he considers it unnecessary to respond verbally.

The first job of the day is normally to take Matt for a walk – an am-eazing walk of course – from which we return to his am-eazing breakfast. Commonly he will consume it am-eazing quickly, but on occasions he doesn't fancy eating and can leave the food in his bowl for an am-eazing long time (I've never known him actually to forgo eating it entirely though!). He is, of course, am-eazingly clever, which he demonstrates ably each time the phone or doorbell rings, whereupon he is entitled to an am-eazingly tasty treat as a reward for doing his job. Of course, because he knows he is due this reward, he can sometimes be am-eazingly evil and alert me and lead me to the phone when it has not rung, in the hope that I will reward him anyway. When this happens I tell him there is no reward, and that he must eschew evil and embrace righteousness. Of course, he understands every word I say, because he is an am-eazing dog.

On particularly warm days he can easily become an am-eazingly hot dog (non-edible variety, of course) though he never seems to feel am-eazingly cold (something to do with the speed at which he moves I think). On days that we go to Hurst Manor he is am-eazingly well behaved in the car – at least he is until we arrive, when he becomes am-eazingly excited at the prospect of seeing Auntie Brenda. Then, because generally he's not in uniform when he enters the office, he will give her an am-eazing kiss and cuddle before settling down under my desk for the morning. Sometimes I have to slip into the next office for a few minutes, but if I am gone too long he will pursue me and cry am-eazingly pitifully until I let him in, whereupon he becomes am-eazingly happy.

And when all said and done, there's really only one comment I can make about it all... Am-eazing! ☺

Moving to The Oaks

As April rolled into May my thoughts were increasingly absorbed by our forthcoming moving date. All concerned were hoping to complete the deal in early June. Over the weeks leading up to exchange of contracts Barry and Annette had invited us to visit several times, which had created an opportunity for Matt to become used to what was to become his new home, and hopefully make the transition easier for him. It also gave him a chance to socialise with Barry and Annette's two golden retrievers and to pinch toys from their toy box. So endearing is this little dog, that Annette never had the heart to separate him from his new found acquisitions when the time came for us to go home. Accordingly, Matt amassed a noteworthy collection of pre-owned soft toys over the weeks before we moved that were no doubt delighted to be repatriated when moving day finally came.

I arranged for Matt to spend the day of the move itself with Penny. His carrying capability is limited to his mouth, and most of what he picks up he is prone to dropping somewhere inappropriate when he gets bored so I didn't see him being too much of an asset while the rest of us struggled with packing cases and such like. He would have a far better time being looked after at the home of an indulgent auntie. The move itself proceeded as most moves do – not without hitches, but essentially smoothly, and a few hours after packing up at my flat in New Milton the furniture van rumbled into down town Godshill carrying all my possessions. I'd briefed the driver on finding the house, and set off before the van, so as to arrive and open up the house before it did. Unpacking was the usual, chaotic, "I-can't-find-the-kettle, where-did-you-put-the-coffee, who-saw-the-tea-towels-last" kind of experience. The removal men, my friend Geoff who'd come from London to help me move, and I, worked continuously to unload and unpack and get the place into a semblance of order. By six o' clock the van had gone, the most important boxes were unpacked and Penny had arrived with Matt, who, as expected, took childlike delight in dashing round the house and garden at break-neck speed investigating everything of interest and a considerable amount that wasn't.

Despite the busyness of the day we did find time for a walk that evening, strolling up the valley in the same direction as I had walked with Barry on that day back in March when I had first come to see the house. On that day Barry had advised that by June we should be able to see the marsh orchids. Crossing a little bridge (which we later came to christen 'Jamie's Bridge') over into the area of the valley that Barrie and Annette had nick-named 'Little Scotland,' we hunted a while but never did find the orchids. Instead, we came across innumerable hare's tail cotton grass flowers, which dotted the marshy sides of the valley with little white cotton wool buds of flowers for several weeks from June into July. And as the sun began to drop a little lower in the west on a gorgeous June evening, we gradually made our way home... to our new home.

Feeling Sheepish

I've moved house enough times in my life to know what a demanding and chaotic experience it can be, and I had decided some weeks earlier that we would benefit from a short break once we'd had an opportunity to unpack. Of course, as far as the AD was concerned moving was a doddle, and living at The Oaks just about as close as life on earth gets to doggy heaven. We'd slipped quickly into the habit of taking an hour's walk in the morning before launching ourselves on an unsuspecting day, and had identified a dozen or more different routes we could take by doing nothing more complicated than strolling out of our front garden gate. Matt, no doubt, would have been content to continue the routine indefinitely, but I for one was in need of a break.

So just about a week after we'd moved in, when we'd finally emptied all the boxes and found homes for most possessions, Matt and I set out in the car to the Peak District for a couple of days break from moving matters. We'd rented a small cottage, which I'd found on the Internet by typing into a search engine the words 'National Park' 'holiday cottage' and 'dog.' Quite naturally, rather a lot of sites came up, but I'd never been to the Peak District before, and this seemed and interesting and relaxing destination for a few days break without going to the ends of the earth.

We arrived at the cottage at about 4.00pm on the designated day and introduced ourselves to the owners. Matt made several attempts to introduce himself to their elderly cat, but for some unfathomable reason she wasn't having any of it. Of course, the majority of cats will turn tail and run from the presence of a dog, but this particular feline was made of sterner stuff. Whenever the AD got too close she would do the usual back-arched-fur-on-end thing, then take a swipe at him with her paw. Though she never inflicted actual bodily harm, the threat of hostilities was sufficient to make him undertake a dynamic risk assessment, and a strategic withdrawal. Perhaps the ignominy of the situation created some sense of hurt pride that contributed to the crisis that was shortly to arise.

We passed an uneventful evening and settled in for an early night, intending to wake early, as usual, and head out for a walk before the day got out of bed. Now, I suppose with the benefit of hindsight, I ought to have taken more notice of the fact that I was in unknown territory and therefore kept Matt attached firmly to his lead. Perhaps I should have paid more attention to the fact that as his weeks of forest experience had proceeded, he had shown an increasing propensity to chase animals – not only squirrels and rabbits, but on occasions even horses that happened to be running anyway. However marvellous a facility 20:20 hindsight is, it suffers from our inability to bring it into play before an event. As a result, I didn't give too much thought to the matter of letting the AD off his lead as we strolled the narrow tracks and footpaths of the Peak District National Park. And accordingly, when we were climbing a high path between the stone walls of two fields, I gave no thought to the contents of those fields. And when Matt ran on ahead as he always does, I paid no more attention to his excited chasing around and snuffling in the hedgerows than I normally would. In fact, it was only when I looked over the wall of the field to my left and saw Matt disappearing over a hill at maximum speed in hot pursuit of a small flock of sheep, that I realised all was not entirely as it ought to have been. The colour drained from my face (well, I assume it did – I had no mirror to check, and was a tad preoccupied to think about it anyway), my heart rate shifted up to panic level and I yelled at the top of my voice "Matt!!" No response. I kept calling. "Matt!! Matt!!" The AD kept ignoring me. Well, I assumed he did - he was nowhere in sight to enable me to judge what was actually going on for him. I looked around in near panic for anyone that might look like a farmer pointing anything that remotely resembled a shotgun in the direction of my beloved companion. Mercifully, the area was deserted. Aloneness can have its benefits. I took out the whistle I'd been given at The Grange and blew hard on it. Nothing. I blew and blew and blew in short bursts – an emergency signal. Still nothing. And then I stood in complete despair having absolutely no idea what to do next. Though I couldn't have been there more than a minute or so, it seemed like the proverbial eternity. Then finally the cavalry came charging over the hill to my rescue. Well, that is Matt came bounding back into sight at full pelt showing every sign of hugely enjoying what was clearly to him nothing but a wonderful, instinctive game.

There was no point in getting angry with him. He'd not have understood, and he was only doing what came naturally. With an enormous sense of relief, I reattached him to his lead where he spent the rest of our short visit to the Peaks National Park. But matters had now gone too far with the chasing behaviour. Something had to be done to stop it – and quickly.

We packed that afternoon and made for home a day early. The experience had left me with the sense that I wanted to keep Matt on familiar territory until I was better at managing him. I also wanted to get some advice from The Grange as quickly as possible. The morning after I arrived home I phoned Nicky and poured out the whole story. She listened sympathetically.

"Don't worry too much, Michael," she said. Some dogs simply do have a chase habit and it sounds like you did everything you could have done under the circumstances."

"Is it correctable, though?" I found myself asking.

"Oh sure," she replied. "In fact we have people here whose job is solely to work with dogs that have specific behavioural problems. I know Sarah's back down with you in a few days and she needs to look at Matt's pattern when she's with you. But from what you've told me I reckon that this is a job for Celina."

I was somewhat reassured, and it was indeed the case that Sarah was due to pay a further visit towards the end of the month. I was resolved that I would do the only thing I could do – wait for advice and keep Matt firmly on a lead in unknown territory in the meantime.

Part Party

Following our move to the Oaks, it seems that Matt had come to his own decision as to making our relationship permanent, for shortly after our arrival my friends began receiving the following letter:

Dear Human Person
16th June 2004

As you may know, some months ago I came to live with Michael in order to foster him with a view to adoption. I am writing to let you know that after much serious consideration I have decided to make the relationship permanent by legally adopting him. However, it became evident during the fostering period that it would not be possible for the two of us to continue living comfortably in his small flat. He has simply become too set in his ways there, and (if I may say this without sounding pompous) I am a dog who is used to certain *standards*, if you understand me (I simply have to have space to roam in and an open fire to meditate in front of at the end of a long hard day – you know how it is). Though I have managed to train Michael reasonably well concerning my food and exercise routines, I have come to the conclusion that the only possible way both to get him out of his rut and for me to return to the degree of comfort to which I am used, is for us to move. Accordingly, I arranged for us to buy "The Oaks" where, as you will see from the top of this letter, we now live.

Knowing that you are a friend of Michael's I should like to invite your dog to a GRAND ADOPTION CELEBRATION at the above address, on 10th July, starting at 5.00pm You and your mate are also invited, together with any current litter you may have (please bring leads, so that your children may keep you under proper control). However, if you are one of those poor unfortunate humans that sadly, as yet, has found no dog to adopt you, I promise that all dogs at the party will be tactful and not draw attention to your orphan status. In fact, you will be made just as welcome as if you were a complete human person, under the care of a dog.

I can reassure any concerns you may as to the venue, since "The Oaks" has a copious supply of bushes for scent marking and backs onto the open forest for the numerous walks your dog will wish treat you to while you are here. Furthermore, you may also be reassured as to food, since a supper of best butchers' bones and barbecued wild boar sausages will be served at 6.00pm, followed by a dessert of good boy choc drops, washed down with lashing of the finest full cream milk. I will try to ensure there's some human food on hand as well, but should any of you require that funny red or white stuff you drink to make yourselves happy, please ensure you bring some of it with you. Without wishing to lower the tone of this missive, I must also specify that cats will NOT be welcome (nasty, hissy, spiteful things – I can't understand why you allow yourselves to be adopted by them in the first place).

So that I might cater for numbers appropriately, would you please signify your dog's intention to attend by returning the tear off slip at the bottom of this letter. Limited overnight accommodation is available for those bringing dogs from long distances and those with young litters that tire easily. Please ask me if you wish to stay over.

A map of how to get to "The Oaks" appears on the reverse.

Yours sincerely

Matt Lawson

Now, clever though the AD is, I reckon he must have had some assistance with this, even if only in sealing down the envelopes. But whoever it was that helped him, the acceptances began to flow in and we started preparations for a joint housewarming and adoption party. Most were from humans on behalf of their dogs, many of whom were gracious

117

enough to accept. However, one in particular bears special mention, since it was from some other animals, and in this case not dogs:

Dear Canine Creature

We received your correspondence of 4th June inviting our Adopters to your official adoption and Heating - up -House Ceremony (whatever that might be ! these humans really are strange). We actually quite enjoyed reading the little epistle, but all that changed of course when we came across your condescending, ungracious and totally inaccurate remarks about our blatantly superior Feline species! Nasty, hissy and spiteful indeed; we'll scratch your eyes out if you are not careful! Unfortunately our Adopters do not share our opinions of the lower species, and they seem quite keen to spend time in your presence, we know not why, yappy slobbery creatures that you canines are! We cannot imagine why any member or the Human race would want to be fostered by one of your kind when it is obviously infinitely preferable to be owned by a feline. However, each to their own! Our Adopters may have some difficulty in confirming their availability to come until quite late on unfortunately, due to complications of the human variety, these particular problems being in the shape of small, foreign people staying at OUR residence at the time. We hope this will not be too difficult for them to overcome, because they were quite upset when they realised this may prevent them from coming to see you (poor misguided fools) and your Adopter (more understandable).

Our Adopters will be in contact nearer the time, and will hopefully be able to come down to commiserate with and console your Adoptee when he finally realises (as we know he surely will) how infinitely better off he would have been if he had been adopted by a Feline.

Yours Disappointedly,

Gizmo & Kitten.

I showed the letter to Matt. He pronounced himself indifferent by sniffing it and walking away. However, before we could throw ourselves headlong into party preparations we had Sarah's visit to address, and the decision that needed to be made about how to deal with Matt's chase habit.

Chase & London

Sarah had already met Matt and me when she came to undertake the placement visit at my flat in New Milton in May. We had scheduled an additional visit partly because she wanted to see how Matt was getting on in his new home and partly to give me an opportunity to practice taking Matt on the train to London – something I thought I would very likely have to do from time to time, if only to visit Naomi, who lives in Battersea.

Sarah arrived bright and early. I explained to her the full circumstances of Matt's growing chase habit, ending up with the sorry tale of what had happened during our visit to the Peak District. Sarah listened carefully to my story without interruption. When I was done she responded, "Right, well we'd better see him in action in the Forest. Let's take him out for a walk and see what happens. Don't try to discipline or control him in any way – we'll just watch how he gets on."

Matt, of course, was his usual enthusiastic self when it comes to walks. As soon as he gets the idea that we're going out he rushes to the garden gate and back then dashes in excited circles until I have my boots on. If he thinks I'm taking too long about it he's not above complaining by whining loudly until I come to let him out of the gate. As soon as we were underway we crossed the little stream that

119

flows down through the forest and into my garden, then found ourselves on the open forest proper. Matt was away like a cork from an over-pressurised bottle of champagne, dashing this way and that, running on ahead then tearing back to make sure we were following. Sarah looked at me and smiled. "I can see what you're up against already!" she said. "Is he always like this?

"Oh yes, " I answered, "this is absolutely normal, consistent behaviour for him. I'm told that with luck he'll settle down to a reduced energy level somewhere between the ages of two and three."

Sarah gave me a sympathetic smile in response.

A little later in the walk the inevitable happened. Matt spied a large black crow. Without the slightest delay he was off, and wholly unresponsive to Sarah's calls or blasts on the whistle. She watched him a while then said thoughtfully, "I think that when he sees something to chase he simply has too much adrenalin to be able to respond to you. It's not that he's being disobedient, it's more that generations of breeding have produced this response when he sees a bird, or whatever. It's natural to him to go after it and he switches off to everything else while he's in pursuit."

That at least made a little more sense to me. And it certainly meant there was no point in getting cross about it. He simply had no idea of what he was doing wrong. "So what's the solution?" I found myself asking. "In fact, *is there* a solution?"

"Oh yes," said Sarah. "We can train this behaviour to the point where it's under control. In fact we have a member of staff at Hearing Dogs called Celina…." and I knew that Sarah and Nicky were seeing eye to eye! "I'll talk to Celina of course, but I think we need to take him back to The Grange for re-training for a while."

This was new departure. Immediately I was worried that I'd not get him back. "How long will you keep him?" I asked doubtfully.

"Only a couple of weeks, I should think," replied Sarah. "And don't worry, we'll bring him back! I'll talk to Celina and phone you later in the week to arrange a time to collect him." Relieved, I accepted the position as stated and we returned to the house before setting out on our train trip to London.

I was concerned that the city might prove to be a significant challenge for both of us. Many dogs find the bustle and crowds too much, but Matt had been given particular exposure to city circumstances for the very reason that I had told Hearing Dogs I'd likely need to take my dog into town. Accordingly, Matt had been selected for me because the selectors believed he would be able to take it in his stride. Getting on the train was no big deal in itself. Matt was familiar with trains and settled down quickly under my seat to sleep through the whole journey. Of more consequence was getting off at the other end and in particular, heading down into the tube system on the escalator.

"If you're able to," said Sarah, you can carry him down the escalator." I looked dubious. I'd never picked Matt up before, never mind tried to negotiate a moving escalator with him balanced in my arms. I had no idea how he would respond to being carried. "On the other hand, if you're carrying bags or whatever, you can ask for the escalator to be stopped so that you can walk up and down it." I was equally unsure about wanting to draw attention to myself by making such a bold request. But nevertheless, this was the world I now inhabited, and I had had no shortage of training in deaf assertiveness myself. One way or another we would make this tube train thing work for us.

At the top of the escalator under Sarah's watchful eye I leaned forward and lifted him, whereupon he promptly jumped straight into my arms as if we'd been executing this manoeuvre forever! This completely unexpected development made it obvious that however unfamiliar I was with the procedure, Matt was an old hand at it. So we stepped carefully onto the down escalator and the AD surveyed the world of passing passengers in a somewhat superior manner from his elevated position, with no sense of being the centre of attention on the Waterloo escalator that he clearly was that day! And at the bottom as I leaned forward to return him to earth he jumped out of my arms and looked up at me as if to say "Next instruction please?" This dog was clearly one step ahead of my game – but then again he often is. As this was only a practice run, we travelled on the tube train a few stops to check that Matt was ok with it (which he clearly was), then retraced our steps to Waterloo. There, it was back up the escalator in a reversal of our downward journey, an admiring public smiling and staring on. Finally we made our way out onto the Embankment to look for a suitable place for a pee-break before catching the late afternoon train back to Southampton Central where we'd parked the cars.

"I'll talk to Celina and be in touch later in the week," said Sarah as we said our goodbyes."

I made my way home with growing confidence that we would be able to overcome the challenge of the chase habit in the same way as we had all the others challenges – with the help and support of the seemingly inexhaustible patience and skill of the staff at Hearing Dogs. If Matt is the Am-eazing dog, then all I can say is that these are pretty Am-eazing People!

He did the crime... he does the time

A few days later Celina telephoned.

"I've heard all about Matt from Sarah and Nicky," she said. "He certainly sounds like quite a character. I'd like to bring him back to The Grange for some further training. I'll come and pick him up on Thursday 8th July if that's ok with you.

I hesitated a moment. This, of course, would clash with the party. On the one hand we had a lot of guests coming and it wouldn't seem the same if Matt, the star of the show, was absent. On the other we really needed to get to grips with this problem without delay. "Would it be ok if I brought him up to The Grange myself on the Monday morning," I asked. "That's 12th July. We have something on at the weekend I'd like him to attend with me." Somehow admitting to what the event actually was seemed just a tad too naff!

"No problem," came Celina's reply. I think in truth she was glad that I could save her a journey!

So Matt's attendance of the party was safeguarded and we were free to proceed with the preparations. Thus it was that on 10th July at around 5.00pm some 20 VIP visitors descended upon the Oaks for social interaction, party eats and drinks, games and rambles. They were a decent, restrained crowd and I'm glad to say no fights or nastiness broke out as can happen at these gatherings. In fact, judging by the body language I was able to observe, some pretty good friendships were established, and possibly in one or two cases the beginning of true intimacy. Overall, I think I can safely say that each and every one enjoyed themselves immensely. As a grand finale we rounded off the evening by supplying each delighted guest with a surprise doggy bag of a top quality chew-bone. Oh, and I think the human guests had a pretty good time too.

Then, come Monday morning, I ferried Matt back up to The Grange, bade him a sad farewell, not quite believing 100% that I'd ever see him again, and set off for home alone. As I got out of the car back at The Oaks and slammed the door I suddenly felt very alone.

If you've brought up a family and ever spent any length of time away from your children, you might remember that the first week of their absence can be quite a positive experience. You have time to do all those things you can't get to when they're around. You're free to come and go without thought to their needs. But after about a week you begin to realise they're not there and really become aware of their absence. One of the first things I noticed when Matt had been away about a week was the silence. It's not that he makes much of a noise – quite the opposite. Rather, when he's around I spend the whole day talking to him – usually some nonsense about him being am-eazing or some such, but nevertheless, talking. And after a week I realised that what I was noticing was the absence of the sound of my own voice. It was a useful reminder of how much life has changed since he came to live with me – and how important it was to me that this state of affairs should continue. With the first week out of the way and all the chores done that were difficult to execute with a dog around, I fell into missing Matt seriously. Life without him was manageable, but somehow much of the joy had gone out of it. I functioned, and got on with what I had to do, but I wasn't enjoying myself in the way that I do with him around.

Once or twice I e-mailed Celina to ask after his progress. Always she responded promptly to the effect that he was progressing, but gave little away as to any anticipated return date. Then finally, at the end of the second week she telephoned. "We're all done," she said. "I'd like to bring him back next Thursday if that suits you."

"Perfect," I said, not bothering to look at my diary. Whatever was in there would have to be postponed. Getting my best friend back was top priority.

I have to say that I still harboured some doubts as to how much difference it would be possible for the training to make to Matt's chase habit though. It seemed to me that there are some instinctive tendencies that are just there in a dog's behavioural pattern and we simply have to manage them and live with them. But I was to be proven completely wrong. Celina arrived back with Matt who tumbled out of the car and threw himself all over me in an excited bundle of licks and cuddles and yelps and whines. Then, with the welcome over, we set out immediately into the forest to put the new training to the test.

"What I've done," explained Celina, "is to work with him to distract him when he's inclined to chase something. We started with two tennis balls. As soon as I saw a bird or animal get his attention I'd call him and throw a ball for him. But that wasn't enough. His inclination to chase is very strong."

'Tell me about it!' I thought.

"So after that," she continued, "I started using an electronic collar with him. I have a remote control that allows me to give him a puff of compressed air from the collar at any time. It doesn't hurt him, but it does distract him. So when he made as if to pursue some other creature I'd give him a puff of air. As I did, I would blow this." Celina held out to me a referee's whistle that I later learned was called a 'Thunderer.' "What I've done is to set up an association between the compressed air and the whistle. If it works properly he should respond to the Thunderer and not need the air collar. If you ever need to blow the Thunderer you should find he stops dead in his tracks because of the association."

I listened with interest, but still felt dubious as to how much difference it was possible to make to Matt's chasing

125

behaviour. Maybe he'd behave for Celina or another professional trainer, but I couldn't see myself getting the required behaviour from him.

"What you should now find," continued Celina, "is that he doesn't have the same tendency to chase as he did. But if he does set off after something, try calling him back or using your own whistle. Then if neither of those works, use the Thunderer."

So off we set to find a test to prove the point either way. It took no time at all – the forest is pulsing with wild life. At the sight of the first large bird Matt hesitated instead of launching into a chase. Celina had both whistles at the ready, but to my amazement he responded to a simple call. A little later it happened again with another bird. Then later again the procedure was repeated with a rabbit. I was utterly speechless. Not only had it been possible to create the association with the compressed air and the whistle that Celina had aimed for, she had even managed to get him to the point where he knew he wasn't supposed to chase anything at all. From that point forward Matt's first reaction to the sight of something he would like to chase has been to hesitate and look at me. Then all I need to do is say "No," and miraculously he leaves it alone and moves onto the next interesting smell or sight.

We returned home and Celina made ready to leave. "I can't thank you enough," I said to her as she got into the car. You've made a tremendous difference to his behaviour and my management of him. I'm truly amazed."

We said our good byes and Celina drove away. For some weeks afterwards I kept the referee's whistle closely to hand, but found I didn't need it. Matt was a reformed character. My regular whistle is now attached to my key ring, so it's always with me and occasionally I do need to call him with it if he's out of sight or out of the range of my voice.

The Thunderer now lies in the car, unused. I've never so much as found out what it sounds like.

Meet the Gang

It was a beautiful sunny week in late June when I saw the large notice board appear on a tree at the edge of a field in downtown Godshill. "Fordingbridge Show," it announced, specifying a long weekend in a few weeks time when the world and his fashionable wife would descent upon our little village in pursuit of country crafts and rural idyll. Being new to the area I'd not heard of this particular show before. Noting that it was actually within walking distance of home and aware that I ought to do something to begin to participate in local life, I phoned Aunty Penny and invited her up for the day on the Sunday – the final day – of the show.

M'Chicken!

The three of us strolled up the hill from The Oaks, Matt in full dress uniform, the July sunshine making it a pleasure to be out in the Forest. As we neared the showground I smiled in a rather self-satisfied kind of way at the long queue of cars waiting to get into the parking field. It was unusual and very nice, I reflected, to be able to go somewhere interesting without having to take the car for a change. Penny, Matt and I wove our way through the parking lines to the ticket booth. £7.00 per person of hard earned coinage passed from palm to palm and we strolled into the show ground. For a local country show, it was actually quite impressive – tents and display, show ring and animal pens stretching off in every direction, flanked by stalls selling every imaginable product from jam to Jacuzzis. If you've not been to a country show before, they're definitely a worthwhile day out. Their origins lie in the farming community – a colourful annual amalgam of competitions for the best bottled beetroot and the coolest Cornish cattle or whatever, with sage like judges wandering round attaching bright rosettes to the ear of some nonchalant animal. But these shows have evolved far beyond their original remit now, with all comers taking the opportunity to ply their wares and publicise their own particular brand of must-have heaven. The whole effect is great fun, and in our neck of the woods, anyway, the shows seem to be thick on the ground during the summer tourist months.

As we strolled round between guinea pig display and second hand CD stalls, Penny tapped me on the shoulder and pointed. Coming towards us was a lady in an electrically powered wheelchair and trotting along beside her was a dog in Hearing Dog uniform. We stopped, introduced ourselves and chatted for a while. Matt introduced himself in the time honoured, non-verbal, dog fashion (well, actually he's not really supposed to pay attention to other dogs when we're out and about and he's in uniform, but I thought that in the case of a fellow traveller like this one we'd let him make an exception). Suzanne, as she introduced herself, was local, and was at the show for the day to help staff a stand for the local fundraising chapter of Hearing Dogs. Now, I'd heard from the Vet that there was some local activity of the Fraternity, but I'd not yet managed to make contact with the people involved. Here was the perfect opportunity to do so. So having passed some of the time of some of the day with Suzanne, we sauntered off in the direction of the Hearing Dogs stand. Sure enough, there it was, just inside the entrance to one of the general marquees – a display of pictures and leaflets and some rather weary looking helpers – well it was the afternoon of the third and final day of the show, so they were fully entitled to look weary. We introduced ourselves to the stand minders and pointed out that I'd just come to live in the area and was looking to get a involved to some degree. Three pairs of eyes lit up simultaneously. Then it happened. The dreaded c-word was thrown into the conversation – committee. Now, I have to tell you that one naturally occurring geological feature to which I'm congenitally allergic is that infamous structure known as the Committee. The very word strikes terror into my poor deaf heart. Not only do committee members have a tendency to discover I'm a chartered accountant and hence prime Treasurer-fodder, but these days the ol' cloth ears make it harder to hear and easier to fall asleep when matters about as scintillating as the treatment of left toe-nail rot in pregnant ants reaches the top of the average agenda.

I've also discovered over the years that the world is divided into two groups – those whose primary enjoyment comes from doing things, and those whose comes from talking about doing things. Now, I'm not trying to suggest that thems wot talks never does, nor thems wot does never talks. We're talking tendency here, inclination, genetic disposition . But I do have to say that if I gathered together every member of every committee on which I've sat over the years and placed them end to end, I rather think they would have only a marginally slimmer chance of arriving at a decision than they did when I spent my happy evenings with them talking about… well I was generally never really sure what we were talking about, actually. Clearly the fault lies with me, for there must be many wonderfully managed, lean, mean fighting committee-machines out there, whose achievements are legendary and whose effectiveness is dented only by committee-cynics such as myself.

Nevertheless, at the mention of the c-word my heart headed swiftly for the soles of my shoes. I smiled sweetly at the nice gentleman who had uttered the profanity and made as if to move away. But I'd reckoned without the launch of Hearing Dogs' very own thermo nuclear deterrent. "Oh Michael," said Penny brightly, "why don't you give your phone number to David? Then he can arrange for the local organiser to get in touch with you." Now that wasn't fair. Everyone knows that the whole point of a thermo nuclear deterrent is you never actually fire it. But the Exocet had been launched, it had made a direct hit and I was well and truly sunk. I put the coat hanger back in my mouth, handed over my ex-directory, top secret, need-to-know-only-basis phone number and left, tail between my legs. I was once again a fully-fledged committee member (pending). Matt trotted along behind me. He at least was carrying his tail high. I couldn't see the angle of Penny's tail from where I was walking but I reckon it must have been pretty near vertical as a result of a job well done. ☺

The afternoon fading, we made our way back towards the car park via the few stalls and tents we hadn't visited. One along the way made us linger a little. Fordingbridge, if I've not told you already, has a rather excellent health facility. On one large site lies a big GP surgery, a small cottage hospital, a dental practice and a private alternative therapy clinic – the Arch clinic. And who should have taken a tent at the Fordingbridge show, but the Arch clinic. Penny and I both have an interest in alternative medicine and holistic therapy, and we lingered a while at the tables bowed under the weight of literature on opathys and ologies, diagrams of bone structures and leaflets on all manner of therapies. One caught my eye in particular. A course on meditation would be starting in September.

Now, I'd become regular in my daily meditation during the previous year with tremendous attendant benefits, but since Matt had come to live with me in April, my routines had changed and I'd allowed the meditation to slip out of my daily schedule. I was a tad irritated with myself for having allowed it to happen, as well. After all, I'd managed to ensure that every day I showered and ate, and that on most days I watched TV, so there was no real excuse for letting something as fundamentally important as meditation drift out of my life. Here was an opportunity to get back into it. We picked up the leaflet with the intention of booking onto the programme.

Homage paid to country living and a full afternoon thoroughly enjoyed, we ambled off towards home, clutching leaflets on alpacas and meditation, Hearing Dogs and rambling routes through the forest.

I was looking forward to September.

Jamie's Bridge

As you'd expect, with the summer in full swing and being new to the area, Matt and I took many, many walks in the forest and heath land around our new home over those months. There were innumerable places to explore, and we never seemed to run out of new routes to follow. One that became a firm favourite took us east out of the garden gate and up the length of the largely undisturbed valley where our home is situated. The main tourist road through our area runs along the top of one the ridges that shelters the valley and the

other ridge is covered by Godshill Wood. Presumably
because there are few stopping places on our side of the road,
and because Godshill wood is itself off the main tourist
routes, we get relatively few holiday-making visitors. This
valley remains a secret hidden treasure, much loved by the
local dog walking fraternity, the horse riders and, of course,
the forest animals who linger here largely undisturbed.

The valley is perhaps two miles long, and down the
centre of it runs a slow meandering stream that makes its way
lazily down to the River Avon at Fordingbridge. Of course,
that's in summer. As we were to find out later in the year, in
winter the water the water cascades down the sides of the
valley and all the little stream-lets that feed the central stream
become fast flowing brooks (including the one that passes
through the garden at The Oaks). Then the hillsides become
saturated and every indentation turns into a quagmire with
anything up to a foot of mud to be negotiated. Now, that's
enough to cope with in Wellington boots, but when your two
feet tall and your doing it in bare paws the circumstances can
be challenging. More of this later.

About a third of the way in from each end of the
valley with perhaps three quarters of a mile between them, lie
two picturesque little wooden bridges over the stream. That
summer it became our habit to walk up the valley, crossing
the stream on one bridge, then continuing on the other side of
the stream and crossing again on the other bridge, before
climbing the hillside and turning for home. On one occasion
when we were following this ritual we approached the second
of the two bridges to find a pony crossing from the other
direction. Not being in the mood to mind his manners, Matt
stepped onto the bridge, so that neither he nor the pony could
pass without someone giving way. I held back from involving
myself in the confrontation for a moment, intrigued to see
what might happen. They stood about eight feet apart,

looking for all the world like gunslingers confronting each other at the OK coral.

("ok Urpp – there ain't no room on this bridge for both of us ta pe-ass, so yer jess gonna hev ta turn beck."

"Me turn beck Marshall? I thenk yer gonna have to re-*can*-sider that one. Neow, kindly stip aside en lit me pe-ass."

Ok Urpp, draw!).

The pony became impatient and stamped his foot. Matt apparently had no notion of what the gesture mean and stood there wagging his tail. As usual, play was on his mind. The pony stamped again and took a step forward. Matt stood his ground. At that point I became concerned that the confrontation might turn physical and weight might confer an unfair advantage in the pony's favour. So in the end it was me that turned chicken and summoned Matt back off the bridge. As he sauntered haughtily forward, the pony snorted, tossed his head up and returned his gun to his holster. ☺

On another occasion when we were walking the same route we arrived at the bridge to find that someone had stepped down into the water just a few days earlier to write his name in the mud on the bridge supports – "Jamie Cowie – done 19/7/04," it said. As these things sometimes do, this harmless little act started the cogs whirring in my head with the result that by the time we returned home I had the basis of my first – and as it turned out – only poem of the year:

Jamie Cowie

When Matt and I were walking in the Forest
we came upon a bridge that crossed a stream,
and on the bridge's pillar was inscribed:

"Jamie Cowie done 19/7/04."

This Jamie Cowie made me think about
the tendency we have to want to leave our mark
beyond the limits of our days.

When I am done and all my days are passed,
I want to leave no mark on bridges,
nor any epitaphs on cenotaphs.

If I have done the work I came to do,
then I will leave no footsteps on the Forest grass
and whispering winds will not exhale my name.

But Jamie marked my thoughts today.
And leaving marks on souls of other men?
Well, that is quite a different matter.

It was also my first poem to feature Matt. Somehow
seemed a fitting way to mark our return to Forest living and
his arrival in my life.

You no blind

Shortly after Matt had come to live with me I had
come to the conclusion that there was little point in keeping a
cramped convertible car if I wasn't to be permitted to drop

the top when Matt was in it with me. It had, in any case, become impractical for work purposes, and in June I had exchanged it for a Skoda Octavia estate. It was now 13th September and, given my high mileage, it was time for the car's first service. Matt and I drove into Southampton and dropped off the car at the dealer's. We now had a couple of hours to kill over the lunch hour before we could go home again.

I was unfamiliar with this a part of Southampton, so decided to go for a stroll and look for somewhere for lunch. It was one of those warm, sunny September days when you get the sense that Summer is trying to resist forever the ascendance of an inevitable Autumn. As we walked around the streets, Matt in full dress uniform, as usual, we found that we attracted a range of stares and benevolent smiles. With shopkeepers' wares piled up on the pavement in every direction, the traffic fought its way slowly round the obstacle course of delivery vehicles, pedestrians crossing the road and market traders called out their best offers of the day. Against this pleasant general hubbub, we made our way slowly through the stalls and shops, coming eventually to a fish & chip shop. Essentially a take away outlet, it offered just a few tables for the casual lunch time diner to take a few minutes off their feet before continuing with their day. I looked inside, then looked at Matt, wondering what the response would be to his presence by the owners. We stepped inside the door to see a middle aged Greek-looking couple serving behind the counter, and no customers anywhere in sight.

"Sausage and chips, please" I said to the woman. Before she had a chance to answer, a gruff, Mediterranean voice called from the far end of the shop, "No dog!"

I looked at the woman. She didn't respond. I moved further down into the fish bar so as to be able to talk more easily to the man who addressed me. As I did, I was confronted with a very large Greek gentleman in a greasy white overall, clearly suffering form the combined heat of the day and the tools of his profession, perspiring profusely over the fish cabinet. He looked at me out of the corner of his eye. "No dog," he repeated.

"He's a hearing dog," I answered, "an assistance dog."

"No dog," came the predictable reply. Clearly, I wasn't making myself plain.

"He's a hearing dog, "I repeated. "A guide dog. Like a guide dog for the blind."

This got a different response. The Greek gentleman leaned across the counter and looked at me closely and suspiciously. "You no blind," he said, clearly thinking I was trying to pull a fast one. Evidently as far as he was concerned I was some strange individual who, for reasons best known to myself, spent my days pretending to be blind so that I could get my dog into places he wasn't supposed to go.

"No," I agreed, "I no blind. I mean, I'm not blind. But I am deaf, and this dog is my hearing dog and he is allowed to go into the same places as guide dogs for the blind. The culinary professional behind the counter muttered something to his wife (well I suppose it was his wife) and ambled off into the back room.

She smiled at me and motioned for me to sit down. I did so, and Matt curled up under my chair in his normal fashion whilst I consumed a hasty and not particularly tasty lunch before making a swift retreat from the field of battle.

The confrontation was not a pleasant one, but I accepted that it was necessary, and that it would more than likely be repeated from time to time. As well as the personal benefit I derive from having Matt with me, I accepted that to some extent I was in an ambassadorial role for other and future users of assistance dogs. Unless someone stands up and presses for change it will never happen.

Om, lip reading and meditation

August had passed off pleasantly enough, with human guests visiting in the Chalet, and forest creatures visiting in the garden. I'm delighted with how popular I am with friends and relatives over the summer. "Might it have something to do with my location and accommodation," I ask myself on my more cynical days? "Naahhh, no way," I answer when in more rational mind. I love the coming and going of old friends and new friends that the availability of accommodation in the forest stimulates, and I love to watch the deer and the foxes, the rabbits and the woodpeckers visiting the garden. And just over the garden fence there's the annual spectacle of New Forest Ponies feeding their foals, and coming to the window to be fed carrots or whatever they can cadge from me. I sit at my desk in the sun room, with a commanding view from the picture window down towards the stream at the very bottom of the valley, and watch the comings and goings of the local population against the back drop of an ever colourful, ever changing country garden, so intelligently planted by my predecessors at The Oaks.

Come September, the human visiting season was pretty much over, and life began to quieten down. Still advised by Barry and Annette on the idiosyncrasies of the house, I'd begun to prepare for winter with a delivery of logs for the wood burner, and survey of necessary works on the house.

But September also heralded the commencement of the new academic year, when many organisations open up again after the summer. Busy-ness attributable to a multiplicity of summer visitors gave way to busy-ness attributable to taking on too many activities. Within a week or two of the beginning of September I suddenly found myself attending three writers groups, a lip reading class and a meditation group. "Who puts all these commitments in my diary?" I find myself asking when I look at an ink-covered page. "It can't possibly be me, can it?"

To Matt, of course, this was all grist to the proverbial mill. He loves companionship in any form, and meeting new people comes high up his list of priorities. So to each of these gatherings he would accompany me in full dress uniform, be fussed over and admired by the assembled multitude, then slip quietly under my chair for the duration of the event.

Having allowed lip reading to slip under pressure of business the previous year, I knew it was important that I recommenced as soon as possible. I reckoned that in the few years I probably now had remaining before my hearing capability dropped too far, I really needed to apply myself assiduously to acquiring a skill that in the long term could make the difference between maintaining human contact and living a life of not-so-splendid isolation. I'd made enquiries during the spring about lip reading classes near to work, and discovered one that met in Yeovil. So over the summer I'd signed up, and in early September I rolled up for the first session of the new academic year. Parking in the car park of the church where the group was held, I got out and walked round to Matt's door to get him into uniform. As I opened the door, another car pulled up in the space beside me. Now, this made it somewhat harder to get Matt out of the car of course, and I acknowledged a passing thought about the number of empty spaces in the car park ("of all of da spaces in all of da car park, ya had to drive into da one next to mine... park it again, Sam"). Nevertheless, we managed to get him out of the car and into uniform. As I was about to walk away, a muffled voice came from behind. Now, I'm about to attend a lip reading class, and I'm holding the lead of a dog whose coat says "Hearing Dogs for Deaf People." Might it be a safe bet to assume that I can't hear you if you talk to me from behind? Apparently not. I turned to see who was addressing me. A Rubinesque lady of a certain age was emerging from the driver's seat of the car that had pulled in so tightly next to me. I looked enquiringly at her and she repeated her question. "Are you training him for me?"

Now, I'd quite often been mistaken as Matt's trainer over the preceding few months. His coat sports the words "Hearing Dog *in training,*" so I guess its not altogether surprising that sometimes people think I'm training him.

"Err, actually no," I answered, "Matt and I are in training together."

"Oh," she said, sounding disappointed. "I'm waiting for a new hearing dog and I was rather hoping this might be him." There must be a lot of ways to establish a first meeting with your new hearing dog, but unarranged and in an anonymous car park in the middle of Yeovil doesn't seem to me to top the list.

Undeterred, my newfound friend continued "Well, I'm sure you'll do well with him. Any advice you need, just let me know. I've had a hearing dog for *years.*" Now, call me an old cynic, but wasn't there just the merest hint of a patronising tone in the voice here? (Eat your heart out Hyacinth Bucket). I sighed inwardly. How come minding your own business just ain't enough to ensure a quiet life any more? "By the way," she continued unperturbed, "do you know Janet?" The question carried all manner of possible implications, but still managed somehow to sound a tad sinister.

"Err, Janet who?" I asked, trying not to sound inferior, and already wishing I'd not risen to the bait.

"Oh, Janet's the class teacher. I've known her for *years.*" Yup, definitely heard it in the tone that time. (Hyacinth II – just when you thought it was safe to get back into the lip reading class). I know I was supposed to genuflect and bow low at that point, but I had a prior with my lip reading teacher. So as quickly as we could without causing offence, Matt and I slipped off to meet the other new class members.

The format was much the same as I was used to in Lymington – a horseshoe-shaped group of a dozen or so members with a teacher in the centre, who was indeed named Janet. This time there were two other Hearing Dogs. Intriguingly, the group had never had a hearing dog in attendance before. So once again, Matt came in for much admiration and attention, which he bore stoically until the formal class commenced, whereupon, true to style, he disappeared under my chair to snooze peacefully until coffee break. Of course, he would have been delighted to cadge biscuits *a la Sage* if I'd let him, but being new to this game I felt the need to play by the rules. Matt remained fully attached to his halte collar and well beyond the outer perimeter of the biscuit exclusion zone.

Two hours later we headed back off to work where the Matterhorn-sized pile of phone messages awaited attention.

Later the same week we were due to attend our first Meditation group at the Arch clinic. This posed a somewhat different challenge vis-à-vis Matt, as it would likely call for complete silence, which I couldn't be sure he would observe. Discussing the position with Penny, we decided it would be best to leave him at home. Hearing Dogs had given me a device called a Kong – a hollow rubber conical-shaped object that you fill with food to keep the dog busy while you're otherwise occupied. I filled his Kong with dog food, and smeared the edges of it with butter as I'd been taught to do when I needed to leave him. The idea is it's supposed to keep him busy while I'm away. So we shut him in the kitchen with some soft fabric to lie on, some toys to play with and his Kong to eat from, and made for the front door. He was whimpering before we even got out of the house. Penny and I looked at each other uncertainly. "Well, he's got to get used to being away from you sometime," said Penny, wistfully. I nodded and we left, locking the door behind us.

Meditation group was fascinating. Facilitated by Sandy, a lady from Romsey, it was to be a six-week introductory programme, focussing on a different meditation method each week. So over the coming Thursday evenings we would try using mantras, colours, walking meditation, sound induction technique and so on, each time preceded by a series of physical, breathing and chakra exercises, designed to clear the energy centres and to tune us in as effectively as possible to the meditation process.

There were about eight of us in the group, about half and half male and female and about as physically different looking specimens as you could possibly imagine. We were all a little on the quiet side to start with, none of very sure what the others would be like. But Sandy co-ordinated the evening perfectly, and we all seemed to leave feeling better. For my part, by the end of the hour and a half session I was feeling more energised that I'd done for months. It was a salutary lesson as to the importance of meditation in my life. Penny and I agreed we'd hit upon something really worthwhile and were excited about the prospect of returning for more the following week. We headed home to see how Matt had fared and were greeted at the glass front door by an open mouth, a lolling tongue and a waging tail. Further investigation revealed that Matt had emptied his Kong, but that doing so had not stopped him getting bored. He'd apparently then started scratching at the kitchen door (which was damaged but at least still on its hinges) and pushed against it until he got out. Evidently he was happier on the outside of the kitchen than he was inside. Penny and I looked at each other, not quite certain of how to handle the matter, but Matt had made it abundantly clear that as far as he was concerned, kitchen doors do not a prison make. Wherever else he would be left in future, it wouldn't be in the kitchen.

The next week we decided to try leaving him in the car outside the Arch clinic. His wait would be shorter, and I knew he was usually happy to be left in the car. This worked perfectly well, and we returned to an undamaged car and a relaxed, happy dog. We then headed off to sample an evening meal in some hitherto untested local hostelry, where Matt took in his stride the whole routine of sitting quietly under my seat in a food-serving establishment. I also have to say that, to their immense credit, the vast majority of the local restaurateurs and publicans didn't bat a communal eyelid in permitting a hearing dog onto the premises either. Clearly, we were making progress in educating the locality into the whys and wherefores of assistance dogs generally, and Hearing Dogs specifically – not to mention *Matt The Dog* uniquely!

So, leaving Matt in the car during the mediation became the pattern for the next couple of weeks. But I did wonder how we'd manage the situation when the weather turned cold. However, the matter actually came to a head sooner than I'd expected - on Guy Fawkes Night. As soon as we got into the room we were using for mediation, I realised it would be unwise to leave Matt in the car with fireworks going off all round. As it turned out, Sandy was happy for me to try bringing him in. And lo and behold, he placed himself contentedly under my chair for the whole evening, completely ignored the fireworks outside and the meditators inside. From that week forward, Matt became a valued and respected member of the group, and I was instructed by the assembled meditators to bring him in with me week by week. He remains, to this day, the only hearing dog in the country whose infrequent but distinctive bark sounds incredibly like an 'Om.' ☺

Once the initial six-week programme was up, most of us wanted to continue meditating. Sandy agreed to run the group for another four weeks to see how it progressed, which took us up to December. Ten days before Christmas we brought the year's meditation sessions to a close at Sandy's house in Romsey, with a meditation for planetary peace and goodwill, followed by a shared supper. Various of Sandy's friends and connections joined us and the meditation was deep and meaningful. But somehow on this occasion the social side provided me with something even more useful. To my amazement, after so many years of shunning social interaction for fear of mishearing and misunderstanding and the embarrassment caused by so doing, I hugely enjoyed a series of conversations with complete strangers. Some of these were predictably about Matt, so my easy management of them was perhaps nothing remarkable. But others were on subjects chosen by the other party to the conversation, yet I found myself remaining relaxed and content to talk against a noisy background. Was this down to the type of company I was in? To the meditation? To the effect of Matt being there? It's hard to say really, and it's very likely that all three played a part. At the end of the evening as I was about to leave, a middle aged man approached me and said, "You know," you don't really behave like a deaf person, just how much hearing do you have?"

I smiled, wondering how deaf people were supposed to behave! But I thought carefully about the question and answered, "When I have my hearing aids in I reckon I rely about 50/50 on sound and lip reading now, because I know I can't hear without seeing you speak, but equally, I'm not yet good enough at lip reading to understand you with getting some sound as well."

"That's amazing," came the reply. "Have you always been like this?"

I was thinking about the answer, when Penny interjected. "No, she said," "in fact he's only been like this for the last six months. He'd be almost entirely reclusive and unable to communicate socially if it wasn't for the dog."

I looked at her, taking in what she was saying. Being me, and therefore being with me all the time, it's difficult to calibrate how I am now to compared to how I used to be in the era before Matt was with me. But if Penny was right – and she was in a much better position to observe this than I was – then Matt was making a much bigger difference to my life that I could possibly have anticipated. I swallowed hard, as the tears began to edge into my eyes. Perhaps unusually for a man, I do cry easily. But quite honestly, this little dog gives me an enormous amount for which to cry tears of gratitude.

Big Al

By Autumn I was beginning to get tired. Fifteen months or so of renovations at work, climbing the learning curve of living with a hearing dog and moving house were all beginning to have their impact. I'd not taken a holiday since being in the Amazon in January and my inner child was beginning to talk quite firmly to me about taking a break! As care homes tend to be administratively quiet over the Christmas period, I determined that I'd take a long haul trip over the New Year. This would be nothing new to me of itself, but there was now, of course, someone else's interests to take into consideration. And this particular someone had a clear preference to be around me as much of the time as he possibly could! The question, therefore, was how to ensure that Matt was properly catered for while I was away.

In years gone by, Hearing Dogs had offered to take dogs back in for retraining when recipients were away. But with the numbers that were out working around the country by this stage in their growth (something around a thousand at this point, I'm told), it was no longer practical for them to do this, and they were therefore recommending that recipients use kennels. I had a long conversation with my placement officer, Sarah, about how to choose a good kennel, but still felt slightly uneasy about leaving Matt in such circumstances. Not that I had any real reason to worry, of course, since he had spent a great deal of time in kennels during his training at The Grange. But something came up that resolved the issue anyway.

When I next visited the Vet I saw a notice on the wall that read:

4 acres roaming space adjacent to the New Forest.
we look after dogs in our own home in xxxxx
Call Lorna on xxxxxx

I called the advertiser, and Matt and I went over to visit the next week. Following the directions from Fordingbridge to Alderholt, we arrived at a large, hedge-fronted property, tucked away down a country lane. We got out of the car and looked around us. The description I had been given was accurate- before us we saw several acres of open fields stretching in every direction, with stables and barns and outhouses and a distinct air of country life. And as I rang the doorbell, out of the house came a sound of excited barking. I warmed instantly to the prospect of boarding Matt in this kind of environment.

To the door came Lorna, a woman in her mid forties, and dressed every inch as the practical country lady. She ushered Matt and me round to the side entrance, Matt, of course, was more than intrigued to see who was barking. As we came through into the back garden, a posse of excited dogs inside the house threw themselves at the back door, yapping. Lorna gave Matt a few minutes to acclimatise to the

145

garden then allowed his new companions to tumble excitedly out of the door to get acquainted. Lorna had four dogs of her own, all of which were rescue dogs. Leading the pack was Big Al, an enormous, golden coloured Béarnaise Mountain Dog/Collie cross who stood almost waist high against me. Following were his entourage, Tasha, Cassie and Max, ranging in size from approximately Labrador to approximately terrier. But regardless of size, dogs are dogs, and Matt was in his element. Lorna explained that in addition to her horses (she was into eventing and show jumping in a big way), she had four dogs of her own and boarded up to two others at any one time. All got treated the same, and in particular all of them went on a long forest walk every morning. For me, that was enough – Matt would be as much at home here as he was at The Oaks and these were clearly people who loved animals. I would rest assured that he would be well looked after while I was away. I had almost to drag the AD away when it was time to leave, agreeing with Lorna that she would let me have some dates for a trial stay for him before my departure at the end of the year.

Sure enough, a week or so later a letter arrived with some proposed dates for Matt's weekend break and I phoned Lorna to confirm Matt's first visit as 10th December. The phone was answered by a trembling voice, and even with my degree of hearing I could tell instantly that the person answering was distraught, close to incoherence. I managed to glean that it was indeed Lorna I was talking to… something about an operation… With little hearing I couldn't get more and didn't want to intrude too far on the grief of someone I'd only just met. I managed to get her to confirm that she was not alone, and ended the conversation as gently and quickly as possible. Obviously, though I didn't yet know her well, I was worried for her.

A few days later she phoned back, much clearer, to explain that one of her horses, Little Nell, had taken a kick in

the knee from another horse at an event. The kneecap and
lower leg had been broken. I had a minimal knowledge of
horses, but even I remembered the westerns in which the
cowboys frequently had to shoot horses that broke legs. I
understood the seriousness of the situation. Given that horses
are on their feet the whole time a leg break is one of the most
challenging and dangerous conditions to address. With
impeccable timing, I had managed to phone at the very
moment that Little Nell was under anaesthetic, when Lorna,
of course, was distraught at the possibility of her not
recovering. Well, to end the sad story, the vet had given her a
40% chance of success. Sadly, this particular animal fell
within the 60% majority and didn't make it. By the time of
the conversation a week or so after the operation, Lorna was
composed once more, but still very sad and upset at her loss.
I confirmed the date for Matt's overnight trip and let it go at
that. Putting the phone down, I thought about how attached I
had become to Matt in just eight months, and how I'd feel in
comparable circumstances. Truly, we become as emotionally
joined to our animals as we do to other people.

Well, 10th December came, and I rounded up Matt's
bed, food, and a few toys and drove over to Alderholt once
more. Lorna came out of the house, smiling, just as I was
extracting an excited Matt from the back of the car. I gazed
around the surrounding fields admiringly once again, and
spied a horse with a coat on, segregated from the main group
of horses that were in another field. I looked enquiringly at
Lorna. She smiled again and nodded. "He's called Dan," she
said. "I didn't intend to get another horse," she said. "He
just… appeared" I smiled back and didn't press the matter
further. I know how it goes. But then she started gushing
about him… how Dan had come into her possession, how he
was a more experienced show jumper than she was herself,
how she had hopes that he would lift her own competition
standard. I smiled again, and wondered inwardly at the

amount of healing energy animals can offer. Lorna would do well with Dan. He would also do well with her. That's how it goes when we get the partnership right.

Going through the same routine as on our previous visit, we ushered Matt into the back garden, where he sniffed around, intrigued, for a few minutes, though he appeared to have no memory of being there before. Then Lorna opened the kitchen door and out tumbled Big Al plus camp followers, and life was suddenly all wags and sniffs and yelps and barks. I thought to make a hasty exit before I was noticed. But as I turned for the gate, Matted spotted me and dived after me. I looked down on his anxious little face from the other side of the gate and felt like I was deserting a small child. Sometimes, this assistance dog that has come into my life to help me can seem pretty helpless himself! So gathering my emotions in to a tight bundle around me, I turned around and walked smartly to the car. He'd been away from me for an extended period before, of course, when he'd gone back to The Grange for re-training. But that was home territory with the same professionals who had trained him before he ever came to me. How would he fare during this first real separation, and what would that say about my impending trip away for seventeen days at the end of the year?

I fretted somewhat overnight. Would he be all right? Would the other dogs bully him? Would he eat anything? Would he sleep anywhere other than at the foot of my bed? And if he didn't settle, what was I going to do with him when I went on holiday over New Year? And as I drove around completing a few errands without him, it felt distinctly eerie not to have him settled quietly in the back of the car. My mind would drift off to this task or that, but always I'd come back to consciousness of there being something unusual around me. I could feel his absence.

The day passed easily enough for me, and the next morning I headed back over to Alderholt at the appointed time. I turned the car around in Lorna's drive and got out to ring the door bell. But before I got the chance, a large 4x4 rolled in through the gates with Lorna at the wheel and a bevy of excited dogs in the back. I looked at her anxiously as she got out of the car.

"How's he been?" I asked anxiously, half expecting her to tell me he's been savaged by this posse of powerful canine flesh.

"Absolutely fine," came the obvious answer as she opened the door and carefully disentangled him from the rest of the pack. She smiled at me and handed me the lead. "See, nothing to worry about."

Matt jumped down from the car and paid me some cursory attention, before turning back to the pack where he'd obviously become quickly accepted. As Lorna and I talked for a few minutes, a young girl accompanying her evicted the rest of the excited, yelping bundle of dogs from the car and ferried them round to the back garden. Matt's head bobbed from looking at them to looking at me, and back again. Though lacking the benefit of words, he managed to make it perfectly clear to me that he was asking to go and play again! So much for my worries that he'd pine for me. I thanked Lorna, confirmed that we'd be back on 28th December and attached Matt's harness to the safety belt in the back seat of the car. I drove away, confident that I had made the right decision for his welfare when I went on holiday. There was no real question as to how he'd fare when I was away. With four play mates and daily walks in the forest he'd get at least as good a time as he would at home. Maybe the real worry was how I'd fare without him!

I'm getting married… probably

My younger daughter, Vici, had been seeing Tom since February. She'd known him for some six months before that but they'd caught each other's eye in the way these things happen and he had appeared in her conversation regularly from February onwards. I'd had to ask if they were romantically involved – she's not the type to announce information that is not requested. She confirmed that they were indeed "an item" and I duly took note in the way father's are supposed to.

"What does he do?" I'd asked at an early stage of the proceedings.

"Err… he's working as a landscape gardener at the moment…." The sentence tailed off. I looked at my gorgeous, twenty two year old copper-haired daughter enquiringly.

"But?" I added helpfully.

"Well, he's a musician really," she said.

Now I'm thinking Yehudi Menuhin, or James Galway, or at the very least Acker Bilk.

"Yes," she continued, "he plays bass guitar in a rock band and they're going to be really, really big."

I tried not to look crest fallen. "That's err… nice I said, "and if it doesn't work out at least he can be a landscape gardener. Good to have something to fall back on."

Needless to say, it wasn't quite the comment she was looking for!

That had all been back in February or March. I'd awaited further developments, non-judgementally, I hope. Come the summer I'd had my first opportunity to meet Tom. Being a fully paid up, card carrying coward, I'd arranged for Naomi to visit to meet him for the first time as well - not to mention Matt, who loves meeting absolutely anyone!

Vici kept me posted on developments in Tom's impending musical take off over the following months. Having initially been signed by a small record label, after much angst and uncertainty, Tom's band, "Morning Runner" had been taken on by Parlaphone the largest record labels in the world (not that I'd have had a clue about that if I'd not been told!). That in itself was promising. But they were also being managed by a manager whose only other client were a band called Cold Play – and even I had heard of them! I reckoned that anyone astute enough to be managing a household name like that must have their wits about them. It was another useful pointer that my (maybe) future son in law would have sufficient readies to keep my daughter in the quantity of Cadbury's Chocolate Buttons she was used to. So by the time I actually met the rock star in waiting, my fatherly concerns had already been subdued to a reasonable level of decibels and I could concentrate on meeting the man that would likely become a long term fixture in my future. Clever girl, my Vici!

As it turned out I needn't have worried. Tom turned out to be a pleasant young man, laid back and easy going, and he rather reminded me of me at twenty-six. He even had the good grace to be slightly shorter than me – not too many people manage that one! We passed a pleasant few hours together, talking about this and that and the music business in particular at the end of which the happy young couple upped and offed to visit Vici's mum.

Naomi and I looked enquiringly at each other.

"Do you reckon it's long term then?" I asked her.

She eyed me for a moment, seeing if she could detect my own opinion.

"Definitely," she said.

I nodded my agreement. This was him then – my future son in law. The only question was whether they'd hold off getting married until I could afford to pay for a wedding.

On the other hand, sooner rather than later could be a good idea, as I'd never be able to afford to pay for a rock star's wedding!

Over the next few months the news kept coming through. The first tour; the recording studios; publicity photo shoots. Then in early December I received a text from Vici. "Look at the Guardian G2 section and you'll see someone you know," it said.

Dutifully I bought the said newspaper ('tis the rarest of rare events for me to buy the Guardian, being a Telegraph man, meself), and there on the front cover was Tom's smiling face in a crowd of twenty or thirty other musicians. G2 was running a series on artists in general and musicians in particular who'd likely be public property in 2005. Tom's band got a good write up, being referred to as Parlaphone's main priority for 2005. Fatherly fears receded still further.

When, in December, Vici announced she wanted to see me I had a reasonable idea of what she wanted to talk about. It was the first time since I'd moved in The Oaks that she'd visited me on her own.

Matt and I were clearing up the leaves in the garden when she arrived. At least I was clearing the leaves with a blower and Matt was racing round the garden, into and out of the leaves and having a thoroughly good time getting filthy dirty. And that was after an hour's walk that morning, which of course is probably about 10 miles for him. This dog's energy levels defy the laws of physics.

Vici came striding down the garden wrapped up in scarf and coat against the winter cold. My heart melted at the sight of her, as it does every time I see either of my daughters. As soon as he saw her, Matt dived at her in excitement. I tried to do the usual thing of stopping him jumping on people, but its hard when he's so excited, particularly when the person actually wants to be jumped on. I'm not sure he remembered her, but we don't receive many visitors at The Oaks, so any new arrival is a squeal-inducing event.

After the statutory hugs and kisses and cups of tea and chit chat, we headed off to the Forester's Arms for lunch. The Forester's is a highly dog-friendly pub, but normally you're only allowed to take dogs into the bar. I'd not tested them on allowing Matt into the restaurant until now, but this time there were no bar tables left. When I asked for a restaurant table, initially there was resistance. Then I pointed out Matt was a guide dog (so much easier to use that term – people actually know what it means!) and after that nothing was too much trouble. We were shown immediately to a table and after I'd attached Matt's lead to the leg of chair, he duly went to sleep awaiting further instructions.

Seated in the restaurant, we awaited the arrival of our meal, and the conversation turned to the town of Reading and Vici's home circumstances. She had already told me she was considering buying a house with someone else the following year. One thing led to another, and finally I asked if it was Tom she'd been considering buying with. The house purchase idea itself had been dropped in light of the apparently tumbling housing market, but the reason behind it was obvious. I knew my younger daughter was an old fashioned girl, and nothing would induce her to live with her boyfriend before marriage. I also knew she was having difficulty getting round to the subject. So I asked. "Are you and Tom planning to get married then? I asked.

"Yes... well probably..." she said. "That is, given his tour commitments its very hard to be sure of anything. But he's expecting Morning Runner's first Album to be released no later than July next year and the chances are that for 18 months after that he'll be off and about at the drop of a hat." If we don't get married before that, it's likely to be almost another two years before we can."

I looked at her, gathering my thoughts. It's one thing to anticipate your daughter telling you she's getting married but quite another when she actually does so.

"Anyway," she continued, "nothing's certain yet, and this is just early warning. I thought you'd probably prefer to hear it now rather than at short notice next year!"

"I'm delighted," I said, truthfully. "I know I've only met Tom once, but I really like him, and I don't think he's the type to let fame go to his head. "I take it he gets an invitation to the wedding?" I said, motioning towards Matt. On the basis of 'love me, love my dog' I rarely go anywhere without Matt now.

"Absolutely," she said "he will be issued with his own personal invitation," she answered.

"Which he will respond to personally" I finished off.

As we left the restaurant my head was filled with all sorts of fatherly, wedding-type questions, which I had to refrain from asking. I had to remember this was only 'probably' getting married. Details would have to wait for later.

We finished the afternoon by buying a Christmas tree, which Vici decorated for me (I am fully inoculated against good taste) before she headed home. The new year, with a whole host of developments, was approaching fast.

Muddy Friends

The next day Matt and I spent in the garden. I still
needed to finish disposing the enormous quantity of leaves
that had come down with the late autumn winds, and he
needed to continue his self appointed task of running around
in and out of the leaf blower jet, and leaping into the leaf
piles. This was seriously important work – his, I mean, not
mine! We came in tired from our labours just as the afternoon
light was fading to the sound of the phone ringing. Matt did
his usual and I spread my hands open in a gesture of enquiry,
asking, "What is it?" He took me to the phone.

"Hello?" I answered.

"It's me." People still do that to me, and you know I
even still recognise one or two voices enough to know who
'me' is! In this case "me" was Vici and after a few moments I
recognised the voice.

"Hello Sweetheart, what's up?" I asked

"I'm ringing to tell you I've just got engaged." I let
out an appropriately constrained but fatherly 'whoop' at my
end of the phone. "I really didn't know it was going to be so
soon after I told you, but Tom bought the ring and asked me
today."

I congratulated my lovely daughter with genuine fatherly delight and let her rush off to tell twenty-seven or so other people. At least I'd had some warning! New Year seemed somehow even closer than it had done five minutes before.

The next day Matt and I continued to clear up leaves in the garden, just for a change. In a house called "The Oaks" you can make a reasonable assumption about the quantity of leaves to be dealt with at Autumn. The steady, repetitive motion of swinging the leaf blower backwards and forwards is trance inducing, and several times during the day I found my mind drifting away from the task in hand to this or that thought process. But wherever I drifted, I kept coming back to the same issue. Vici's announcement would inevitably lead to contact between my ex-wife and me, on the day of the wedding if not before, and there had been over eighteen months of silence between us. If we left it till the day of wedding to meet, at best it would feel strange and at worst it would lead to uncomfortable exchanges. I owed it to Vici to give her the very best possible day I could, even if that meant confronting any potential difficulty between my ex and me early on.

So that evening I sat down and typed a letter to her in as open hearted a manner as I could. I wanted her to feel as relaxed as possible in the context of any contact that was made, and I wanted her to know I wished her well, regardless of what either of us felt about the past.

One evening about a week later, the phone rang. Matt and I were in the kitchen, and after long day he can sometimes be slow in responding to sounds he's supposed to alert me to, particularly if sees any body language from me that indicates I may have heard the sound myself. So when it got to the second ring I looked enquiringly at him. He stood there, looking back at me as if to say "You heard that, what do you need me to do for you?"

"Come on," I said, tapping my thigh. He mad three quarters of an effort to give me an alert signal, which I took as sufficient. If I don't get to the phone quickly enough the answer phone takes it. I arrived at the phone just as the caller was leaving a message.

"Hello Mike," it started "This is Margaret."

My hesitation was only momentary. This was the contact we needed to move forward for Vici's sake. I picked the phone up and said "Hello Margaret, this is Michael," listening as closely as I could for the tone of her voice (voice tone is one thing that's hard for me to tell with reduced hearing – amplification gives me the words, but sometimes a less good idea of where the caller's coming from emotionally).

As it turned out, we were fine with each other. She updated me a little on her life events over the last year and a half, and asked about Matt. I responded by telling her about Hurst Manor (after all, she'd once been joint owner of it) and suggesting we meet in the New Year so as to ensure we were singing from the same song sheet when it came to getting on in each others' presence at the forthcoming wedding. As you might expect, after 18 months silence which followed the most difficult time in our lives, there was a degree of awkwardness and the conversation was a little stilted. I'd have been surprised if it had been any different under the circumstances. But when I put the phone down and exhaled long and deep, I looked down at Matt and smiled. "We got that one right kid," I said to him. "Vici'd be pleased with me." His tongue lolled out of his mouth as he wagged his agreement.

As December wore on, Vici telephoned again. Her feet were beginning to touch the ground with regard to practicalities. "Dad," she said, "We're thinking of getting married next year on either 27th May or June 4th. Is either date a problem to you?"

"Either's fine by me, Sweetheart, I answered, "I just want you to have a wonderful day and I'll do anything in my power to make that possible. Mum's probably told you already that we've spoken, and everything fine."

"I know," she said, sounding relieved. "But I was wondering… could we hold the reception in the garden at The Oaks?"

Now she'd taken me by surprise. Here I was expecting to be well and truly on the periphery of the most important event in my life for many years, when she slides the carpet neatly from under my feet and asks me for something that would make me feel very much involved. "I'd be honoured, Sweetheart," I answered.

"Tom and I would like to come round to talk about it in a couple of weeks' time."

Great! I was going to get to see more of my younger daughter than I had for months, over this – just as well since a delightful and soon-to-be-famous young man was about to take her away from me!

The happy couple appeared on the doorstep about a week before Christmas. Tom had been busy recording and away on tour, and they'd not seen as much of each other as they might. Now the news of the engagement was public, they were being a little freer in their expression of affection to each other and it was clear that they were very much in love. After a quick coffee we tugged on Wellingtons and, much to Matt's delight, headed out to survey the garden for suitable sites for a marquee for 200 people. Tom had a little laser machine that measured distances and while I stood several metres away from him to fire it at me to get a range, Vici took down measurements in a note book. In my excitement I was full of thoughts to contribute, and worked hard not to go over the top. I remembered my own wedding back in 1976 when every relative this side of Mars seemed to think it was their entitlement to dictate how they thought the arrangements should be handled. I wasn't going to do the same to Vici and Tom. Full of ideas, they set off to see Vici's mother and then to have dinner with friends before looking at Churches the following day. Matt looked at me as I waved them off in the car and then ran off in the direction of his favourite forest walk. I looked down at the Wellingtons still on my feet from the garden and then looked back at him, just about to cross the stream that defined the boundary of commitment to an outing. "Oh all right then," I said. "I guess you come next." I picked up his lead and treat bag and followed him off in the direction of one of the longer regular walks we take. They may not be able to talk, but boy do they make a good job of telling you what they want!

The year in decline

The late November colour was fading. Our traditional walks had become mud baths, leaving tide lines shin deep on my Wellington boots. Matt literally took the mud in his stride as he leapt anything up to six feet across the dirtiest streams. Not that it stopped him from getting himself filthy though. Each morning on returning home I had to hose him down before drying him and letting him into the house.

On 26th November I heard by letter that Matt had been allocated to the Fordingbridge Hearing Dogs fundraising group as being their sponsored dog. Earlier in the month we had taken him to the skittles fundraising evening. The inevitable questions arose, just as they do wherever we go, and people with benevolent smiles pointed him out to one another. "Aren't they marvellous... Such clever animals...

he's so beautiful..." - all of which of course goes completely over Matt's head. It doesn't go over mine though, and I hope I never tire of hearing it. It serves as a perpetual reminder of where I have come from with deafness and to whom I owe so much of my fortune in making the journey. Matt was content to sleep the evening away under my chair, but was overwhelmingly good natured when people want to meet him & pat him. In more ebullient mood he'd become prone to jumping up and I knew we had to eliminate that before he could pass assessment, which was set for 9th December. We'd already been taught the standard procedure by Sarah: getting people to ignore him until he's on four feet. It's easy to get the right behaviour from the dog if you get it from the people first!

Perhaps I've said it too many times now, but looking back over the preceding eight months it was quite clear he had revolutionised my life. He had become a permanent presence of a friend in an otherwise largely solitary existence, and a catalyst to social interaction at so many levels. "The best bird puller in the business," as my friend Caroline had remarked one day. She meant Matt, of course, not me!

Assessment

November turned to December and the light continued to fade, bringing early morning darkness and later forest walks than Matt and I had been used to. We had two note-worthy events scheduled for December –Matt's final assessment on the 9th, swiftly followed by the trial sleep-over at Lorna's on the 10th that I told you about earlier. I had some concerns about both events.

Sarah, Matt's placement officer had paid a final pre-assessment visit in November. After some general testing of his obedience and of his sound work, and after watching him working around town, she had come to the conclusion he was fine to be assessed. I had slight misgivings, but accepted that she had an infinitely better appreciation of the standard required for the final test than I could possibly have. Matters were slightly complicated by the fact that the day before the assessment happened to be the staff Christmas party at Hurst Manor, so Matt and I would be leaving Somerset extremely late. However, to complicate matters still further, I found myself coming down with 'flu on the day of the party. Now, this party was a seriously big deal to all involved (I'd even brought a jacket and - wait for it – *a tie* - with me to do due honour to the occasion) and there was no possibility of my cancelling my attendance. So I reconciled myself to having to be there regardless of my state of health. Matt and I duly turned up at the seriously posh (bouncers in DJs, bar staff in evening dress) venue of the Westland Helicopters Social Club at around 8.00pm. I was ready for the usual objections ("Sorry, we don't allow dogs in here, sir") and had my responses all prepared. After all, in October the Disability Discrimination Act had come into force and there was now just about no one who was legally entitled to turn a hearing dog away. However, nobody official batted so much as an eyelash as we strode into the building, brandishing our ticket (well *my* ticket, actually). As the evening commenced, Matt curled up under my chair on a rug I'd brought especially for the purpose and, despite the amplified music and general din, would have contentedly stayed there for the rest of the night had he been required to. But by 9.30, given the progress of the 'flu, I was beyond my limit, and had to bow out, thus sadly missing the delights of the disco and the appearance of the Four Tops (even I remember them!). This was one night when I would gratefully have flopped into my bed at Hurst Manor for an extra night and thus avoided the long drive home. But alas, not only was the assessor coming the following day, but I'd also arranged for Matt to go to the groomers in a vain attempt to disguise my failings in matter of attending to his furry *toilette* frequently enough.

Consequently, I made my way home as carefully and safely as I could, arriving at The Oaks not long before midnight, and dropping into bed in confused exhaustion. Nevertheless, the next morning I needed to be up bright and early. I was going to do my very best for Matt in his assessment. I owed it to him, given how much he consistently did for me with genuine joy. So we were up before the light dawned, took a swift thirty minute constitutional into the Forest, then it was home just in time to meet Jane, from 'Super-clean dogs.' Jane's pretty good with dogs – she has twelve of her own! Matt trotted happily after her and just as she pulled away in her van I noticed the light flashing on the answer phone. I had an hour to myself before the assessor came, so I turned it on to try to retrieve my messages – often a touch and go procedure, since around half of them by this time were unintelligible to me. The first was exactly that, but the second was perfectly clear.

"Hello Michael," said the voice. "This is Debbie from Hearing Dogs. I'm really sorry to tell you this at such short notice, but Julie who was coming to do Matt's assessment has had to cancel – her daughter is ill. Can you please call to re-arrange for another day?"

I felt like an over-inflated balloon that was having its air slowly. Frankly, given the way I was feeling I wasn't that sorry about the postponement. I just wish I'd known about it the day before so I could have stayed in Somerset – or even that I'd listened to the message before Jane had whisked Matt off to make him a super clean dog for no particular purpose. Still, what could we do? I remembered the many, many cancellations either I or my ex-wife had had to make when our children were ill. So I did the only thing I could do. I rang The Grange and tried to re-arrange. It wasn't as easy as it sounded though. The next available slot fell bang in the middle of my holiday over the new year, and the one after that wasn't until 3rd February. I took it, little realising the complications that would be imposed by the intervening two month gap.

Butchers and Admiration

Later in the month, Matt and I drove into Fordingbridge one morning at the start of a very busy few days before Christmas. As I went to get him out of the car and put him into his uniform, he turned his nose away in a gesture of resistance. The halte lead means work and Matt doesn't always want to work. But I was short of time and placed the lead firmly on him, to be quickly followed by the maroon coat, which he never does resist. Although the halte lead is not the most desirable of accoutrements as far as Matt's concerned, it does make it clear to him that he's to be in work mode. As a consequence he goes through an instant personality change every time I put it on him. Gone is the ebullient, playful puppy-like creature who believes life was invented exclusively for the purpose of enjoyment. In its place appears the poised, profession assistance dog, that virtually never puts a foot wrong in public. You'll think I'm over-stating the case of course –everyone does. But I assure you its absolutely true – it's like having two completely different dogs around me.

That morning we headed first to the butchers. I had wondered on my previous visit there with Matt if there would be difficulty persuading the butcher to let him in the shop, but to his credit he's never mentioned him. So once again that morning we stood in the long queue, waiting our turn to be served. The AD, of course, quickly became the star turn, attracting smiles and benevolent looks from adults and strokes and giggles from children. After ten minutes or so of this I was wondering if he would become tired of it and whether I'd need to ask for him to be left alone. But we arrived at the head of the queue in the nick of time, collected the Christmas turkey and departed. I decided it was time for a break in our favourite coffee shop, The Coffee Pot. We'd been in many times before, and Matt was well known and popular with the staff. There'd been the initial "Sorry, we can't allow dogs in here," but a proper explanation had ensured that there was no problem with my taking him in on subsequent occasions. Being near to Christmas, the place was pretty full, and we slipped into a table in the window. Two ladies at the next table were watching him closely. Matt decided to settle himself down between my table and theirs, so I asked if they minded. This resulted in yet another extended conversation about how Hearing Dogs worked and how Matt had changed my life.

I settled down to lunch and a coffee, engrossed in my newspaper. After my meal, I got up ready to leave. Matt reads my body language closely now, and he knows the drawing back of a chair commonly means it's time to go. He roused himself and stretched. It was then I noticed a young family two tables away. A little girl of about four was sitting on her mother's lap, looking closely at Matt. I asked her mum whether she'd like to meet the doggie. The answer was a forgone conclusion.

As the child slid off her mother's lap to get down on the floor and become acquainted with Matt, the woman asked me how long he had been in training. It was a common question, and I once again explained the hearing dog training process. She then asked me how long he would be with me before going on to be with a deaf person! I smiled and explained that I was actually the deaf guy and Matt would now hopefully be with me all his working life! We smiled, wished one another "Merry Christmas," and I left the restaurant, marvelling and how far I'd come in my ability to communicate, all courtesy of Matt, of course.

But that evening there was another communication issue that needed some further exploration. I quite often get asked questions about the rate of hearing deterioration I experience and whether I'll eventually lose all of my hearing. The honest answer here is that I don't really know, nor, it seems does anyone else, for no one will give me a firm prognosis. It's also not that easy to calibrate the rate of deterioration I've already experienced, since I am with me all the time, so to speak. But from time to time I get a yardstick that tells me to some extent what's going on and that the decline is continuing. Last year it was the telephone, and I began to notice that some voices were getting harder to hear. I had replaced my telephones with more powerfully amplified models and gave the matter no further thought. But during the course of 2004, I was finding it harder and harder to decipher answer phone messages. Of course, living in two places and commuting between them means I get quite a lot of messages left. At work these are transcribed for me, so there's no real problem beyond pushy sales people trying to force their products onto me. But then that's something everyone in business has to live with, and in fact, being able to say I can't hear them can actually be quite useful!

The real problem is with the answering machine at home. I'd not really noticed earlier in the year when I had begun to find the odd message with a difficult voice or sloppy articulation unintelligible. But by the later part of the year I was becoming aware that I was unable to hear a larger and larger proportion of messages left on the phone. So that evening when both Penny and I were at a loose end, I invited her out to dinner. Of all the people I knew she seemed to have the most pragmatic and down to earth approach to matters associated with my hearing. We headed off to The Tudor Rose pub just outside Fordingbridge where Matt stretched out in front of a roaring open basket fire while we enjoyed a main course and debated whether our waist lines would cope with a dessert so close to the festive season. Then, on returning home, I put to Penny the matter of the answer phone. We tossed the issue this way and that for a while, debating the personal and business consequences of simply doing away with it. How tied we all are to communications technology these days, and how alien it feels to be without it! Eventually we hit on a solution. As soon as I was back from holiday in the New Year, I would record an introductory message that asked people not to leave messages, but instead to call me on my mobile phone. A simple enough solution, you might think, and at the technical level it certainly was. But that night as I got into bed I pondered on this significant change to my communication strategy. It constituted an acknowledgement that yes, my hearing was continuing to decline. The fifteen-year-old question sat down in front of me, cocked its head on one side, and smiled enquiringly at me once again. Would the decline be continuous until I became profoundly deaf, or would it bottom out at some point? I had no more conclusive an answer to it that even than I'd ever had. So I simply smiled my uncertainty back at the question, turned over and went to sleep.

Toys–R–Matt

When Matt and I were first introduced he was eleven months old – still very much a puppy and I, of course, knew very little of puppy behaviour. Essentially I had not a clue of what to expect of him. But then neither did he of me – we were both flying blind. At that first meeting Fiona, Matt's original trainer, had given me a handful of food with which to attract his attention and when all said and done, our first encounter didn't last all that long.

When we got together for the second time, at the beginning of our week's training together at The Grange, and they left us alone in the farmhouse for that first real get-to-know-you hour or so, they left me with a handful of food again, but this time also a box of toys and chews and so on. After his initial curious sniff around the farmhouse and sniff around me, his attention began quickly to wane. I had therefore needed some device to keep his focus. The obvious solution was the toy box. We'd been given a whole selection of bits and pieces to play with – a rag knotted at each end, a big heavy bone impregnated with something or other that definitely attracted his attention and a couple of soft toys from which the squeakers had very carefully been removed. In the hearing dog world, squeaks are very definitely about sound training and not about play!

To keep him happy on that occasion I tried just about every toy in the box. We settled on the knotted rag. I tried throwing it first, but Matt's never had the "I-am-a-faithful-hound-and-will-bring-back-what-you-throw" attitude to life. As far as he's concerned possession is ten points of the law, and if he can hold onto something and stop me from getting it off him, that's far more fun than handing it over to be thrown round the garden or wherever. His trainers, I have noted, don't seem to have this problem with him. At The Grange and when they visit me at home, they've consistently been able to elicit model behaviour from him, including the traditional drop-throw-retrieve routine. He's clear about who's in charge when a true professional's around, but being a professional himself, is able to spot an upstart rank amateur like me at a hundred paces. No sooner have we shut the door behind a trainer after a disciplined and obedient day's work than he reverts to type, safe in the knowledge that he can

push me a lot further down the road to dog's-in-charge-ville
than he'd ever dream trying with the trainer.

Thus, when we first came home to my little flat in
New Milton in the Spring, he was swift in establishing full
authority over the waste paper basket (if you're a dog it's
amazing how much fun you can have tearing up old paper
and tissue, then watching your human clamber round the
floor on his hands and knees clearing it all up. And you know
what? Your human only does it 'cos he knows how much
pleasure you get out of emptying the basked again as soon as
he goes off to make a cuppa. This, of course, is axiomatic,
for were it otherwise, your helpful human would signal his
intent by covering up the wastepaper basket, thus indicating
you should find more sport elsewhere. His failure to learn to
do so despite your repeated forays into said basket can be
taken as firm confirmation that the basket and its contents are
wholly within your domain. Of course, it's dramatically more
fun when the contents of the basket include mummified
banana skins or other questionable organic material. Once
having savoured the pungent delights of such fare you can
drag it triumphantly round the floor, thoroughly impregnating
the carpet with its delicate aroma in preparation for the next
time you wish to re-explore any particular corner of the flat
that takes your fancy. And naturally, you human's failure to
empty his waste baskets on a regular basis confirms beyond a
shadow of a doggy doubt that this is actually the primary
purpose of the waste bin itself).

So did I ever learn to cover the waste paper baskets
and empty them regularly? Did I hell. What kind of a writer
would I be if my bins weren't permanently overflowing?

Gradually though, Matt and I did begin to approach a
common understanding of what was his to play with and
what was mine and thus (usually) beyond the boundaries of
play. Courtesy of several forays into the pet shops of the New
Forest, and the kindliness of several self-appointed aunties

and uncles, he managed to acquire a pretty comprehensive collection of ropes, rags, soft toys, former squeaky toys with squeaks removed and sundry bits of rubbish that he claimed as his own personal property and were sufficiently unimportant to me to re-establish territorial authority over. Of course, said collection of possessions was easy to add to when we visited other homes with doggy occupants. For instance, during the early summer we made several visits to The Oaks, in preparation for our eventual purchase of the house. Barry and Annette's two dogs were extremely friendly, extremely large golden Retrievers, who were old enough, slow enough and friendly enough that they were regularly willing to share the contents of their toy box with the young upstart who periodically came to visit with them. And as far as Matt was concerned, the presence of any given soft toy at floor level implied axiomatically that he was entitled, nay *expected*, to take possession of it and run at maximum velocity round the house and garden with it until dropping exhausted into a puppy sleep at my feet. So wistful and endearing was his look at home-time and so cute did he look with someone else's soft toy hanging from his jaws, that invariably he was invited to retain possession of the item when we returned home.

Then again there was the time we were running a bring-and-buy stall at Hurst Manor. When Juliette, one of the nurses, came into the chalet one morning carrying an armful of children's cast offs including a small, but perfectly formed teddy bear, Matt stood in front of her bright eyed, wagging his tail and panting in cute expectation until the lady was forced to concede ownership of said teddy for a small consideration that found its way from my pocket into the bring-and-buy fund. The look of delight on his face when she bent forward and handed it to him was worth all of the 50p involved. Objective thus achieved, he retreated to his normal haunt under my desk and fell asleep with his chin on the bear. Cute or what?

By such fair means and foul Matt soon acquired two collections of possessions that he was allowed to treat entirely as his own. One for our visits to Hurst Manor and the other for day-to-day use at home. Thus we had "M'rag" (not to be confused with "M'rope") "M'pup" (one of the thousand and one Dalmatians that he'd pinched from I can't remember who), M'sheep (soft toy ram donated by Auntie Penny) together with several unlikely looking creatures, legitimately purchased from pet shops and of such appearance as to make it impossible for us to arrive at a suitable name.

Now, I've said earlier that I'd given Matt ownership of all these items and in my book ownership means you get to do what you like with something without unreasonable interference. Matt's version of doing what he likes can be pretty destructive. Thus, the routine for an evening when we're at home alone is that I'll settle on the sofa to watch some TV, whereupon he'll bring up M'rag or M'rope to play tug of war. When we've done that for a bit and he's bored, he'll then proceed to dismantle a toy of his own choosing. Accordingly, over the summer the menagerie became progressively more and more depleted, as M'pup first lost his stuffing (and boy it's such great fun crawling round picking up soft toy stuffing from all corners of the house, I just *so* wish he'd tear his toys apart more often), then his head, then various bits of limb and torso until his very existence was reduced to a few scraps of material of a dirty grey, slightly greasy consistency. For whatever reason, to Matt these were just as much fun as the whole toy had been in the first place and would be extracted from the toy box for play just as regularly as the original toy had been when in possession of its full faculties. Naturally, M'pup was rapidly followed swiftly down the road to perdition by M'cow, and M'sheep and anything else in the box that doggy teeth could pleasurably dismember. Come Christmas, therefore, the toy box at The Oaks was sadly close to being empty, sporting only those items that had been beyond my wayward puppy's capacity to destroy, together with a few sad and tasteless reminders of the glory that had once been, prior to the acts of destruction.

Clearly, therefore something had to be done if I didn't want Matt to start claiming other items round the house as his own (he'd already removed the odd tree decoration from the Christmas tree, and the sharp "No!" he'd received for doing so didn't reduce his interest in said interloper into the house one iota). But fortunately that cute little face is enough to launch a thousand shopping trips by kindly self-appointed uncles and aunties around the various parts of the globe that we frequent. Accordingly, on Christmas morning Matt was the proud recipient of several new toys not only from me (yeah, I can be kind hearted too, ya know) in the form of M'chicken, another M'ball and a M'Humphry (well what else am I supposed to call something that's made out of Zebra striped fur, is 70% mouth, has elongated green ears and sports red rope for legs – get a dog and get creative, I say) but prezzies from Auntie Penny (string of plastic sausages) Auntie Brenda (doggy Superchew) and from Matron Sue's dog, Cinders (a book called One hundred muddy Paws for Thought) – remarkably clever the ways these dogs advise one another on what its possible to get away with if they learn how to mange their owners just *so*). Touchingly, he'd remembered to buy me a present (copy of The Dog Listener – was he trying to tell me something tactfully?), but I reckon he must have asked Auntie Penny to help him wrap it up. There are some things you can't teach even a hearing dog, you know!

Christmas day was thus negotiated with considerable pleasure and tail wagging at new possessions, the cadging of slightly more indulgent food than usual (ok, I confess, I gave him some turkey which is not Hearing Dogs-approved fare, but what the heck, it's Christmas, isn't it?). Remarkably, by Boxing Day he had yet to throw up or make unapproved deposits on the floor, the toys were fully intact and accounted for, and he was asleep under the desk instead of tormenting Naomi and Vici who were both snoozing peacefully upstairs. How normal can a hearing dog household get?

Boxing day morning brought the arrival of Vici's fiancé Tom, negotiations and debates over whether to have a fry up breakfast or a buffet lunch (inevitably the former, of course, since I had made provision for the latter) and a healthy post Christmas constitutional in Godshill Wood. Given the quagmire into which the lower part of the valley had turned, we took the car up to the top of the hill. The car park was fuller than I'd ever seen it. Evidently, everyone else had decided to pay lip service to the need to walk off Christmas day lunch. Matt of course, was exuberant at the prospect of a walk any time or place, but the presence of large numbers of people and dogs raised the excitement level several notches. And he knows precisely what he can get away with. While I was a tad preoccupied with trying to follow the conversation (not easy to lip read someone when you're walking next to them and therefore not facing them) he was off, charging at full throttle towards some unassuming party of people we'd never met as if he was going to throw himself at their legs full force and knock them clean from the ground. Then at the last moment, just when it seemed inevitable that he would break someone's shin bone, he'd change direction and run deftly around them instead of straight into them, thereby endearing himself to said group and engendering a series of benevolent 'oohs' and 'ahs' before running off to do the same thing with the next unassuming targets amongst the Boxing Day walkers. Once I'd got the drift of what he was up to, I called him away and he charged back to me with a look on his face that I can only describe as a giggle. Can dogs giggle? He certainly has a pretty fair handle on what he can do for fun and what elicits a positive response. They tell me that around two years of age (three months away as I write this) the energy level will begin to ease off and he'll settle down. That's a tad difficult to believe just at the moment.

Towards the end of the day my human guests disappeared off to spend the evening with the girls' mother, and Matt and I headed out to have dinner with Auntie Penny and her parents, Cyril and Betty. We'd not met them before, but I knew that Cyril was a former submariner and Betty a former nurse, trained under the old school philosophy of nursing. Clearly these would be people of some formality and behavioural standards. We had to make at least some attempt to demonstrate that we were capable of conducting ourselves appropriately for a few hours! I wasn't at all sure how Matt would be received, given his rather laid back approach to life and his inclination to inflict death by licking upon anyone who shows him the least bit of attention. Of course, added to that was his habitual propensity to go unreservedly bonkers whenever he visits the indulgent Auntie Penny, who always does her level best to ensure that in her home, at least, he has a haven where he's fully off duty, even if he has to behave formally everywhere else in the world!

When we arrived at Penny's house, true to form he threw himself at the front door in excited anticipation. Then, when Penny opened the door he threw himself at her as if he's not seen her in months. As soon as I let him off the lead he charged round the house to investigate the garden and search for the toy box that she keeps for visiting dogs. He was mercifully restrained with Cyril and Betty, which enabled us to carry off a reasonable imitation of being fairly civilised, genteel folks that we're definitely not, nor ever will be capable of being. With our departure later that evening for

Hurst Manor and the final paperwork before going on
holiday, Christmas was officially over. A two week break
would mark the end of 2004. My return would require that I
hit the ground running with regard to work projects, the need
to spruce up the house for the forthcoming wedding and, of
course, Matt's final assessment in February. But for now, I'm
writing this at 9.00am on the morning of 28th December and
as usual Matt is snoozing at my feet under the desk. In a few
minutes I'll pack up his food and his bed and take him off to
spend the next two joyous weeks in the company of Big Al
and Co. on the Costa del Alderholt while I head off to South
Africa for a much longed for holiday. Excuse me if I don't
send you a post card, won't you?

South Africa

Well, I duly dropped off Matt at Lorna's house where
he proceeded to become reacquainted with Big Al and
entourage, paying me the scantest of attention as I departed
with a worried tear in my eye. Would my little friend miss me
while I was away enjoying myself on holiday – would he
heck! He'd be too busy playing with the other dogs and
duffing up unfortunate little interlopers into Lorna's garden
now he had almost carte blanche to do what he liked in the
absence of Dad's stern voice and a hearing dog uniform!
    I took my taxi to Heathrow, met a whole crowd of
"Singles" who were touring South Africa with me, and
settled down to enjoy my holiday. Of course, on Boxing day
we'd had vague news of a big wave hitting some distant
countries to which we didn't particularly relate, but we had
no concept of the scale of the disaster. The word "Tsunami"
was yet to become part of the national vocabulary, and news
broadcasts were packed with minor insignificant bits and
pieces as they tend to be around Christmas time.

I was wondering how I was going to get on without Matt, as he'd become my habitual companion in almost every context since the previous April. Of course, I'd been without him for two and a half weeks while he was off being retrained in July, but somehow that had felt different – a necessary investment in his technical skills and obedience training that I'd need as the future came our way. On this occasion I was travelling without him out of choice for the first time. So yes, I felt a tad guilty, and just a little exposed without the hearing dog that had been the catalyst for so many conversations and interactions over the preceding months. Nevertheless, I arrived after a twelve-hour flight to the sights and the smells of South Africa on my first visit to the African continent. I've written elsewhere of that trip, so I'll not go into too much detail about it here, other than to say that as well as being a holiday, the fact that I was butting up against Third World poverty within the embrace of what is also a first world society, was a deeply provocative and thought engendering experience. I found myself moved beyond words by the overwhelming sense of reconciliation and forgiveness on which that society is based, and I came away with a clear impression that upon such a foundation the country will build walls and roofs, not only of concrete and metal, but also of love and generosity, if its founding spirit can but be maintained.

On returning, we touched down at Heathrow at 7.20 on the Wednesday morning. By lunchtime I was approaching Lorna's house, wondering how Matt had fared. I needn't have worried. As I got out of the car his nose was poking through the wrought iron gate to the back garden, his eyes had caught me in their tractor beam and his tail was well into wagging mode. Lorna opened the gate and he threw himself at me. Clearly I was not forgotten, nor even held at paw's length for the sin of running out on him for two and a half weeks! "He's had three baths while he's been here," Lorna called out,

clearly a tad embarrassed that he was absolutely filthy from
that morning's walk. I resolved yet again that it was time for
him to be clipped, with a view to attempting to ensure he
picked up a little less mud on future forays into the forest.
But overall my first voluntary separation from him had been
successful.

Dry Rot and Sculpture

With Vici's announcement toward the end of the
previous year that she wanted to hold her reception at The
Oaks, I knew that in the first half of 2005 we'd need to
undertake a pretty rapid programme of internal and external
works on the house and garden to get ready for the influx of
some 200 guests for a day in June. I suppose I'm as
competent a DIY-er as the next guy (well, maybe not!) but
there was a lot I was already scheduled to get through in 2005
(not least of all the completion of this book!) and there was
no chance of my undertaking the building work myself. Back
in December I'd finally had a new front door installed. It was
bespoke designed in solid oak and perfect for the cottage. The
day after its installation you could almost hear the house
sighing in satisfaction that it had its front door back after
more than forty years. The change in energy level inside the
house was palpable and I was confident I'd done the right
thing in having it installed. But now it was time to address a
whole range of projects we needed completed before the
wedding. After much thought and discussion I had decided
the most reliable and cost effective way of achieving the
desired result was to take someone on for a few months, who
would plough steadily through the work in a way that I
wouldn't, at a cost that could not be matched by a series of
independent trades people coming in to tackle the work
project by project. So while I was away on holiday an ad had

been running in the local newsagent's window advertising for a suitable person. The ad carried Penny's phone number so that she could note down the calls as they came through and by the time I got home there'd been several hopeful enquiries, two of which sounded promising. The first was from Guy, a general builder with experience of all sorts of project work similar to what I needed done. The second was from Suzie. Suzie had a Czech au pair working for her whose name was Clara. And no, Clara wasn't a strapping six foot builder looking for extra work, but she did have a boy friend who'd just arrived in the country who was exactly that! Suzie did a wonderful sales job on me over the phone and I was all but convinced that we should take Luca (pronounced Lucash) on immediately. Then I thought about the language question. "How's his English," I enquired.

Suzie hesitated. "Well, he understands it quite well," she said "but he's a bit shy about speaking it." I pondered for a moment. Would it be sensible to take on a builder whose English was poor, given that I'd be away three days a week, partly in order to supervise builders at Hurst Manor? "But Clara is free lots during the day," Suzie added quickly, "and she's really good at translating for him. And besides, he's willing to work at reduced rates because of the language barrier and I'm sure he'll pick up the language quickly once he gets stated." She sounded desperate on his behalf. I thought fleetingly of how I might feel in a strange country where no one was willing to give me work because I couldn't communicate effectively. That was enough.

"I'd like to meet him on Saturday," I said, and an appointment was made an hour before I was due to meet Guy. "And by the way, if he's interested I'd also be willing for him to stay in the Chalet we have here on site for a couple of months, assuming we decide to take him on."

On Saturday morning at the appointed time the doorbell duly rang and Matt went through his normal routine of self-imposed insanity, before calming sufficiently to inform me of the arrival of guests. I toddled off to answer the door. "In your corner," I said to Matt, and he duly withdrew to the other side of the room, super-obediently awaiting an "off you go" command from me and a dog biscuit reward. As expected, Luca was on the doorstep but was accompanied not only by Clara but also by Suzie's husband, Ian.

The three visitors made an intriguing sight. Lucas was about twenty-three or so, about six foot two tall (the younger generation make me feel so short these days), dark, good looking, and quietly reserved. Hanging on his arm and looking perpetually up into his face with an adoring smile and the biggest eyes I had ever seen was Clara, a very attractive blond girl of perhaps nineteen or twenty, with cascading golden hair falling about her shoulders. "Ahh, I though, how the years have flown by!" Penny and I invited them into the lounge where Matt determinedly planted himself at Luca's and Clara's feet; he always chooses to sit next to the newest arrival – some doggie perception of new energy, perhaps, or maybe just in hope that he can cadge something to eat off someone new in the house!

It was the first time I'd interviewed an applicant for a handyman's job accompanied by two human references! I found myself gravitating towards talking to Ian, given the linguistic circumstances, and checking periodically as to whether Lucas was understanding. He nodded sagely each time, saying almost nothing. Intermittently, Clara would translate something for him, but in honesty, I got no feel for his level of competence in English beyond what others were prepared to say on his behalf. A little later we waked round the house and toured the garden discussing the various projects, with Clara and Ian nodding vehemently whenever I asked if Lucas had the necessary skills to do something. By the end of the interview I had the impression that if this young man wasn't skilled enough to do the work he had the reputations of several other people about to be ruined by his incompetence! I still wasn't certain if this was a good idea though, and part of me was having visions of holes in the ground, half built walls and spouting water pipes. If it happened I was wondering how we'd recover by the time of the wedding. "Perhaps Guy will be more suitable," I found myself thinking.

Off went Lucas, Clara and Ian with my promise ringing in their ears that we'd phone them later in the day. Ten minutes or so later, Guy appeared on the doorstep. We went through the whole insanity routine with Matt again, who greeted him as if he was some long lost and dearly beloved relative instead of a complete stranger. Then we settled down in the lounge for the second time that morning to talk through the project work with Guy. Now, Guy was a completely different proposition, at least visually. Nearer to my own age (bless him), sufficiently bald that I felt positively hairy, and short enough that I didn't feel intimidated, he was a definite dose of chalk to Luca's cheese. And his approach was wholly different too. He took out a CV and spread a whole series of photographs out in front of us… photographs of sculptures, which he then proceeded to talk us through with enormous (and in my opinion wholly justified) pride. "This one," he said, I did for Richmond Borough council." We were looking at a beautifully crafted piece of artwork in metal, wood and stone. "And this was a private commission," he continued showing us another piece. Then there was another … and another, until I was beginning to wonder if he'd come to the right interview!

"But err, how are your building skills, Guy?" I asked as politely as I could.

"Oh yes," he said "I can do all sorts of building work, internal and external, particularly hard landscaping." Now, he'd said the magic words. The landscaping project was the biggest piece of work we needed doing and the one where I was least clear about what I wanted. To have someone as self starting as Guy clearly was on the project could be a big advantage.

"And bricklaying?" I asked.

"Err, no," he answered, "not too good at that." My face fell. The other big job was the rebuilding of a garden wall that had all but fallen over. Frustratingly, we needed someone like Guy for half the work and someone like Luca for the other half!

After Guy left Penny, Matt and I set off for Salisbury to do some shopping and discuss how to move forward. Guy or Luca... Luca or Guy? Towards the end of the afternoon we found ourselves in Waitrose picking up a few items of afternoon shopping. I've long since got used to the fact that dogs are unusual in supermarkets and in such locations Matt attracts particular attention. An anticipated twenty minutes zooming round the shelves to fill a trolley commonly turns into fifty minutes of stop start shopping, as we break off to spend time with the many people who want to talk to Matt or talk to me about Matt or talk to Matt about me, or simply to admire him and pat him. He takes everyone the same way, happily tolerating the patting, licking the incautious hand that veers too close to his nose, and jumping up to greet people if I don't manage to stop him first! Waitrose on this particular Saturday was no exception, and we were approached by three different sets of people who wanted to admire a working dog, or find out a bit more about his responsibilities. For me, the experience is delightful, and as I must have mentioned before, since as a result of having Matt over the last year, I've probably spoken to as many people I didn't already know as I'd done in the whole of the ten years before that!

Finally, we settled down in the coffee shop to try to arrive at closure on the subject of handymen. I reiterated the dilemma again. "Do we take Guy or do we take Luca?"

Penny looked at me and simply said "Why don't you take them both?" I looked at her for a moment, wondering if I could afford to adopt this very simple and obvious solution. Then realising that it wouldn't actually cost any more and that the work should just be completed earlier, I gratefully smiled back my agreement. As we drove home I wondered if we'd end up with garden walls reminiscent of Prague Airport and a patio with sculptures on each of the four corners. But banishing incredulity and cynicism from my mind, that evening I phoned both Suzie and Guy and proposed the arrangement. It was agreeable to all parties and start dates were agreed for Luca the following Thursday and Guy the week after.

On the dot of 12.00 on Thursday Luca and Clara duly appeared on the doorstep smiling in uncertain anticipation. I showed them down to the chalet and Luca spent the next couple of hours moving in. By mid afternoon he was back on the doorstep looking to get started with the work. Being used to the archetypal British builder who has an inclination to lean on his shovel from lunchtime til sunset, I found that rather refreshing! So we all trouped down to the local builder's merchant's where we managed to establish through hand signals and the occasional word of English what it was Luca needed by way of materials. A promise of delivery was then elicited for the following day. Mission impossible accomplished, we returned home and I let Luca loose on the garden wall that was falling down.

By this time I'd also decided that I wanted to move my study out of the house and into the little bothy in the garden. This beautiful little single-storey, one roomed building, about four metres by four externally, thatched to match the main house, had started life as a cowshed some two hundred and fifty years earlier.

At some point in its history and with innumerable generations of cows long since departed, someone had had

181

the good sense to convert it into useable space. But it was over twenty years since the previous owners of the house had paid it any attention and it needed pretty thorough redecoration (not to mention a new bathroom) before I would be able to use it in the way I wanted to. Needless to say, Luca also had the job of stripping this little building down and bringing it back up to standard before I moved in.

On Friday morning when I set off for work I left him cleaning off bricks and digging back the earth behind the garden wall. I was wondering what it would all look like when I returned home that evening. At least he didn't have time to erect a replica of Prague Cathedral in my absence! By Saturday morning my worried mind was at rest. Luca had all the bricks cleaned off and piled professionally, ready for rebuilding the garden wall. He worked all through Saturday (another trait not common amongst the lesser spotted British Builder) and by the end of the day the wall was beginning to rise out of the ground again. When it was too dark to work outside he had moved into the bothy, stripping tiles and wall paper and taking out anything else that we'd not be able to use again. Clearly this young gentleman knew what he was doing and was determined to do a high quality job. He knocked off work for the day when Clara's car rolled slowly up the lane. As we saw the lights go on in the chalet Penny giggled, and remarked on how their accommodation must surely be a tad more private than they were used to when living at Clara's employer's!

The next day, Sandy, the meditation group leader was coming for lunch and also to talk about helping us with planning out the interior of the house – or so we thought. But when we pushed the chairs back after dinner, we got more than we bargained for. Sandy took out a crystal on a chain and started dowsing the energy in each room. I watched, fascinated, as she held out the crystal and it swung this way and that, in circles or in pendulum fashion, clock-wise and anti clock-wise, as it responded to the flow of the energy around the building. Matt, of course, was wholly unconcerned. All he wanted to do was follow Sandy around wherever she went, since she was the most recent arrival in the house and therefore, by definition, the most interesting.

Outside, we showed Sandy round the garden, ending up inside the bothy, which was now looking decidedly like work in progress. Sandy stood in the middle of the room for a moment and then looked up. "What's up there?" she asked, motioning to the ceiling.

I shrugged. "Just empty space, I think," I answered, then the thatch.

"Have you thought about opening up the space and having a vaulted ceiling?" she asked.

"Wow," I said. "I haven't, but what a fantastic idea. I'll talk it through with Luca and Clara when I next see them."

Sandy set off for home to think through some ideas on the house in the context of its energy flows and the uses to which we wanted to put the space. I needed to spend another couple of days at Hurst Manor at the beginning of the week, so it was Wednesday when I got to talk to Luca about the idea. I explained it to him slowly, careful to use simple common words, though even in the short time he had been working at The Oaks, his English and his confidence had clearly improved. He understood what I was after with little difficulty. "Can we do this?" I asked.

He shrugged his big shoulders and smiled. "No problem," he said. It was becoming his standard answer to every question! So later that week, the ceiling in the bothy came down, scattering accumulated dirt, debris and armies of panic-stricken spiders all over both Luca and the floor, and opening up the space that Sandy's designer's eye had visualised all along. Luca then began the painstaking process of lining the space between the tree-trunk rafters. I left him to

it, buoyed and confident that we were going to get a really
nice result.

That evening, shortly after it was dark there was an
unexpected knock on the door. As was often the case, I didn't
hear it, but I did hear Matt's characteristic squeal of
excitement, so I knew what to expect. He came charging into
the kitchen at a rate that exceeded the Forest speed limit and
made a rugby tackle dive for my shins. Without so much as a
pause he then hurtled back out of the door in pursuit of the
exciting person – whoever it might be – on the other side of
the front door. Then, suddenly aware that I wasn't following,
he dashed back, grudgingly gave the alert signal properly and
promptly flew back out of the kitchen! As I followed at a
more leisurely pace he turned, just as he was supposed to do,
to ensure I was coming. When we finally got the door open
and I'd rewarded and released Matt, Luca was standing there
with a small piece of paper. On it he'd drawn a picture of a
plasterer's float, and written three words that had no doubt
come out of his Czech-English dictionary. "Foam" and "Dry
rot." I looked at the paper and gulped. Visions were already
assaulting me in full glorious Technicolor of dry rot climbing
malevolently up the timbers and walls of the bothy, the whole
building swaying on the edge of collapse, and in immediate
need of being propped up with buttresses all round. I tore out
of the house and over to my beloved little bothy, wondering
if the rot spores were even now wafting their way over to the
main house, under dry rot air traffic control, in deadly in
pursuit of their next target which would within seconds leave
me homeless. So ok, I admit it: I'm prone to panicking when
it comes to builders and building work.

Luca followed at a more sedate nothing's-gonna-
shake-my-cool kind of pace, wondering what all my fuss was
about. I looked quickly round the little room but could see
nothing terminal. Reminding myself that the little building
had stood up quite contentedly without assistance from me

over the last two hundred and fifty years, I turned to Luca and asked "Where's the dry rot?" He looked at me quizzically, clearly not understanding. "The dry rot," I repeated. "You wrote it down on the paper?" He shrugged his shoulders and looking somewhat confused and embarrassed. After numerous further questions I managed to elicit from him that what was required was a plasterer's float with a foam plastic base (and hence his drawing – but I'd never heard of one of those before). What Czech word he had translated as 'dry rot' I wasn't able to establish, but clearly what we didn't have was a situation of panic magnitude on our hands. My heart rate slowed and I wished him good night and returned to the house. The following Saturday I went to the DIY store and bought a large can of wood treatment fluid just to be certain!

Three steps forward, one step back

Something was beginning to concern me. Since my return from South Africa, Matt's sound work had not been as good as it was before I had gone away. We'd had that frustrating incident back in December when his assessment had had to be postponed due to the assessor's illness. That was a shame, because Sarah had been really confident he would have passed at that point. But something had changed in the meantime. In particular he wasn't as diligent at alerting me as he had been. When one of Matt's sounds occurred, if I was apparently preoccupied with doing something, such as washing up at the kitchen sink, he would hang back from alerting me, seemingly not having enough confidence to disturb me. Then, if encouraged to give the alert signal, he would sometimes then mix up the responses he was supposed to make to the different sounds, perhaps leading me to the wrong source of sound, or dropping to the floor in an emergency signal when it was only the phone ringing.

I phoned Nikki. She invited me to spend some time with her at The Grange in order to assess Matt and do some sound training work with us. So that Friday morning at the end of January we arrived back at Princes Risborough. Of course Matt immediately knew exactly where he was and started looking around for old friends. Every person we passed, everyone who came into reception as we waited, all were potential targets for his most effusive of greetings. It almost didn't seem to matter if he actually had met them before or not!

It felt quite eerie, almost like stepping back in time. It had been ten months since Matt and I had last trained there. But the old routines came back quickly, and Matt was soon chasing round the house in response to doorbells and squeakers, alerting me beautifully to the various sounds. I'd also mentioned to Nikki that I'd not pressed him on alerting me whilst I was in bed, as he seemed to be having enough trouble with the basic sound work. So as part of the session we headed of to the first floor for some bed-based sound work. With a little time for Matt and a lot of guidance for me from Nikki, he was right back to where he needed to be, jumping onto the bed to "wake" me in response to the alarm clock and alerting me to danger when the smoke alarm rang.

At the end of the session I turned to Nikki and asked "Well, do we go ahead with the assessment on Thursday or not?" Nikki wasn't certain, and neither was I.

"It's more important to get it right than it is to do it quickly," she said. "In fact, nothing really changes when he's passed, other than the fact that he gets a new coat. But it's really up to you. If you want to run with it we will, or if you prefer we can postpone."

I pondered this for a moment. She was right, of course. The important issue was to get him doing the sound work correctly and to keep him up to the necessary performance standard with it. "How about I take him home, work on it with him over the weekend and we decide on Monday," I suggested.

"Fine," Nikki replied. I'll phone you on Monday at 4.30 to see how you've got on."

So we headed home, with me clutching a new alarm clock in my hot little hand, whose sound Matt was familiar with. That evening Penny and I worked with Matt on fire bell (recorded on the CD), smoke alarm, doorbell, telephone, cooker timer and the call. Frustratingly, the alarm clock didn't work, so we were limited to working with the squeaker in the context of bed work. Each time he got the alert signal right, he'd be rewarded with a "Meaty Treat" - "*all the variety and flavour your dog could want in one re-sealable pack*" (not that we needed to re-seal it terribly often!) Essentially he was fine, if a little hesitant on the question of "waking me" in bed. I was beginning to think we would be ok to proceed with the assessment. On Saturday Penny had gone away for the weekend and Naomi came to visit. Once Matt's usual hearty welcome was over, Naomi and I once again worked through the repertoire of sounds again. Amazingly, overnight he seemed once more to have lost his edge, and to my concern he was leading me to danger sounds instead of dropping to the floor to alert me to the danger. Logic suggested a postponement of the assessment.

When Nikki phoned on the Monday. I reported our experience and my concerns. It didn't take long to arrive at the slightly disappointing but fairly obvious conclusion that a postponement of the assessment would be in everyone's best interests. Nikki agreed to send me a replacement alarm clock and to ask Sarah, Matt's Placement office to arrange a visit.

Building structures and building confidence

Arriving home after another three days away at work, I found that Guy and Luca had made enormous progress on the landscaping. New walkways and patios were emerging almost before my eyes. However, Guy had discovered the dastardly dry rot that Luca had been referring to. It hadn't been a mis-translation – it really did exist. Mercifully it was quite limited both in its extent and in the damage it had done. What was more, on further investigation the roof timbers of the bothy were showing distinct signs of their two hundred and fifty year age and several were cracked. We spent half a day discussing and designing a solution that finally entailed building a supporting structure without disturbing the existing roof and Guy and Luca set to, carrying and cutting large pieces of timber to slot in as supports. I love work – I could watch it all day long. ☺

I was also pleased to find that the new alarm clock had arrived from Nikki. That night we tried it out in bed. I set it for a minute or so ahead of the real time, and lay there, clutching a Meaty Treat in one hand ("*All the variety....*") and a squeaker in the other, lest Matt need some persuasion to jump on the bed. Ninety seconds later the alarm duly rang, and Matt became considerably more animated, dancing round the bed and round the room. But he still wasn't quite confident enough to make the leap (literally!) on his own. I pressed the squeaker. He put his paws on the edge of the bed. I pressed it again. He licked and chewed my hand! I pressed it a third time. "Come on Matt," I said encouragingly. Then he did it. He actually made a leap, but jumped straight over me to land on the other side of the bed then ran off in the opposite direction! Finally, with encouragement he jumped back on the bed and lay down on top of me. The point of principle had been established, and I felt sure he would respond to the alarm clock for real the next morning.

On no account are Hearing Dogs allowed on the furniture!

As it turned out, the point of principle had been so firmly embedded in my dear little friend's psyche, that he now considered it appropriate to jump on the bed at any time of his choosing. Hence, around 3.30am he wandered around to my side of the bed and licked my hand which was poking out from under the duvet. Getting only a slurred "GobacdasleepMatt" from me, he returned to his sheepskin. But with the alarm set for 8.00 the next morning and a blessed lie-in in prospect, Matt was by no means finished with me for the night. At 6.35 he decided it was high time I was awake and without the aid of alarm clock or safety net, he jumped on the bed and licked me until I was 100% free of that tiresome lie-in sleep that he just *knew* I didn't really want. Meaty treat? Not bleedin' likely! The only variety and flavour he got from me for that one was verbal!!

The next day I received the following e-mail from Nikki at The Grange:

"A few suggestions for some practice for the alarm clock.

Begin with a week of just practicing the sound. Once a day (we don't want Matt going the other way and start leaping on the bed at other times)............."

Yup, that was definitely good advice, that was.

Well, we were up and about, so I thought I'd get ahead of schedule and take Matt for his morning walk early, despite this being a day to be spent at home. We struck out into the forest in the direction of Jamie's Bridge. When we came in sight of the bridge Matt stopped, his body holding a certain unusual tension. I looked up, following his line of sight. Further up the valley he had spotted a herd of maybe twenty deer. "No, Matt," I said to him quietly, sensing that he was just itching for permission to run after them to see if they wanted to play. "Let's just stay here and watch them quietly." He relaxed, correctly interpreting both my tone and the word 'No,' even if he didn't understand anything else. I'd seen many deer in the forest, and indeed, even in the garden quite frequently – but only in ones and twos. So here I was confronted with an unusual and delightful sight with no camera to record it. I reprimanded myself mentally for being foolishly lazy in such a small matter. Timing, as a friend of mine says, isn't everything – it's the *only* thing.

We continued on up the valley, crossing the stream by the further bridge and climbing the hill up towards Godshill Wood, before turning for home. As was normal, we met numerous dogs and their owners along the way, some familiar friends, others new acquaintances. By this time, stopping to talk to people was no longer a big deal to me, and I had words for everyone along the way who wanted to exchange them. The minor miracle Matt had worked seemed commonplace now, and I needed to remind myself of the importance of it periodically. When we were perhaps fifteen minutes from home, we found ourselves approaching an elderly lady with a West Highland Terrier. When she saw Matt she bent forward and called him, despite the fact that, as far as I could remember we'd never met her before. Obviously he took this gesture as an invitation, and dashed towards her. Before I had a chance to utter my customary "No, Matt!" in stern tones, he'd jumped up on her. She didn't seem to mind, though. However, the same could not be said of the terrier. Jealous of the attention being afforded another dog, he made a loud and aggressive bee-line for Matt, who, sensing that he was no longer quite so welcome, darted off in the other direction. Now, you'd think that an aging terrier would be no match for the dilithium-powered rear legs of our hero. But on this particular occasion the high-octane adrenalin-driven terrier was a bit too much, and Matt couldn't shake him off. So round and round they went, the terrier snapping at Matt's heels and barking excitedly until I arrived close enough to the scene and summoned Matt away in the direction of home. As we made our swift exit the terrier dropped away, satisfied with seeing off the interloper. I saw the elderly lady patting and fusing him proudly. Could I really have heard her right when I thought she said "Well done, boy"? Presumably the dog was being resoundingly praised for protecting his mistress against poor Matt, who, two minutes earlier, had been the focus of her encouraging attention! As it's oft been said: there's none so queer as folks. Ahh well, beam me up Scotty!

The Good, the Bad and the Unexpected

I'd like to be able to tell you that Matt's behaviour is always perfect. Once in a while, however, he reminds me that no matter how well trained he is as a Hearing Dog, he is still, and always will be, a dog. Now, that might seem obvious to the educated, but sometimes I just get so used to a certain standard of behaviour from him that I'm surprised on the few occasions that I don't get it. Of course, it's also important to point out that nothing he does is ever negatively intentioned – I don't think this creature has a malicious bone in his body. Bone idle at times? Certainly. Surreptitious on occasions? Unquestionably. But malicious? Never!

One area of behaviour that's always been a particular difficulty with him, though, has been a tendency to jump up. Matt, at just less than two years of age, was a dog full of exuberance and the unutterable delights of being alive. High on the list of his priorities come people, whom he assumes always want to be friendly and always, without fail, will want to play with him. For Matt, the belief that he is universally popular is axiomatic. Well, when seen from the dog's point of view, you can understand it. When we meet other dog walkers they take interest in him. When we're out and about around town and he's in uniform, innumerable people want to admire him, talk about him, talk to him and pet him. The odd occasion that arises when people really don't want to know truly are few and far between.

I'd long since discussed the jumping up problem with Sarah during one of her many visits over the months Matt had been with me. Quelling his inclinations whilst in uniform had not been particularly difficult. By agreement with Sarah I tried always to have him sitting before allowing people to pat and talk to him when he is in uniform. On the odd few occasions on which someone makes a bee line for him and starts fussing and cuddling him without asking, a jump up might have occurred. But a stern-sounding "Off!" has always been enough to get him back onto four feet where the human 'oohs' and 'ahhs' have been permitted to continue to gush until they abate naturally. What's decidedly more difficult, however, is when he is out of uniform and he decides someone wants to play before I realise what he's doing. For instance, the other day I was talking to Luca and Clara in the garden about some aspect of the building work that needed better communication than Luca and I could achieve alone. Without warning Matt, who had been sniffing around happily somewhere a few moments before suddenly hurled himself at Clara from behind. Up went two more-than-adequately muddied paws on the back of her nice clean trousers at a pressure of several Gs. Not surprisingly, Clara let out a brief scream. That, plus my more than adequately firm reprimand was quite sufficient for Matt to be aware that his assumption had been incorrect and no, the young lady did not want to play just at that moment. I mused on the event afterwards. Of course, ultimately the responsibility was mine. But in fairness I can't have my full concentration on him the whole time – life has to be gotten on with. So the matter passed and I allowed it to drift from my thoughts.

But on the first weekend in February it raised its unexpected head again. Penny and I were out walking with Matt just before lunch on Sunday. It was one of those beautiful late winter mornings when the daffodils were straining at the leash to break through the soil and the energy of new growth was beginning to promise that Spring was pressing home its advantage. We were deep in some conversation, with me addressing my usual challenge of lip reading someone walking next to me. Matt's never terribly far away on such occasions. Indeed, he tends to become insecure if he drifts too far, so generally I'm not concerned so long as I can see him. But on this occasion, coming towards us from the other direction was a young family, with two little girls of about 9 and 5 years of age. Matt decided one of the little girls must surely want to play. Whether it was the encouragement he had received to jump up by the old lady several days earlier I'll never know. But unfortunately he jumped on the older girl from behind. Once again, up went two muddy paws on the back of a very pretty and exceedingly clean pink anorak. As soon as I saw what was happening, I let out a very stern "MATT!" at the top of my voice and he charged back towards me, completely oblivious to the wrong he had done. Though I put him straight on the lead, unfortunately the damage was done. We were now facing one extremely surprised and very tearful little girl and two parents with faces like thunderclouds. They said nothing, but I could hear "Why can't you keep your dog under control?" anyway, and "If you can't control him you shouldn't have him off the lead." There was no way whatsoever of getting out of this one, so I walked Matt purposefully forward towards the little family group where mother was comforting her little girl and father was looking decidedly irate. Mentally dropping to my knees (but not physically this time) I apologised profusely. I offered to buy the little girl some sweets to make up for it, but she wasn't going to be bought off that easily. I received a rather cool "It's all right" from father, who seemed to feel that adequate penance had been done by my metaphorical roll in tar and feathers. Duty discharged, we proceeded on our way. I resolved to talk to Sarah about how to deal with Matt's excessive enthusiasm when she next visited.

On the Following day we set off for work as usual. This time I was taking with me the new alarm clock to ensure I continued to concentrate on Matt's sound work as far as possible while I was away from home. For the preceding few nights Matt had woken me in the night. Evidently this was just for the fun of doing so since he had now established territorial claims over the bed. It was clear he had no practical reason, since when I came to offer him the chance to go out at 3.00am he consistently refused. Thus, I had resolved that from that night forward I would ensure he had a proper opportunity to go into the garden at 11.00pm to do what every little doggie needs to do, and thereafter I would disregard all pleas for attention until the next morning when the alarm clock bleeped. Now, I have to say that the plan was far from foolproof, since I can't hear the beep of the alarm clock. I'm therefore left to assume that it's rung when a certain little doggie form bounds onto the bed at a heightened level of excitement. But fortunately, I can tell the difference between the darkness of 3.00am and the sky beginning to lighten on a February morning at 7.00am. So that night when I went to bed I look at him. "Right Mate," I thought, "I'm ready for ya!". But of course the artful Matt was, as always, one and half paces ahead of me. We slept peacefully until said alarm clock rang at 7.00, whereupon he bounded onto the bed, ran all over me in excitement and licked every part of me not covered by the quilt until he received his meaty treat. And on this occasion there was no need for my language to be as varied and flavoursome as the treat!

Space Invader

I've made no mention so far in this story of interactions between Matt and the feline species. In his first year with me, Matt had certainly had many *close encounters of the first kind* - sightings of cats – and one or two *close encounters of the second kind* – getting a cat to spit at you and arch its back. However, up until now *close encounters of the furred kind* –grabbin' a cat by the scruff of the neck and shakin' the living daylights out of it – had thus far eluded our gentle hero. Accordingly, he tended to view this glowing-eyed alien species with particular interest (*"it's life Dad, but not as we dogs know it"*). Matt is a creature who believes that the sole function of all intelligent life such as himself is to play. It thus does not come easily to him to understand that not all entities in the universe are as naturally besotted with him as I am. Consequently on several occasions when we have been out walking he has approached felines at his usual pace - warp factor 10 - only to find to his amazement that either the *Species* concerned exits at warp factor 11, or it arches its back, makes its fur stand on end and spits venom at him from 50 paces. In the later case Matt's warp factor 10 forward has, generally speaking, morphed instantly into warp factor 10 backwards. *Resistance, clearly has been futile.*

The next weekend had long been booked for a visit to my friends, Chris and Dilys, who live in Kent. (It was their cats, Gismo and Kitten, who had written in protest at Matt's innocently intended comment (☺) about the inferiority of cats compared to dogs at that time when he had issued his invitations to my surprise adoption party).

Accordingly, this weekend we were about to enter the very home space of the aliens, with whom he had hoped for so long for First Contact. It was Matt's presumption that, when on home territory, The Species would surely feel sufficiently confidence to enter into the rough and tumble and leaping and lurching that true intelligent life such as dogs indulge in constantly.

We arrived about lunchtime on the Friday to our usual tumultuous welcome by Chris, Dilys and their twenty-year-old daughter, Hazel. Matt had barely set foot inside the door when he became aware of the smell of The Species, whereupon he began tugging forward on his lead. Though we were in a private home, I had taken the precaution of putting him into full dress uniform, so as to ensure he felt in work mode, in the hope that this would offset the enticing attraction of cats to some degree. Uh huuh

Indeed, it must also be stated that this was a first, not only for Matt, but also for Kitten and Gismo, who had never had a canine traveller in the home space before. This, of course, would undoubtedly be a source of tremendous honour and intrigue to them. Uh huuuuuuuuh.

Now, as every space fleet admiral knows, it is easier to defend territory from above the enemy, thus forcing him into the disadvantage of fighting upwards. From such an advantageous location one can launch one's most spirited defence with whatever weaponry (laser cannon, photon torpedoes, spittle etc.) is available. Upon our arrival, both cats had retreated to the back of the house, where there was some eminently defendable high space and – last line of defence – a worm hole into the alternative universe of the garden (i.e. a cat-flap). Gismo (grey and white, small), less experienced in the arts of feline-canine inter-dimensional warfare, had not waited for an opportunity to assess the strength and weaknesses of the earth-bound enemy but from the moment of our arrival had opted for the fall back position preferred by every alien - the shed roof. Here she proceeded to spend most of the weekend until our departure. Kitten (black and white, bit larger), evidently the more militarily experienced of the two aliens and clearly a seasoned Predator of numerous campaigns, had adopted some of the more defendable territory inside the house - high up on a wall unit behind a cheese plant that acted as an invisibility suit against the enemy.

Welcomes, cups of tea and other preliminaries having been duly completed, Dylis decided it was time that the aliens were introduced to their new visitor. She retrieved a somewhat reluctant Kitten from behind the cheese plant and brought her through into the lounge. Whilst she was gone, though he was shut inside the lounge and some twenty paces away, Matt was acutely aware of what was happening. He sat in front of the closed lounge door, wining desperately for an opportunity to achieve First Contact. When Dilys was ready (I can't speak for whether Kitten was ready or not) slowly, the lounge door opened, and step by careful step, emerged Dilys, in Mother Ship mode, with Kitten perched high up on her shoulder, present only for the purposes of assessing the strength of the enemy's battalions and fire power. From the safety of her high and highly manoeuvrable control module

197

(i.e. Dil), she peered down at the invading earth creature, invoking that innate attitude of superiority that cats always have over dogs when they know they have them out-foxed, out-reached or – as in this case - out ray-gunned.

Matt, for his part, sat bolt upright, rigid and quivering in excitement, barely daring to move his tail, wholly possessed with the prospect that he might actually have here the potential of making First Contact with the much admired and deified species that for so long had remained frustratingly beyond his reach. After a couple of minutes it was clear that Kitten had finished her reconnoitre, and she scrambled to get away and back to the safety of the cheese plant. From here, much to Matt's frustration she spent most of the weekend peering down at him from the ray-gun slits of the plant's leaves, periodically stretching enticingly but oh so frustratingly, so that the invading earth-bound dog could see what he definitely was not going to be permitted to touch.

Come Sunday lunch, and clearly somehow aware that we were shortly to depart, curiosity got the better of Kitten. As we sat, finishing off lunch and lazy conversation, she gingerly stepped over the cheese plant, and jumped down onto a part of the wall unit that was just feasibly within doggy reach. Matt, immediately aware of her change of strategy, again sat frozen in the light of her Tractor Beam at the prospect of genuine First Contact. I watched him carefully, ready to yell "No!" should he make a light speed move in Kitten's direction. But the Bark Side of the Force was clearly not strong with him that day. He sat perfectly still, muscles quivering, tail flicking almost imperceptibly, yet seemingly totally unable to move. Confident that she now had not only the upper hand, but also complete control over the invading force, Kitten boldly went where few cats had gone before and jumped onto the seat of an empty chair, where she proceeded to annex the space on behalf of the Feline Empire, by washing her front paws nonchalantly, monitoring the disdained enemy from the corner of her eye. Matt, completely bemused as to what on earth to do now that First Contact was now a real possibility, simply sat, awaiting further initiatives from what he now recognised to be indisputably a Higher Intelligence. The Higher Intelligence, however, was having none of it. She had now demonstrated her innate superiority to her own satisfaction and it was beyond dispute by the assembled party. She therefore returned to safety behind the cheese plant where she remained, much to doggy disappointment until we left. Was it her Drone that buzzed us as we reached the M2 on the way home? I'm not sure – but at the time of writing First Contact remains enticingly just out of reach. Anyway, what can you expect? After all, Matt is from Mars and Cats are from Venus. ☺

"I'm reviewing the situation…"

After that visit to The Grange earlier in February and with the decision to postpone Matt's final assessment, we had elevated sound work to the very top of the agenda. I worked Matt daily on doorbell, telephone, alarm signals and so on and watched him gain noticeable ground each day. The week after the Close Encounter we had arranged for Sarah, Matt's Placement Officer to visit once again. With the progress that he was making I must admit that my main concern was whether she would think I'd been making a fuss about nothing. But there again, Nikki, Matt's trainer at The Grange, had concurred in the decision to postpone the assessment.

Bright and early on the Thursday morning, there was a ring on the doorbell – at least I assumed there was, since Matt squealed in excitement, dashed for the door then rushed back to alert me. By now he knew he would get nowhere unless he did the job correctly. He dropped his bottom elegantly to the floor (*CAN* a dog drop his bottom elegantly?), and put his front paws around my knees in a perfectly executed alert signal. I spread my hands enquiringly and asked him in the time-honoured response "What is it?" whereupon he rushed for the door, checking behind him to ensure I was following. Sure enough it was Sarah. I instructed Matt into his corner where he proceeded to wait patiently until I had invited Sarah in and said hello. As soon as I released him though, he wanted to be all over her. As he jumped at her, Sarah raised her face upwards to break eye contact and stood with her arms folded, completely ignoring Matt until he returned properly to the approved position of all four feet on the floor. It was a good start to the day.

We filled the rest of the morning with tests on his sound work to which he responded well, but sufficiently short of perfection to demonstrate the need for further improvement. The afternoon was spent walking him in the forest, with me holding tight onto my whistle lest he decide to demonstrate his jumping problem by terrorising some unsuspecting passer-by with an unscheduled leap at them. But though he roughed and tumbled with every four-footed creature that came within playing distance, his behaviour around people remained impeccable.

At the end of the afternoon we sat down to review where we were. "Well, he's not perfect," said Sarah, "But I reckon he's ready for assessment."

I'd heard this before, several months previously. "Are you sure he'll pass?" I asked with some reticence.

"No, you can't be sure how he'll behave on the day," she answered, "but he needs to average 75% across all assessed areas of performance, and if I'd been assessing him today I would have passed him."

"OK," I said slowly, "can we arrange for the assessment sooner rather than later then please, because I'm due to go on holiday with Naomi at the end of March, and if we delay 'til after that there's a good chance he'll deteriorate again while I'm away."

Sarah phoned The Grange immediately. Matt's assessment was arrange some three weeks hence on 10th March. Clearly, We still had some work to do to ensure his performance continued to improve right up until the target date.

Bar & Barred

I've written earlier of some of the encounters Matt and I had had with various establishments that were less than wholly happy to admit him. But in October of 2004 a major change took place in the law that affected the position fundamentally - the Disabilities Discrimination Act came fully into force. One of the aims of the Act is to ensure that disabled people receive no lesser a service from suppliers of all types than fully able consumers. And in the case of assistance dog users such as me, it is clear in requiring virtually all establishments to permit the entry of assistance dogs. On the Saturday following Sarah's visit, little did I know that we would be testing the Act to its limit.

Periodically, my brother Richard and his son David come down from London to visit my mother who lives in Lymington, and we all go off to have lunch together. The pattern was well established that I would meet Richard and David from the station, from where we would go to collect Mum and then head out to lunch in some local restaurant. On this particular occasion I'd overbook my diary. (I'm sure there's a little gremlin inside it that adds extra entries when I'm asleep at night – I'm absolutely certain it's not me that puts every appointment in it that I find there each morning). As a result I had a relatively small window for lunch. To save time I collected Mum first, then made for Brockenhurst

Station to meet Richard and David. With hugs and kisses
duly dispensed all round, I said, "I hope you don't mind, but
my time is really tight today. Is it ok if we make for the
nearest hotel or restaurant for lunch?" Everyone was in
agreement and within five minutes we were turning into the
driveway of a hotel near Brockenhurst.

We all piled out of the car with much zipping of coats
and donning of hats and gloves against the ravages of the
February wind. As is often the case, due to the time it takes to
get Matt out of the car and into uniform, I found myself
bringing up the rear of the party as we entered the restaurant.
Consequently, Matt was not visible as the maitre d' led our
little party towards a table. Arriving at the table, he turned
around and I watched his face fall as he saw Matt and me
bringing up the rear of the group. He said something to my
brother that was inaudible to me, shaking his head and
glancing at Matt and me uncertainly. Now, if there's
something I hate it's being talked about when I'm present as
if I were absent – especially if it's talk of the 'Does he take
sugar?' variety that many disabled people suffer. I called out
to the gentleman concerned "If you're talking *about* me
would you please come here and address your remarks
directly *to* me. I am hearing disabled, not intellectually
challenged."

Quickly he approached and led me away from the
restaurant area lest I create any further disruption (disruption?
Wot *moi*?). He said something inaudible to me.

I looked at him, beginning to feel a little irritated that
someone who now knew quite clearly that I had a hearing
impairment would not take the trouble to adjust his speech
for me, particularly given what he was trying to achieve – i.e.
my departure! I looked straight at him and interrupted his
mumbling. "Stop, please!" I said. He looked at me
uncertainly. "If you want me to understand what you're
saying," I continued, "you need to slow down and speak

directly towards me so that I can read your lips. It's the only way I'll understand you."

Some restaurants are happy to accept us

To give him his due, he responded appropriately immediately. Slowing his speech down and facing me directly, he said, "I'm sorry sir, but I am instructed that I may not allow dogs into the restaurant."

I looked at him a moment, gathering my resources as my heart rate rose – I hate confrontation of any kind and will go to enormous lengths to avoid it. But if there's one situation for which I make an exception, it's this one. When I'm out and about with Matt I feel like an ambassador for everyone else who's apt to receive inferior treatment by reason of their disability, and I simply will not back down any longer. And yes, we are talking red rags and bulls here. "Are you aware," I answered in slow, measured tones, "that the Disability Discrimination Act came into full force in October last year, and that if you turn me away because of my Hearing Dog you will be breaking the law?"

He hesitated a moment, caught between his orders and an uneasiness that this awkward customer might just be telling the truth about the law. Then his training and obedience regained the upper hand. "I'm sorry sir," he replied, "there's nothing I can do. These are my instructions."

"Then please understand, "I responded carefully, "that before I leave I will require details of the ownership of this establishment and that I will report it for contravention of the Act and as a result you may be prosecuted." He didn't respond, clearly feeling uncertain of how to proceed. I pressed home the point. "Would you turn away a blind person with a guide dog?" I continued.

He hesitated before answering. "No he said, but we do have special provision for them." He motioned towards the seating in the bar area. "As you are now telling me your dog is a guide dog," he continued, "I can offer you seating here."

I looked where he gestured. I was feeling embarrassed, rejected, marginalized and more than a little upset. He had already ensured I was not going to enjoy lunch. But time was tight, I didn't have long enough to try anywhere else, and I was now impinging on the goodwill of my family a little further than I felt was reasonable. I wasn't going to walk out, but I needed to push the point further to be absolutely clear about what was going on. I continued, "So if it's possible for us to sit here, why are we being denied access to the restaurant?"

But in asking the question, I had given the maitre d' the escape route he needed. "Why, because someone might trip over the dog in the restaurant," came his swift reply.

I looked down at my little dog who stands about eighteen inches at the shoulder and who spends every available moment curled up unobtrusively at my feet. Obstruction is not the first word that comes to mind when you look at him lying motionless behind my chair in a public place. I looked into the bar area I was being offered which was too dark for comfortable lip reading and where the tables were closer together than they were in the restaurant anyway.

"Then you surely must agree that there is more chance of his being tripped over here in the bar than there is in the restaurant," I answered. So what's the real reason you won't let me in?"

I wasn't expecting an honest answer, but something had clearly clicked for the maitre d'. After a few moments he replied in a softer tone, "Because someone might object to a dog in the restaurant."

I looked directly into his eyes. Even I could hear the raucous noise of the only occupied table in the restaurant a few yards behind me where several excessively lubricated diners were making more of a nuisance of themselves than Matt would ever be capable of doing on his very worst possible day. But my time had run out. "Then I have to tell you that although I am accepting your offer of a table in the bar, I believe I am still being discriminated against by reason of my disability and I still intend to report this establishment for a breach of the Act." At that moment I had no idea how to report a breech of the Act, or for that matter, to whom it should be reported. But I fully intended to find out first thing Monday morning!

Nevertheless, the maitre d' had won – or at least his problem had gone away. He said nothing more, opening his hand in a gesture towards the awaiting table. We sat, and Matt proceeded to fall asleep in the corner behind my chair in his wholly inconspicuous and non-intrusive regular fashion. Not much chance of his being tripped over there. To add to the pain of the event we were then offered the bar menu instead of the restaurant menu, presumably in an attempt to get rid of us as quickly as possible! I objected once more, feeling as though I was going to have to fight every inch of the way for decent treatment.

In truth, I really didn't know at that moment whether the restaurant was in breach of the Act or not. They had accepted my dog, albeit requiring me to accept an alternative and arguably inferior location in the bar. But the maitre d' did have at least a presentable argument – less chance of the dog being tripped over – even if I considered it spurious. My intention was to let whichever authority was responsible resolve the issue. But during the meal an unexpected development took place. Just as we had finished ordering dessert, into the bar walked a gentleman in black tie, looking more than a little fazed. He glanced around nervously. Sensing this was about Matt, I caught his eye and looked enquiringly at him. He began addressing me inaudibly from the far side of the table, adding to the sense of frustration I was already feeling. OK, I accept I can't expect people to know what my needs are as a hearing disabled person until I tell them, but when you've been abused by reason of your disability it tends to ruffle the feathers a little, leaving you less inclined to be sweetness and light than you might normally be. I swallowed hard and controlled the urge to turn into an uncannily accurate imitation of The Hulk having a very bad day.

"Could you come over here and talk directly towards me please," I asked, trying to sound polite, "so that I can lip read you and hear you more clearly?" He complied with the request immediately.

"I'm sorry sir, there seems to have been a misunderstanding." I looked at him enquiringly. "I gather you were refused entry to the restaurant because of your assistance dog. That was a mistake on the part of the restaurant manager. He's been told that dogs are not permitted, but that instruction was never intended to include assistance dogs."

Well, at least we were now getting somewhere. "So if I come here with my dog again," I asked, "I will be permitted to sit in the restaurant?"

"Yes sir," came the swift and unequivocal reply.

I thought for a moment. I had retrieved just about everything from this frustrating and painful occasion that I could, and there would be little to be gained from pressing the matter with the authorities (or so, in my ignorance, I thought). "Then there is no further complaint, "I found myself answering, surprising myself with my reasonableness. He nodded, thanked me and slipped away in that unobtrusive manner that is common to excellently trained service staff at the quality end of the hospitality industry.

As we rose to leave, the maitre d' said to me apologetically, "Well, I learned something today."

'Yes,' I thought. 'Unfortunately your learning has cost me a rare, otherwise enjoyable family meal and a waste of £80.00.' How come I never say these things, even when I think of them in time?

I've not yet been back to test out whether the restaurant's policy really has changed. Clearly, even with the full force of the law on their side, disabled people will face discrimination for some time to come.

The Haze Begins to Clear

Quite co-incidentally, on the Tuesday following this incident, we were having a disability audit at Hurst Manor. It had not escaped my notice that my business, too, had to ensure it was complying with the requirements of the Disability Discrimination Act. The RNID had offered us an audit and, given the fact that we still had time to make any necessary changes to the new building we were constructing, it seemed a perfect opportunity to make sure we were getting it right.

Jacqui from the RNID appeared on the dot of 11.00am as arranged. I had cleared my diary and my desk in order to spend the rest of the day with her if necessary, running through our policies, procedures and premises. I guess it was inevitable that my experience at the restaurant should come up in the course of the conversation. Jacqui, a veteran campaigner for disabled rights, was incensed. When I told her the detail of the story, her response was, "Michael, there's no question but that you were discriminated against. When we've finished here today, I'm going to e-mail you details of the Disabilities Rights Commission (DRC) who are the body responsible for enforcing the Act. You'll find case study after case study on the site where they've taken up the cause of a disabled person given inferior service by reason of their disability. And what's more, the position regarding assistance dogs is now very clear. Any exclusion of an assistance dog, or provision of an inferior service because of an assistance dog is a clear breech of the Act." Maybe I now had a route forward for avoiding the unpleasant feelings associated with confrontation. I waited eagerly so see what the DRC web site had to say.

Jacqui finished her visit with us, made several helpful recommendations and life proceeded in its normal manner. Forty-eight hours later I had the promised e-mail – in fact I had four of them from her! One indeed took me straight to the case studies on the DRC web site where one case-study on an excluded guide dog for the blind sounded remarkably similar to my own experiences. In each case-study a DRC worker had contacted the supplier concerned, explained they were breaking the law and agreed compensation for the disabled person who had suffered inferior service. That compensation commonly ran to several hundred pounds.

My confidence shot up - not that I'd be looking for confrontation, but rather that should there be another attempt to exclude me by reason of my assistance dog I now knew exactly what to do. Of course, I had no reason to know at that moment that I would very soon be offered an opportunity to put my new found knowledge to the test.

Deputy Dawg

We were now into March and, given the rate at which I knock up mileage on the car, it was time to have it serviced again. I'd arranged an early morning appointment and dropped car off at the garage at 8.00am, giving myself a couple of hours to kill in Southampton before I was due to pick it up. Clearly, it was too early for a fish & chip lunch, so I was hopeful there'd be no more experiences of the "You no blind" variety that day!

Now, at 8.00 in the morning, downtown Southampton doesn't exactly rival Las Vegas on a busy night. What's more, we were having a seriously cold spell, so the one thing I wasn't up for was wandering the streets window-shopping. After a swift trip to the cash point I found myself approaching a sandwich board standing outside a café, advertising such culinary delights as English breakfasts, deli sandwiches and take away Cappuccino. Now, as those who have had the opportunity to observe my waistline first hand may suspect, I'm a tad partial to the occasional traditional English breakfast. And walking the streets in temperatures of minus-something-pretty-cold was a sure fire way to get me visualising sizzling sausages snuggling up to crispy bacon in the pan, contemplating a ménage a trios with a nice helping of mushrooms on the side. Accordingly, Matt and I followed our noses in through the door of the café. Inside it was warm, and bright and buzzing with activity – clearly an eating-house at the leading edge of petit-dejuner cuisine in central Southampton. Of course, given my recent experiences of exclusion I knew there was a possibility that someone would have something to say about Matt's presence. But after my surfing of the Internet a few days earlier, I had my response well prepared. I slipped into John Wayne mode and *walked kinda lazily up ta the counter* (I find it really helps me to slip into John Wayne mode when I want to look confident).

There were three young men serving. The youngest, a lad of about twenty, turned to me, glanced down at Matt and said, "What can I get you?

Now the yung'un, he was the meanest lookin' boy a ever saw. He looks up slow from the bar and snarls at me. "Waddle it be?" he says.

"An English breakfast and a black coffee, please," I replied.

I was sure thirsty from ridin' all day and ma faithful hownd dawg Matt, well, he was plum tuckered out from runnin' beside me in the noonday heat. "Gimme a beer," I said, "an' a wawder for ma dawg."

"OK." He said, "Where are you going to eat it?

*Well, the yung'un, he screws up his eyes kinda funny and looks straight at ma dawg's coat – the one with the HEARING DOGS logo right in tha middle of it." Aint he a **diputy** ?" he asks. " We don' like diputies in these parts. We likes to make our own lore here."*

"Over there" I answered, motioning with my head towards some empty spaces in the seating area to my left."

Now, I din' cum there looking fer a fight. But the lore's the lore an' its ma dawg's job to enforce it. "Oh yeah," I sez ta him " well we're jes gonna hev ta see about that." An' ma dawg, Matt, spat some a hes chewin' ta-baccy straight at the yung'un's feet.

"Sorry, we cant let the dog in here," he responded.

"Now you jes' git on yer hoss, ride odda te-own 'n make sure yer dawg goes with ya," he says, gitting a mite riled.

I felt tempted to point out to him that strictly speaking he had already let the dog in!

I sighed. "you may not know," I said, "but the law changed in October. You're not allowed to exclude an assistance dog with a disabled person."

So I looks at him kinda long and slow. And then I sez ta him, "Ne-ow, ma dowg's comz in here, peace-luvvin and lore-abadin' like, to teach you fellas the lore, 'n peaceful's hows we wan' it ta stay. I'm a-givin' you jes one chay-nce ta surrender, boy."

He hesitated. "OK, but you've got to think of everyone else," he said, motioning to a pretty full seating area behind us.

Well, I wuz clearly gittin' ta him, coz he hesitates, then he sez a bit softa, like "Now marshal, the citizens of this here tay-own, they jes don' wan' ya and ya dawg here.

211

*They's jes quite happy with
the lore they got now, n'all."*

I was ready with my
response. "If you exclude me
because of my assistance
dog," I said "I will indeed
leave. But you need to know
that the first thing that I'll do
on leaving here is report you
to the Disabilities Rights
Commission and you will be
fined for breaking the law."

*Then he looks at me even
meaner, like. 'An that's when
it happenz. Quicker 'n a
jack-rabbit he undoes his
holster, an' draws hez finger.
Hez jess about ta point it at
the daw ta make us go. But
ma faithful hownd dawg
Matt, he's fester still.
'Quicker than you ken say
Hearin' Dawgs fer Deaf
People, ma dawg Matt slips
the safety catchs on his twin,
pearl handled copies of tha
Disabilities Discrimination
Act. Then he points em
straight at the boy's business.
He fair took ma breath away,
I ken till ya.*

*"Son," I sez, lookin' at the
yung'un all serious like, "ma
dawg don' wanna use them
there copies of tha
Disabilities Discrimination
Act on ya, but if ya force him
ta he will. 'An ya betta look
at the notches on the pearl
handles too– one fer every
business that he's had ta
report on coz they tried ta
turn him away. 'An if ya ever*

saw a business sufferin' from a DDA report, you'll know it's a slow an' painful process – an' not at all a purdy sight. So I'm advisin' ya to put yer finger away 'afor someone here gits hurt."

I stood looking at him, wondering what the response would be. He stood looking at me, not responding! High noon at the OK Corral? Finally he spoke. "OK," he said (yup, there was a certain consistency to his conversation!) "What do you want?"

I was thrown for a moment. Was that it? No more confrontation?

"An English breakfast and a cup of black coffee," I repeated. I probably sounded surprised.

"£4.35," he said.

Then ya know what? That yung'un, he jez crumbles right in frona me. "OK sheriff," he sez, soundin' real scared. " I jez can't take no more. Tell yer dawg ta put down his copies of the DDA – I'll a' give in quietly."

Finally I sez to him, "Son, yer law-breakin' days are over. We're-a gonna make an honest cit-zen av yer."

"Why sure sheriff," he sez, sounding all meek n' mild now, "anything you sez. I'm real glad you'n the dawg walked in here today ta show

213

me the error of my ways 'n all."

And that was it. Confrontation over. No more arguments. I'd found a form of words that was workable – that people – even those that didn't understand the Act or the need of disabled people for equal service – could understand. From now on I'd know exactly what to do when there was an attempt to exclude Matt. A major problem was solved.

So me 'n ma deputy dawg settled right de-own ba' the yung 'n's camp fire 'n paid fair 'n square for a honest meal.

The breakfast came, the sausages sizzling on the plate, just as envisioned. My only disappointment was that I couldn't offer a share of it to the little dog lying quietly and unobtrusively under my chair.

Then, with our beenz 'n cawfee still hot in our bellies, ma faithful deputy dawg 'n me rode oudda town to bring the lore to some other godless corner of lore-less wild west Hampshire. ☺

Assessment

Of course, the major event that was coming up in March was Matt's assessment. Unfortunately the whole process had turned into something much more complicated and daunting than it was ever intended to be. Back in December I'd accepted, on Sarah's advice that he'd pass. But the assessor, Julie, had been unable to come on the appointed day and we'd had to postpone. Her next preferred date fell slap bang in the middle of my newyear holiday, so we'd eventually settled on the next available time as being in early February. But by the time I'd come home from holiday in mid January, Matt had lost ground on his sound work to the point where at times it seemed he just couldn't be bother to make the effort. As a result, I'd taken him back to The Grange for that top up training day in late January. And as a result of that we'd taken the decision to postpone yet again. Assessment had finally been set for 10th March, which gave me a month to work hard with Matt on his areas of weakness. As far as I was concerned, there'd be no more postponements. We absolutely had to get it right.

From late January right through February and into March, with Penny's help I worked with Matt constantly to get his responses to his trained sounds exactly as they ought to be. Sarah, Matt's Placement Officer had left CDs with me, recorded with the sound of the fire alarm and the smoke alarm, which meant that I could also work with Matt when I was alone. Virtually daily we'd play the CDs and I'd wander round the house until the sound of the fire alarm or the smoke alarm stimulated Matt into work mode. Then we'd try activating the phone or the doorbell or the cooker timer. With increasing frequency, he would get the responses right, distinguishing correctly between emergency signals where he was required to drop to the floor, and other sounds where his job was to lead me to the source of the sound. Then we'd go through the whole routine again with me lying in bed, so that he was required to jump onto the bed to simulate waking me in response to one of his trained sounds.

As the month of February drew on I became increasingly confident that he would be ready for the assessment. But that was also that nagging uncertainty as to whether something would go wrong on the day. If it did, the consequences would not be terminal of course. I knew that in the event of a dog failing assessment, Hearing Dogs' policy was simply to continue Placement Officer visits and continue training the dog until the required standard was achieved. My darkest fear – that someone would take my beloved dog away from me – was thankfully long since behind me. It would, however, be irritating and time consuming if some unforeseen event took place on the day that caused him to behave out of character.

Well, on 10th March, Spring woke and got out of bed at the same time on as it did on any other morning. It rubbed its eyes and examined its progress on the crocuses and the daffodils before coaxing the reluctant sun up to its 6.30am rising position. And with 6.30 comes the sound of my alarm clock. Although I'm not able to hear it, some time ago I'd learned the wisdom of setting it for 6.30 – if I don't, Matt wakes me at 6.30 anyway!

So at the appointed time my little friend leapt on the bed, licked my face and walked systematically all over me until he received his treat. Then he settled down on me for his morning cuddle, which he continues to impose upon me until the point where I'm absolutely awake and realise there's no point in staying in bed any longer. His faultless performance in ensuring I was awake that morning was a good omen for the rest of the day. I went through the normal getting up and getting ready routine and by 9.00am we were set. Matt looked just the part. A late afternoon visit to the groomer's the day before, itself the source of enormous excitement, had

left him looking perfect for Julie's visit. It remained to be
seen whether his behaviour would match his appearance.
Still, nothing was going to go wrong, was it?

Assessment? Wot Assessment?

I made a cup of coffee. I tapped my fingers
impatiently. We did a bit more practice work with the CDs
and cooker timer. But 11.00am steadfastly refused to come
any faster than it normally did. However, eventually at about
five to eleven, there was ring on the doorbell. Matt went
manic with excitement as usual. I waited in my chair for his
eventual recollection that the door doesn't get opened until he
comes to tell me the bell has rung! Finally, as he always does,
he got the message, and came to alert me. So far, so good. I
opened the door and Julie and I introduced ourselves to each
other, as Matt sat obediently in his corner until I released
him. Amazingly, he made no attempt to jump up at her. This
was looking promising.

Julie, an attractive blonde lady in her early thirties,
was dressed in the standard maroon sweater and relaxed
professional smile sported by virtually all the Hearing Dogs
people I had met over the preceding year. We headed for the

lounge where coffee was consumed and pleasantries exchanged for a few minutes. Then Julie explained the structure of the assessment to me. First we'd cover the sound work, then she wanted to see him working around town. Finally she wanted to take him out for a walk with me and observe his general obedience work. At least we would get the potentially tough part – the sound work – out of the way first. I reckoned that the rest of it would go smoothly.

We started with the cooker timer set to four minutes. He responded perfectly. My hopes started to rise. We moved onto the CDs of the alarms: again, a perfect response. "OK," said Julie, "I'd like to try the smoke alarm while you lie in bed." Now this one could have been a problem. I lay down on the bed and Julie proceeded to activate the smoke alarm at the top of the stairs. I held my breath, unable to hear the alarm at all, and waited to see if Matt would do his stuff. There was a moment's delay. I became worried. Then without further ado he leapt from the floor and landed squarely on top of me – another perfect response. I pushed him gently off the bed and got up. "What is it?" I asked, spreading my hands wide. He dropped to the floor – a perfect response. I rewarded him with a treat accordingly We were passed the danger area and I was hopeful of a relatively easy ride on the rest of the sound work.

Next, Julie tried a call. She stood in the kitchen and put me in the study. Matt disappeared in her direction, evidently responding to her calling him. A few moments later he scampered back into the study, alerted me then turned dashed back off in the direction of the kitchen. Another success. Finally we tried the phone. But Matt knew what was happening and knew the reward system. He pre-empted the phone and alerted me to no sound at all! Julie spotted his mistake instantly, and we repeated the exercise. This time he acted perfectly, leading me to the ringing phone in the exact prescribed manner. I sighed. Sound work was complete and

Julie didn't seem too disturbed by his jumping the gun over the telephone. We were not yet home and dry, but the omens were decidedly positive.

"OK," she said, "I'd like to see him working around town, please."

"Right you are," I said, "I need to run some errands anyway."

I strapped Matt into his car seat and we drove off in the direction of Fordingbridge. On arrival, I extracted Matt from the car, placing him in uniform. I was careful not to let go of him at any time – quite a tricky manoeuvre when I have to remove him from his harness and get him into uniform. Nevertheless, the task was achieved and we made for the first stop – the bank. No problems in here. He stood patiently while I awaited my turn at the cash machine. With cash retrieved, we made for the supermarket. For most dogs this is a more testing environment, as the food smells coming off the shelves can be tempting. Matt's never really displayed a problem in this area though, and I was hopeful that we'd sail through this test without difficulty. If I had a concern it was that someone would bend down and distract him without warning, raising the possibility of his becoming excited and jumping up. Mercifully, though, the population of Fordingbridge was on its best behaviour that day, and we left the supermarket unmolested.

"Wow," said Julie "he completely ignored the food! I'm really impressed."

'Just keep it that way m'dear' I thought. Not that I said anything, though.

Our final visit was to Tony and Anne's hardware shop where I needed to buy kindling. It's here that Matt always gets a treat from Tony. I did wonder if that might cause a problem, but thought 'Well, it's what happens every time we go in there, so if Julie doesn't think it should be happening I'm sure she'll tell me.' When we got into the shop, though, matters were a tad more complicated. A shopper at the till turned and looked closely at Matt.

"Oh," she said, "Are you involved with Hearing Dogs? I've been wanting to get in touch with them for some time. I own a local kennels and we often get given stray dogs. I was wondering if they might be of interest to Hearing Dogs."

"I'll very happily pass on your details to them," I said. And then she was all over Matt, fussing and fondling him. Not that I mind that particularly. My concern was that he'd get excited and jump up. But no, my angelic little friend behaved perfectly. Soon we were out of the shop and heading for home.

The last test was to walk Matt while Julie to observed his general obedience. On returning home we set out into the forest. When we'd gone far enough and Matt was far enough ahead of us, Julie said, "Call him back now please," and I duly complied. His response again was perfect. He turned towards us and dashed back at warp factor 10 to the power of 10. I was beginning to think we might get through this and finally put the assessment behind us at last!

Warp factor 10

Walking a little further Julie said, "Right, I'd like to test the 'stay' command with him please." I had no concern over this one – we'd practiced it frequently. I instructed Matt to sit which he duly did. Then I said firmly to him "Stay", held my hand up to him and walked a dozen or so paces away. Matt sat motionless. I turned and made my way back to him. If it was going to go wrong it would be now – he might break away before I released him. But no, he remained rooted to the ground until given his treat and release command.

"One more," said Julie. "Get him to lie down and stay."

I must have looked blank. We'd never done this before in the whole of the year Matt and I had been together. I had no way of knowing how he'd deal with it. But there again, I really had no option but to do as Julie asked. With a degree of uncertainty, I instructed Matt down into the lying position. As I walked away he lowered his head down onto his paws and remained motionless as if we'd done this a hundred times before. With my back to him, I counted a dozen paces. Would he break and follow me? I'd known him to do so when we were working at the 'sit-stay' command. I really couldn't say if he'd stay put now we were trying something completely new. At a dozen paces I turned. He was still there, motionless on the ground, head on his paws, eyes fixed intently on me. I made my way back, trying to keep to an even speed that would give him no reason to be roused. As I closed the gap between us he remained perfectly motionless. And as I released and rewarded him, I heaved a huge sigh of relief.

"Perfect," said Julie. "I really can't fault him in any way at all." Evidently, she had forgotten or discounted the excessive enthusiasm he'd shown over the telephone earlier.

We turned and made for home, talking of this and that, with Julie sounding like she was going to pass him.

221

"Would it be premature of me to ask if he's passed?" I asked.

"Yes," Julie replied quickly, "because if anything goes wrong between here and home I might still have to fail him." I zipped my lip.

As we approached home, my alarm bells started to ring. Out of the garden came Clara, a particular favourite of Matt's, who had obviously been visiting Lucas. There was a serious chance he'd make straight for her, and very likely jump up on her. I was all but ready to call or whistle Matt back, but before he noticed her she got into her car and drove away. Danger was averted. As we arrived at the garden gate Julie giggled. "Right," she said, "He's passed." I sighed and relaxed inwardly.

Finally there were a few formalities – another form to sign (inevitably) and a brand new uniform without the words 'In Training' emblazoned on the side. And after that I put Matt immediately into his new uniform and took him outside for Julie to take our graduation picture. And that was it. After almost a year of working together, Matt was a qualified hearing dog and we were an inseparable team.

A few days later I wanted to e-mail Sarah to thank her for all her efforts that, more than anything else, had been responsible for Matt's success at Assessment. Because she didn't have an e-mail address of her own, I wrote to her care of her line-manager, Philip Biggs, whom I'd never met. A day later he wrote back, saying:

Dear Michael,

I most certainly will pass your very kind comments onto Sarah. I too suffer from hearing loss and am well aware of the frustrations attached. I am delighted that Matt has had such a positive effect in your life, and that you are reaping the benefits. Blending your life to accommodate a working partner such as Matt can at first seem traumatic as one literally has to change many lifetime habits, but hopefully the road wasn't too long, and you can now look forward to a rewarding partnership

with your canine friend who doesn't judge, doesn't lie or have hidden agendas and only asks for care and companionship in return. I have worked with dogs for over 25 years and still never cease to be reminded of their choice to associate with and help human beings. May I offer my congratulations to you, as I am well aware of the time and effort that you will have made available to Matt in order for you to now work in harmony together. I always think of it as two individuals at opposite ends of the dance floor who eventually come together to waltz through life with instinctive anticipation of each others movements.
Kindest Regards
Philip Biggs
Placement Manager Hearing Dogs for Deaf People

On retrieving that e-mail and I sat and looked at the words on the screen for a very long time, so succinctly had Philip summed up the efforts and rewards, the pitfalls and the gain that had been my and Matt's lot for the preceding eleven months together. He was right. There was just no more that needed saying.

The Pace Speeds Up

There was little opportunity to bask in the sunshine of Matt's success, though. We were half way through March now. We needed to complete the works on the house and garden in good time to clean up before Vici's wedding on 4th June.

As soon as I arrived at work I'd be taking calls from the builders at home - "Where's the lights for the path? Which outside white paint is for the cob walls and which for the rendered walls? Which inside white paint is for the ceiling and which is for the walls?" I'll never understand why we have to have so many different kinds of white paint. Well I ask you!! When I was a boy white was white. Now there are two hundred and ninety seven version of white from three hundred and forty-three and a half white paint suppliers. The world's gone white paint mad.

Over Easter Naomi and I were scheduled to take a short holiday in Lanzarote. Matt was due to visit his old friends at Lorna's house for the week. Immediately upon our return, he and I were scheduled for a formal welcome by the Fordingbridge fundraising branch of Hearing Dogs at a pudding evening!

Lightening Never Strikes Twice

I'd been living for some months with a fault on one of my hearing aids. Most hearing aids carry what's called a 'T' switch setting. You turn on to this setting when you want to use an induction loop, such as when you watch TV, when you're in the bank and so on. It makes an electronic sound source such as microphone or a TV talk directly into the hearing aid. The T-switch on my left hearing aid (left being the ear I have a little more hearing in and on which I consequently rely more) had given up the ghost some time before, but with the incessant pressure on time I'd not valued the facility of the T switch high enough to do anything about it.

About a week before Naomi and I went to Lanzarote I finally got around to doing something about it and book an appointment with my audiologist. I guess I wasn't too surprised when she told me it would have to be sent away and that consequently I'd be without it for about four weeks. 'Not to worry,' I thought 'I have a spare pair of aids and I can use those.' So off Naomi and I toddled with me sporting my spare left hearing aid. Of course, what I'd not reckoned with was the fact that the spare aids, having been supplied by the NHS, were not as robust as the aids I had bought privately. Now, the private aids have been all over the world with me,

and have experienced such adventures as high temperatures
in equatorial rain forests and a thorough soaking under the
immeasurable power of the Iguazu waterfalls in Argentina.
Though I'd been pretty demanding of them environmentally
and they had occasionally faltered, they had never failed to
return to normal functioning within a day or so. Alas, not so
the NHS aids! Within two days of arrival in Lanzarote the
spare left aid (yup, Murphy decreed that it had to be the left
one for which I now had no back up) had spluttered into
dampened malfunction and lain down and expired as a result
of infiltration by perspiration. I was now down to one
functioning hearing aid – and that was on the side on which I
have virtually no hearing at all. I sighed in resignation and
accepted it wasn't too big a deal since I was on holiday and
my daughter was there to interpret for me. Thus the holiday
continued with comprehensive reliance on lip reading and
much translation of other voices by Naomi!

Returning home was a bit more of a problem though.
The day after arrival Matt and I had been booked for our first
official public function. We were to be presented to the major
event of the year held by the Fordingbridge fundraising
branch of Hearing Dogs where Matt had been adopted as the
official dog of the branch! Amazingly though, the event,
attended by almost 200 people, passed off successfully and I
was able to hold a number of conversations with many people
interested to meet Matt, all conducted with me relying almost
totally on lip reading. It's remarkable what you find out what
you can do when pushed into a corner to do it!

I might reasonably have expected the matter to rest
there until my next visit to the audiologist, when I would
have my repaired aid returned to me safe and sound. But I'd
not reckoned with the fact that lightening indeed sometimes
strike twice in the same place. Having returned to work on
the Sunday evening I woke early on the Monday to take Matt
for his morning stroll round the park before settling to the

Everest-sized mountain of paper on my desk. We duly took our morning constitutional and were heading back to Hurst Manor when Matt's attention was taken by something in an abandoned building in an adjacent field. He ran off to investigate, and intrigued, I followed him. Whatever it was had gone by the time we got there, and with time marching on towards 8.00am, I turned once more for Hurst Manor. But emerging from the field back onto the path, I ducked below a low hanging tree branch and, coming up a bit too soon afterwards, got struck on the side of the head by said branch. Now I know this is stretching credibility just a teensey-weensey bit, but what do you suppose the chances are of a low flying tree branch thumping one upon one's cranium at just the right position and angle to dislodge one's behind-the-ear hearing aid? And if you've come up with an appropriate mathematical response to that question then double the odds against it, 'cos if you remember I was wearing only one aid! Now, to this improbably infinitesimally small chance, apply a further discount to establish the odds of not being able to locate said behind-the-ear hearing aid that was so conveniently dislodged from behind one's ear, particularly when one knows precisely where one lost it! Your final answer is now a fraction so small as to be as near to zero probability as doesn't matter..... so if any one can explain why I now find myself the proud owner of but one useful hearing aid out of an original four, I'd be really interested to know. Answers on a post card....... ☺

Lightening most definitely does strike twice!

Well, I reconciled myself to working temporarily with only one aid for the next few weeks and called the audiologist once again to ask for a price on a replacement right hearing aid. The air might reasonably have been expected to turn blue when I was quoted just over £2,000. In fact the air remained very transparent and very silent. I was simply dumb founded, for I had discontinued my insurance some 18 months earlier on the grounds that in 15 years of ownership I'd never lost a hearing aid. So there was no point in paying £80.00 or so a year to cover an eventuality that most definitely never, ever, ever was going to happen, was there? Uh huh.

Rightly or wrongly, I took the decision to postpone the replacement of the second hearing aid until the cash haemorrhage being generated by wedding, house renovation, business extension and so on was over. Suitably chastened, I set out for a few days in France with Penny, primarily for the purpose of buying the wine and champagne for the wedding, leaving Matt to stay with Big Al and friends once more.

Now, I'll bet you're wondering what went wrong in France, aren't you? Well, actually nothing went wrong in France. I even managed to revive my school-boy French and attempt some conversations, with Penny explaining to me the responses of the other participant in the conversation – well, if you can't hear in the mother tongue, the changes of hearing in another langue are even slimmer! We even managed to take a trip to Chartreuse, where we walked the meditative labyrinth laid out on the cathedral floor. In fact, it was a near perfect, hitch free trip… until the phone rang the day before we were due to go home.

"Michael," said a voice. It took me a few moments for me to tune in to the fact that it was Guy speaking to me. "There's been a problem," he said. "Godshill has been subjected to a freak storm. I've never seen anything like it in my life. Lightening has struck twenty to thirty times in the village in the space of an hour. Two of the hits were on your house. It blew a window frame out and the power's off. We can't tell how bad the damage is. What do you want us to do?"

I looked at my watch, my heart sinking. It was late afternoon on Friday. I was 150 miles and a five-hour sea crossing from home. There was effectively nothing I could do until after the weekend. I thanked Guy for letting me know, asked him to secure the house as best he could, grinned stoically and bore it.

When we finally did arrive home late on the Saturday evening there was no point in even visiting the house, since it would be pitch black out in the Forest. I gratefully accepted Penny's offer to stay over at her house. In the morning I collected Matt from Lorna before heading home to try to assess the damage. As it turned out, we had been incredibly fortunate, considering the fact that The Oaks is a thatched house. If the lightening had gone for, say, a TV aerial on the roof, the house could have been burned to the ground. But as we found out on the Monday with the first visit of the electrician, the strike had probably been on some outside wiring. The enormous voltage had passed back up through the system and blown the main fuse, together with all the trip switches. With nowhere then to go, it had caused an internal build up of pressure in the house powerful enough to pop a window frame right out. I was immensely fortunate that I had been absent at the time of the strike. On any normal Friday I would very likely have been there. I breathed my thanks to my angels for protecting me.

The electrician was due to return on the Wednesday to conduct a full investigation and assess the damage. Meanwhile, I had informed the insurance company and obtained their agreement to fund a preliminary investigation of the damage. "What about paying for somewhere for me to stay," I asked in my innocence. "There's no heat or light and no hot water."

"Yes," came the preliminary answer, "we will pay reasonable accommodation expenses. It was about an hour later that the same person phoned back. "Sorry," she said,

"I've got that wrong. The underwriters say they'll only pay accommodation if the house is uninhabitable, and they don't agree that yours is." Accordingly, I spent the Monday night in my very dark, very cold house that in the wisdom of the insurance company was still considered perfectly habitable, wondering how on earth I'd have coped if I had a young family with me. The thought occurred to me more than once as I struggled round the house with candles that insurance companies are more than content to lend you umbrellas – unless of course it is raining. Thanks NFU Mutual, I love you too. ☺

Well, Wednesday dawned at about the same time as Tuesday and Monday before it, to welcome the early arrival of the electricians. Of course, uppermost in my mind was the fact that we were now some six weeks away from the wedding and I had, as yet, no idea of how long it would take to get the repairs undertaken, never mind to get the insurance company's agreement to the work being done. The electricians worked steadily through the day and by evening had a preliminary assessment of the circumstances. Jonathan, the man in charge, was a softly spoken, tall young man, with that somewhat grave look professionals have about them when working. "What's the damage?" I asked.

He looked at me thoughtfully before responding. "I can't be absolutely sure as yet, since I've not tested every circuit. But it seems you've been remarkably fortunate. Most of the circuits are undamaged and are now back on. We've found some faults not necessarily connected with the lightning strike and I'll need to do some further testing to know what the implications of those are. But I'm happy to have your supply turned back on apart from some circuits which I'll isolate."

I breathed some more silent thanks to my angels. The house was immediately back to working status and reasonably comfortable again. Most important of all, there seemed no reason why we wouldn't be ready for the wedding in six weeks time. Nothing else could go wrong now, could it? I mean, we'd had our full allocation of trouble, hadn't we? Surely we could expect a reasonably smooth ride down to 4th June now. Uh huhhhhh.

On the home straight

Actually, for the most part, life moved forward pretty predictably after that. The remaining chaos around the house gradually morphed into a semblance of order and eventually the builders left. My weekends were occupied with final touches such as putting up new curtains, awaiting the delivery of furniture and liasing with Sandy the designer about finishing touches. It all seemed very domestic, very calm... in fact all far too normal! Wedding preparations accelerated, and I seemed to be perpetually on the phone to Vici, to caterers, to various parties who had information I needed or needed information I had.

Matt, of course, at the overt level, was blissfully unaware of all of this. I say 'at the overt level,' for he is particularly prone to responding to atmospheres around him. If I, or others he cares for are elated, he will be elated. If we are worried, he will sense it and look for re-assurance himself. If we are sad, he will seek to comfort us. He doesn't have the verbal language skills to communicate his close involvement in all that goes on around him, but he finds other ways of expressing himself. He was very much part of the chain of events that were unfolding at this time, and greatly valued for being so.

By the time the electricians left us in early May we were some four weeks away from the wedding. The pace of events rapidly increased to a frenetic level. Final preparations included a thorough cleaning of the house after some four months of building work, letters to warn the neighbours of the likely disturbance the wedding would cause, suit delivery for me, suite deliveries for the house and a final clip for the AD.

BTW

The following week was to prove to be frenetic. So much was our attention focussed on the wedding that we had come to refer to all of time as being either BTW (before the wedding) or ATW (after the wedding). It was still, of course, BTW but the arrival of the crucial day for which so much preparation had been made was imminent. The last few mind blowing-ly busy days were to hold both frustrations and the source of great mirth.

I'd arranged for Tuesday to be my last day at work before the wedding, so as to have a few days in which to put the final touches to the preparations at home. On the Tuesday afternoon Matron Sue and Auntie Brenda presented me with an enormous card, signed by all the staff at Hurst Manor, for me to pass on to Tom and Vici. Though no one at Hurst Manor had ever met either of them, clearly everyone felt as if they'd known them both all their lives. Evidently, virtually my only topic of conversation at work for several weeks had been *the wedding*!

On Tuesday evening I arrived home to a somewhat surreal sense of peace. Knowing what was about to happen, it somehow seemed inappropriate to have such a quiet evening. Nevertheless, Matt and I spent a few hours quietly dozing in front of a log fire – a favourite evening pastime for both of us. The AD woke me early the next morning in the time-honoured fashion. By six we were out and making our way up the hillside towards Godshill Wood. As we climbed, I looked back down the valley in the direction of the house.

Once again, the hare grass cotton tails, little white flowers like cotton wool buds, were strewn carelessly over the valley floor, just as I remembered them almost a year before when we had first moved to The Oaks. There's something about living in the country that impresses the passing of the seasons on me in a way that I never really noticed when I was a city dweller. It seemed incredible to me that on 4th June, the day of the wedding, Matt and I would have lived in the little hidden corner of Godshill for exactly one year. As we reached the top of the hill we looked back not just on a peaceful valley, still sleeping in the early morning light, but also on a year spent in our wonderful forest home. And as we pressed on to take a longer than normal walk through the wood, the opening fox gloves seemed to echo the dance of the seasons, resonating to the rhythm of the gentle passing of another year of my life. Completing our circuit, we dropped down the side of the valley once more to the waiting day and the long list of tasks that needed to be completed before the wedding.

By mid morning the marquee suppliers had arrived and spent the rest of the day erecting the two large marquees that would act as the focal point for the reception. Clearly, they didn't need my help, so I proceeded to Penny's house where I collected an additional fridge for chilling the champagne and an additional chair to ease the pressure on the seating in the house that would inevitably occur. Penny had also pointed out that one of the toilet seats in the house needed replacing. 'Oh yes,' I thought, recalling that one of them had seemed loose since I moved into the house. Some jobs you just never get around to doing until you're forced to. So I made a detour to the local DIY superstore, picked up the required item and made for home.

In the afternoon Sandy, our designer, arrived with the last of the curtains that completed the physical work on the house that we had commenced some four months earlier. She hung the curtains to much ooing and aahing in admiration by yours truly and we both stood and smiled in a rather satisfied way at her handiwork. After she left oohing and ahhing gave way to grunting and groaning as I struggled to loosen the bolts that held the down the toilet seat I was supposed to be changing. Had the toilet not been in the 1960s extension to the house I could quite easily believe that it had been in situ since the cottage was built in around 1750. Nevertheless, with the aid of junior hacksaw and socket set I finally managed to shift the offending bolts. The rest of the job was reasonably straightforward and by the time Penny returned that evening I was able to point proudly to my masculinity-enhancing DIY success. She took one look at it and said "You've changed the wrong loo seat. I meant you to do the one in the toilet in the bathroom next door!" Masculinity-enhancing DIY success slumped its shoulders and slunk dejectedly away to lick its wounds elsewhere.

Nevertheless, we were able to acknowledge briefly the completion of four months work before focussing on the events of the next day. On the Thursday the pace speeded up even further. Without wishing to labour the point, the day's schedule looked something like the following:

8.00 am	Decide there is no time to walk the AD that morning (seriously bad decision).
8.30am	Unbeknown to me AD leaves calling card outside chalet as a result of not being walked.
9.00am	Clean house.
10.00am	AD overcomes life long fear of water and jumps in stream.
10.30am	Immensely proud of himself, AD presents himself for praise and commendation, dripping muddy stream water all through newly cleaned house.
11.00am	Clean house again

11.30am	Supermarket delivers sufficient food and drink to feed the Star Wars Clone Army for the whole of an intergalactic journey.
12.00 noon	Unpack food
2.00pm	Pick up fridge from Penny's to add to wine chilling capacity.
2.00pm	AD gets in stream again (house kept locked – wot do you think I am – stoopid or summin?)
2.30pm	Put booze in fridge & discover I can't remember where I hid last 6 bottles of champagne.
3.00pm	Clean car, ensuring AD keep 30 paces from car at all times.
5.00pm	Caterers arrive to set up tables etc. in marquee. Mistake caterers for daughter's future in laws (well I only met them once before) causing severe confusion and sufficient personal embarrassment to justify banishment to Elba for rest of life.
5.30pm	AD gets in car when I am preoccupied with embarrassment.
6.00pm	Richard (bro) Rosemary (bro's darling wife) & David (sweet 'n innocent lil' nephew of almost 7) arrived while I am still recovering from caterer-induced embarrassment.
6.05pm	Sweet'n innocent lil' nephew treads in AD's calling card by chalet.
6.06pm	Sweet 'n innocent lil' nephew enters into the chalet grinding AD's calling card firmly into carpet.
6.07pm	Sweet 'n innocent lil' nephew renders DVD inoperable!
7.30pm	x-wife arrives for unannounced inspection of marquee.
7.35pm	X-wife pronounces marquee & preparations

	(phew!).
9.30pm	Firstborn daughter Naomi invited herself to stay over and requests lift from Southampton station at 10.45pm
10.30pm	Support drooping eyelids with scaffolding
10.45pm	Collect Firstborn from Southampton station
11.45	Remove scaffolding from eyelids
11.45-6.02am	Blissful sleep til AD decides we should awake

W-day minus 1

By Friday morning Matt was high with the sense of excitement that now pervaded the house. I had already determined that the only way for him to cope with an influx of visitors on Saturday such as he had never known, would be to keep him in full dress uniform most of the day. But until then there was going to be no stopping him.

By lunchtime Vici and her Intended had arrived, together with entourage of bridesmaids and best man, all of whom were now lending a hand to fix lighting, run cables, decorate the garden with candles and drink coffee. By mid afternoon Vici and the bridesmaids had headed off to their manicure and would be staying at my ex-wife's house for the night before the wedding. The rest of us continued the programme of preparations until around 4.30pm, when best man and Intended set out to take their car to Winchester where it would be collected by the newlyweds after their departure from the reception. I looked hesitatingly at my watch, realising they had just two hours to get there and back for the wedding rehearsal at 6.30pm in New Milton. Then I looked nervously at the sky, that had decided to empty itself that afternoon, wondering if the forecast of dry weather for the Saturday could possibly be correct.

Arriving at the rehearsal a minute late myself, I was immediately aware of the absence of the bride groom. Unperturbed, the lady Vicar proceeded with the practice, with Fields, another member of the Morning Runner band standing in for the absent Tom. When we reached the point in the service practice where I had to place Vici's hand into the groom's she giggled nervously. "Well," I said to her, "if you can't have the bass guitarist, won't the keyboard player do?" Vici suppressed another giggle and said nothing. Moments later Tom arrived. The assembled multitude sighed in relief and Vici hugged him thankfully, confident that she wouldn't have to find a substitute the next day. At the end of the rehearsal the bride and groom to be and ten others headed off to the pub for a pre-wedding celebration. I had already explained to the key dramatis personae that noisy environments were difficult for me, as were large group conversations. Putting the two together would very likely make for an unpleasant evening. Everyone concerned understood and I noted how far I had come in being assertive in my deafness. Two years before I would have attended out of politeness and very likely hated every minute. Now I was able to say what I needed and act as best suited my needs. That kind of openness has become a crucial part of making life work well for me in the context of my deafness. So I returned home where Chris and Dil (minus Kitten and Gizmo) had already arrived. Matt and I spent the last evening before my daughter's wedding in the comfortably company of old friends. It was all as it should be.

Will you take this man...

As far as Matt was concerned, Saturday was not expected to be any different from any other day. He pre-empted the alarm clock in the normal way, waking me at 5.30

or so. But given the significance of the day, I was already coming to and didn't mind. I'm not above pushing him off the bed if he wakes me before the alarm, but today it didn't matter. We took our early morning walk up the valley before the rest of the household was up. Then he and I busied ourselves for an hour or so – I by checking everything for the tenth time, he by chasing non existent rabbits round the garden and dunking himself in the stream (just for a change). I let him have full freedom up until 10.30am, since I knew that for the rest of the day he would be expected to behave himself impeccably. On the dot of 10.30am, Jane from Super Clean Dogs promptly appeared, whereupon Matt went berserk with excited expectation of a most enjoyable hour's pampering at her experienced hands!

Starting the day as we meant it to go on, the other seven of us settled down for a celebratory breakfast of croissants, smoked salmon and buck's fizz. Then, all at once it was 12.00 and time for us to make our way to New Milton where Penny would drop me at my x-wife's house for photos and for the final trip on which I would accompany my younger daughter as a single woman. Vici had long since decided that with five bridesmaids to follow us down the aisle, being accompanied by a dog as well would be just too over the top! Accordingly, Matt would be in Penny's charge for the service after which we would be reunited. I had no concerns. All of those romps and tumbles on the floor at Penny's house had so cemented their relationship, that Matt would be entirely settled in Penny's presence.

I arrived to a house buzzing with anticipation that emanated from bride to be, best woman (Naomi), bride's mother, bride's grandmother and five bridesmaids. Naturally, the excitement metre was registering off the top of the scale! So we proceeded with the pre-departure photos in endless combinations of bride and family, bride and bridesmaids, bride and parents, bride and mother, bride and father… and on and on until it was time for the bridesmaids to leave for the church, only some three or four hundred yards from the house. Then suddenly, Vici and I were alone, me in my best suit, she in a long white wedding gown in which she looked astoundingly beautiful. She paced nervously round the lounge while I tried to reassure her that everything would be fine, that everything would go well according to plan. She looked unconvinced until the car returned for us and I helped her in, holding her hand, just as I had done so many times some twenty years before, when she was three years old. If you're a parent you'll understand what that does for you, for the years fly in a way that we cannot really relate to.

In a matter of minutes we were at the church where the vicar was waiting patiently, smiling, and the bridesmaids were waiting nervously, giggling. Then it was a final adjustment of everyone's clothing before the music started and we were into the doorway of the church, with the congregation looking round to catch their first glimpse of the bride. As Vici and I stepped inside the door I caught Penny's eye enquiringly. She nodded slightly, confidently, in confirmation that Matt was, of course, perfectly all right with her. Then it was on down the aisle to the alter where my son-in-law-to-be was waiting, an enormous smile spreading across his face as his bride made her way towards him. Never have I been simultaneously so much on public view and yet so completely ignored! But I was more than content for it to be that way. It was Vici's day and I had already done absolutely everything within my power to make it unerringly special for her. She was the undeniable star of the day as every bride should be. And at that moment I was glad that Matt was not at my side, for he does tend to have this habit of stealing any show in which he participates. It would not have been seemly for him to have done so on this occasion.

The rest of the chain of events you can predict, I'm sure. The service proceeded to the exchange of vows and the exchange of rings, a deep and meaningful kiss and a cheer by the congregation, the signing of the register and a procession back down the isle to the church garden... where it promptly started to rain! Plan B was quickly enacted and the photos took place inside the church, following which Penny and Matt and I leapt quickly into the car so as to be first back at The Oaks to ensure everything was in place. Half an hour later we pulled up outside the garage, and I can honestly say I'd never seen my house and garden looking so beautiful. The rhododendrons were in full bloom throughout the acre of garden, the fences were decked in wedding flowers and the tables in the marquee each carried a single stem lily. As I turned round I saw a long convoy of cars coming up the lane behind us, with the ushers, who had only just arrived themselves, rushing back to direct the parking! I left them to get on with it – they would do a better job of organising it that I would, and my function now was just to enjoy the rest of the day, and watch my daughter have a wonderful time at her wedding reception.

Well, the day proceeded, as we had hoped, without major hitch. Welcome drinks gave way to relaxed conversation which yielded to a barbeque buffet. The skies had long since forgotten their anger and smiled on us for the rest of the day. In conversation after conversation I presented the impeccably behaved Matt to a succession of intrigued guests, each of whom returned home having learned a little more about deafness and the work of Hearing Dogs. Then twilight fell and the jazz band started to play.

The evening slipped all too quickly away, with Bride and Groom taking their leave sometime around 10.00pm – truth to tell I really didn't notice the time and it really didn't matter. And with their departure the majority of guests also sloped off for their drive home, leaving the last few straggles to enjoy the dusk of a summer evening in the New Forest with the jazz weaving its characteristic rhythm around the garden candles and the burbling brook, while the night owls began hunting field mice in the paddocks. Finally, around midnight, in deference to the neighbours both human and animal, we tipped the last of the party-makers out and sent them home.

Penny, the houseguests, Matt and I collapsed in a heap in the sun lounge and tried to take in the day's events. We had worked towards this day so intensively that we had set aside all plans for what would happen ATW. Now it was just about ATW and life would, somehow, have to get back to something we could call normal. Penny slipped away home round 12.30am and Matt and I hit the hay immediately after she left.

ATW

A small black and white form woke me the next morning around seven by jumping on the bed and licking my face until he had me giggling. As we had done so many times over the preceding year, we slipped out of the house before the rest of the world was awake. As always, we made our way up the side of the valley, and as we climbed I turned to look back at the house, surrounded by the oaks trees that assuredly were several hundred years older than the two hundred and fifty year old cottage itself. Matt waited patiently as I once more looked down at the hare's tail cotton grass dabbing the face of the valley with their cotton wool buds, and I looked down on Jamie's bridge that I had crossed for the first time just over a year before. Yesterday had been a life event, a rite of passage. Today was both a time for reflection and for thinking about the future - a future at which, in reality, each of us can only guess. It has been said that there are no certainties in life except for death and taxes.

But to me, more important than either of those is what I do with the years I have remaining.

What will my future hold? More learning opportunities? More growth for, and with the people with whom I work? I certainly hope so. More travel to distant lands to enable me to soak up more of the lessons this planet has to teach us all? I'd very much like to think so. Further deterioration in my hearing? Very probably, and perhaps in due course, the all pervading silence of complete deafness. But one element of the future for which I hold high hopes and expectation is the continuing relationship I have with a small black and white dog who had exploded into my life just fourteen months before. In that short time he quite literally changed the course of my existence. He facilitated my re-entry into a world that has little awareness of deafness and still less understanding of the challenges and demands it imposes. He has made it possible for me to accept my limitation without anger or malice. He has helped me to learn that this condition, though significant, does not need to prevent me from doing anything I want to do or from experiencing the future as I want it to be. Whatever else the future does or does not hold, I have hope and confidence. And as will now be more than obvious to all reading, none of the changes I have made could have happened if it wasn't for that dog.

If it wasn't for that dog...

Michael Forester